Praise for *Tinderbox*

'Simpson sticks the landing with an epic conclusion. Fans of Andrea Hairston's *Master of Poisons* and other secondary world fantasy will enjoy this expansive magical adventure.'
Publishers Weekly

'This promising debut features strong world building and well-developed systems of magic. It will appeal to readers of Kacen Callender's *Queen of the Conquered* (2019), N.K. Jemisin's *The Hundred Thousand Kingdoms* (2010), and L. Penelope's *Song of Blood and Stone* (2018).'
Booklist

'A grisly murder, a missing box, a dangerous task, and a cranky magical talisman. Expect betrayals, intrigue, peril, and romance in this smartly moving fantasy.'
Jacey Bedford, author of the *Psi-Tech* and *Rowankind* series

'W.A. Simpson begins with a simple tale of revenge and quickly weaves a grand adventure bound together with the threads of fairy tales and fey creations...where possessed staffs speak, wil-o-wisps roam, and Jack's giant vine protects the world both above and below.'
Troy Carrol Bucher, author of *Lies of Descent*

'Tinderbox is a riveting tale about personal strength and hidden magic '
Foreword Reviews

W.A. SIMPSON

TAROTMANCER

The Tales from the Riven Isles

Book Two

This is a FLAME TREE PRESS book

FLAME TREE PRESS
6 Melbray Mews, London, SW6 3NS, UK
flametreepress.com

US sales, distribution and warehouse:
Simon & Schuster
simonandschuster.biz

UK distribution and warehouse:
Hachette UK Distribution
hukdcustomerservice@hachette.co.uk

Thanks to the Flame Tree Press team.

The cover is created by Flame Tree Studio with
thanks to Nik Keevil and Shutterstock.com.
The font families used are Avenir and Bembo.

Flame Tree Press is an imprint of Flame Tree Publishing Ltd
flametreepublishing.com

A copy of the CIP data for this book is available from the British Library and the Library of Congress.

1 3 5 7 9 8 6 4 2

HB ISBN: 978-1-78758-788-5
PB ISBN: 978-1-78758-787-8
ebook ISBN: 978-1-78758-789-2

Printed and bound in Great Britain by Clays Ltd, Elcograf S.p.A.

W.A. SIMPSON

TAROTMANCER

The Tales from the Riven Isles
Book Two

FLAME TREE PRESS
London & New York

CHAPTER ONE

Innocent, the cards whispered. They were going to execute an innocent person.

Harper was barely out of infancy when the cards had first spoken to her. They did not speak as a person would, although they murmured words beyond her understanding. Other times she saw things, visions that sometimes frightened her.

She heard them whisper this time and hurried down the crowded street towards the market square. Their voices, which she had learned to distinguish over the years, continued to guide her.

The citizens of Innrone filled the streets even at this early hour. Most of whom hadn't slept or were about to take to their beds after either work or pleasure. The affluent came much later or sent their servants out for whatever it was they needed.

The market square itself stood at the intersection of Merchant Row and Copper Street, which made up the business district. Depending on how far you walked, the prominent shops were closer to the square, but as you traveled farther, that's where you found the less-reputable merchants.

Harper avoided executions. Why would she want to watch someone die? But when a young girl running errands for her boss nearly knocked Harper into the dirt and explained she was going to the hanging, she heard the Lady of Lies say *innocent*. As Harper approached market square, she threaded her way through to the head of the crowd.

At the center was a somewhat new knee-high circle of white limestone bricks with an uncomplicated design. A fountain once stood there, but there was nothing left but crumbled pieces of blue-veined marble. The city officials weren't willing to import the rock a second time, since rising from the rich dark earth was an offshoot of the Celestial Vine. From its roots at Jack-In-Irons to the island of Morwynne, its branches and offshoots were the source of all magic and held the fragile island together.

The central stalk was wide but supple and healthy green, growing twelve feet tall in whatever time it took. Smoother than a baby's arse, as people liked to say. Cordons made branch-like extensions, slimmer than the trunk but enough to support the weight of a teenaged boy. The ones who dared make the climb proved this. Smaller canes and shoots cascaded down in a shower of darker tendrils. It had appeared right in the middle of the noon rush. The sound of stone breaking was like lightning striking many times, and the earth trembled underneath the terrified crowd. The offshoot broke through, continued to grow as it reached into the sky.

Opinions of this happening varied. Some said it was the Vine giving its blessing to Innrone. Others had more disturbing guesses. That it served as a warning for all the people partaking in unlawful or immoral activities in the dark alleys of the square. Harper didn't know either way. Customers asked her a few times, and she gave the same answer. She'd never been able to make a divination about the Vine. Besides being the source of magic, it also birthed the magical creatures, who were more powerful than Harper hoped to be.

Three people stood in the loam. One held the reins of the mare upon which the thief sat with the rope around his neck. A second man was to his left and an old woman near the horse's flank. Harper guessed she would slap it on the rear to get it going.

They'd slung the rope over a lower cordon. Harper pushed closer, recognizing the man holding the reins as the local junker, although the well-to-do liked to call his wares antiques.

"Master Jessen!" she called.

He turned upon hearing his name. "Hello, Miss Harper. Come to see the spectacle?"

Harper did not consider an execution a show, but she didn't say. "You are about to execute an innocent man."

"What's that?" He crossed his beefy arms across his chest. "He was in my shop nosin' around and next thing, a few small trinkets gone."

"You saw him lift them?"

"Who is this brat?" the second man, who Harper didn't recognize, demanded. "Let's get on with it!"

"Be at ease, Felix."

"I will not!"

While the men continued their argument, Harper inspected the would-be thief. He was slight and thin. His skin was an unusual reddish-brown that Harper had never seen before. It was difficult to tell which part of the Isles he was from. His hair was long, fiery, and unkempt as it rested across his shoulders. His shirt, vest, and hose, even his shoes, were red. He wasn't very smart, dressing like that. Despite his position, Harper swore he was smirking. Bright eyes, the color of chestnut, seemed to take the entire crowd into consideration. But for what? Escape? He didn't have a chance without her intervention.

"Now hold on," Master Jessen was saying. "Our Miss Harper is a diviner."

"She fair divined my wife was pregnant with twins!"

"I got good numbers from her!"

"Let her have her say!"

Felix rolled his eyes but kept quiet. Harper stepped over the limestone wall, stood next to the horse, and brought out her deck. The first one she drew was what she wanted. She showed it to Jessen. "Do you recognize this card?"

He peered at it. "Aye, ain't that the Lying Lady?"

Harper smiled. "Yes." Although the proper describer was Lady of Lies. "Would you untie his hands, please?"

"Now wait a—" Felix began.

Jessen shrugged and complied, saying, "I'd not try to run, thief. This lady's about to save yer arse."

"What's your name?" she asked him.

He didn't speak right away. "Red."

"Just Red?"

"Yes."

"Take the card."

"Why?"

"You want to be hanged? Take the damn card."

He did so. The Lady whispered again – *Innocent.*

Just to satisfy her own curiosity, Harper nodded and drew another.

The Jack. Amongst the Major Arcana like the Lady of Lies, it could mean different things. Some diviners thought the Jack referred to the Farm Boy, while those not familiar with tarot assumed it was the same as the jack from a common deck. Within the tarot, it meant greed, unless reversed. Harper let the card fall to the ground. The next she drew was the Martyr. Tempered by the Weaver and the Match Girl. "He is prideful and greedy, but also has somewhat of a heart. If he were guilty, the Lady would have said so." Harper retrieved her cards.

"Then tell us, oh mighty diviner, who did it?" Felix's tone was mocking.

Harper ignored him. "Master Jessen, if I may look at your store? Hold the thief here."

When Harper walked into the shop, Jessen pointed out where the trinkets had been. Harper drew again. The Piper. Someone being led astray. The Deceiver, and the Lady of Lies. Harper pinched the bridge of her nose. "Who was that man out there?"

"That's my cousin." Jessen's eyes widened. "You don't say?"

One last card. The Knot. "Someone tied to you," Harper said. "You'd better have a talk with that cousin of yours."

In no time, Jessen...*persuaded* Felix to hand over the goods and they released Red. Jessen muttered an apology before dragging his wayward cousin back into his store, and the crowd went about their business.

Harper didn't expect Red to stay around to thank her, but he did just that. He approached and said, "Thank you, Lady Diviner."

"I ain't no lady." Harper shrugged. "Call me Harper if you like."

"You seem educated, if you don't slip into that common speak."

"I am," Harper said. "Pops always said an ignorant gambler is a poor gambler."

"Pops?"

"The owner of the…establishment where I work."

"An illegal gambling den," Red said, matter-of-fact.

"Eh," Harper said, noncommittal. "I'm glad I could help. Nothing's worse than being accused of thievery when you ain't no thief."

He laughed, as if he knew a secret. "That is where you are wrong, Lady Harper," he said. "I am a thief."

CHAPTER TWO

Red wondered how he appeared to the quivering mass of human flesh before him, though there were no mirrors nearby. Sharp pointed teeth, glistening in the semidarkness. Hair the color of fire covering his body, with lean muscles underneath. He'd removed that red outfit, keeping only the trousers on, and they strained against his cock and balls. "You didn't believe I'd let that pass, did you?" Red grinned.

The man – what was his name? Felix? – still sporting the bruises visited upon him by his cousin, sat huddled in the room's corner where he'd taken refuge after the junk man had thrown him out of his home. Red assumed Felix had nowhere to go, estranged from his own family, if his stealing from his own relative was any sign of his morals.

The rooming house stood between two prosperous businesses in a dead-end alley. A scar on otherwise flawless skin. It catered to the criminal and the destitute. Red had tracked Felix there. He couldn't let what happened go unpunished. Of course, he wouldn't kill the man. Red hadn't committed murder since— Well, he wasn't about to dwell on that. It was ages ago, and he was a different person now. Sometimes he looked back and experienced…guilt? Yes, he supposed it was. He'd never given his actions a second thought.

When Red arrived at his door, Felix had tried to shut it in his face, but Red, who was much stronger than any human, had forced his way in. Felix was stupidly unarmed. Even a dagger would have given him an air of menace. Red stood over him and widened his sharp-toothed smile. "Now, what should I do with you?"

"Wait!" Felix cried as he pushed his arms out in a warding gesture. "I have something that may interest you."

"Oh, and what might that be?"

"Tonight, I was going to...borrow a family heirloom."

"You mean steal it."

"It's worth a lot of money."

"Why would I be interested?"

Felix didn't speak, his mouth opening and closing like a fish out of water. "I was told—"

"Don't bother," Red said between his teeth, making himself look more fearsome. "What about this heirloom?"

"A mask."

"What of it?"

"Well, I'm not sure."

Red took a step forward and bared his fangs.

"Wait!" Felix's eyes bugged. "All I know is my uncle won't allow anyone near it. It's supposed to be encrusted with gems and made from the finest porcelain."

It didn't seem believable. "This is the junker's father?"

"No, no." Felix calmed. "He is brother to mine." He released a breath. "And likely he'll blame my father for the theft." He said this more to himself. "Which is fine."

Red did not like meddling in the affairs of family. "You have no love for your father."

Felix snorted. "He turned me out."

Red figured there was a reason. Felix was nothing but a common thief and vagabond. "Fine, where is it?"

The woods outside of the city. They didn't have a name. Most people referred to them as Wandering Woods, after two young children who disappeared while exploring. Some claimed they met an evil witch who had them for her supper. Others said a monstrous wolf devoured them. Red felt it was better if he stayed away. He wasn't a magician, although well acquainted with the arts. There must be some measure of safety, if this rich uncle had lived in the woods all this time.

Felix was going on and giving whatever information he thought was important. Where his uncle's manor was, how to get there, and an insulting description of his uncle that called his manhood into question.

"All right then." Despite his misgivings, Red wanted to get moving and for Felix to shut his mouth. "We'll call things even, if I find the mask and it's worth something."

"Oh, it is!" Felix brightened for a moment, then shrank back again.

"It had better be," Red said, "because I will come for you if it isn't."

He turned, but not before seeing the terror return to Felix's expression. He smiled to himself as he made his way out of the alley, taking time to regain his human form. Now what to do? He'd burgled a few large estates in the past but always near or within the city limits. It was uncharted ground for certain. If only he knew a magician....

Red thought of Harper.

He grinned again. When he'd told her he was a thief, she shrugged and replied, "Not my choice of work, but you gotta eat."

"I am in your debt, La— Harper," Red had said. "Someday I will return the favor."

He could visit her and let the cards decide if this was something he might do, suffering no mishaps. And repay his debt by offering her a cut. It might not be a fair cut but killing two birds and such. He'd followed her at a safe distance to watch where she'd go, but to Red's shock, she started visiting some less than reputable individuals and the dangerous backstreets. It didn't take him long to figure out she was paying winning bets. He'd never seen so many people so happy to see one person.

And she did her job without fear of robbery, although only a half-wit would attack someone with the Gift. Red figured it had more to do with her reputation than anything. And wouldn't she see it coming?

Confident in his idea and success, Red whistled a jaunty tune as he moved through the teeming city streets until he came to Pops' Gambling Den. Patrons crowded it in the early evening with the day laborers stopping for the games and drink. Later that night, after sunset, the oh-so-perfect respectable folks would arrive, and the true money would change hands. Red visited these places often, but not to steal. He enjoyed gambling. And there was no way he'd get out of there alive if he stole.

A curvaceous dark-skinned woman approached him. "Evening, love, you need a table?"

"Actually," Red said, "I'm here to see Harper."

Her lips thinned, and eyes narrowed. "You a friend?"

Friend? He'd only had one, but that was long ago. "Tell her it's Red."

Her eyebrows rose. "Oh, you're him." She grinned. "Follow me, handsome."

He did as she weaved amongst the jammed tables, showing surprising skill. The air was thick with smoke, mingling with the smell of unwashed bodies and hard liquor. He'd been in too many places like this, so it ceased to bother him. Harper was in the room's rear, at a rickety old table, but the surface was smooth. She was sitting across from a matronly woman, who was wringing a handkerchief in her plump fingers.

"I'm sorry," Harper said with genuine sympathy.

The woman made a noise like a squeak and buried her face in her hands. Red guessed, unfaithful husband. He was no saint, but he believed any man who did that to a woman was a coward and a whore. The woman pushed back from the table and stood. She would have fallen backwards over the chair had Harper not reached out with a swiftness, grabbed the woman's wrist, and steadied her. She splayed her other hand over the woman's face.

Red would swear time halted.

When Harper released her, the woman stood still. Red moved around to the side and saw her expression of resignation. The woman nodded and reached into her dress at her bosom and drew out a pouch. She opened it and withdrew coins, which she counted out into Harper's palm. Then, without another word, she turned and left. Red got a glimpse of what the woman had paid, five celestials. It would set Harper for the next several months. Almost made him wish he was a diviner.

Harper noticed him standing there. "Well, greetings."

"Miss Harper." Red moved closer to the table. He heard his escort chuckle as she moved away. "I figure you can't tell me, but what happened to that woman?"

"Personal," Harper said, "but let's just say her husband is about to be paid back for his indiscretions."

"He deserves it," Red said.

Her expression brightened, impressed. "I'm glad you think so." Harper gathered up her cards. "Now, what can I do for you?"

"May we sit?" Red said. "Have you eaten yet?"

"You offering to pay?"

Red shrugged. "Unless you are willing? But let it not be said that I'm not a gentleman."

"I eat for free." Harper moved from around the table. "Follow me."

Like the server, Harper knew the smoothest way through the crowd and tables. She and Red slipped into the kitchen, which was small but seemed to manage the load. The enormous man at the stove already had several bread trenchers, bowls, and plates filled with food spread out on the cooking block. And with the man's thick shoulder-length hair and long beard done up in two braids, Red wondered how much of it got into the food. It was with some unspoken signal that the cook whipped up two extra plates and set them down at the end of the block.

"Thanks, Marcel," she said.

He gave a sharp nod and returned to his work. Harper led Red behind the kitchen to a small room with a round table and two chairs.

"He isn't Pops?"

"No, that's one of his sons," Harper said. "His other son works as the bouncer."

"Is this your private eating place?" Red asked.

Harper laughed. "More or less. Coffee?"

"Please."

Her eyebrows rose.

"I may be a thief, but I do know basic manners."

There was a low running board against the wall where an old, dented coffeepot sat, along with several clay mugs. Harper picked up two and filled them with the dark brew. "Sometimes we have sugar and goat's milk to go with it, but not today."

"It's fine. I prefer it black."

Unless you were at least comfortably well-off, sugar and milk, even goat's milk, was a precious commodity. Without certification, getting such a luxury in the den would draw unwanted attention.

Harper set down each cup and slid into the chair opposite. "You wanted to talk?"

Getting right to the point. He liked that about her. "I have a proposition for you." He told her about the intel he'd received on the mask and that he planned on...*appropriating* it that night.

"I'm not a thief." Her eyes narrowed, and her brow furrowed.

"I know, I know," Red said. "But I could—" He didn't want to say 'use', although that's what he was doing. "I mean I would feel safer with you along."

She lifted her cup to her lips. "Oh?" She took a sip and eyed him over the rim.

Red knew people of culture considered it impolite to eat before the host, but he hadn't had a satisfying meal in a week. And the eggs, thick slices of ham, and fresh biscuits were calling to him, so he started in, and after a few moments Harper followed suit, not upset. Red didn't worship any gods, so there was no grace said either and Harper offered none. Gods were for others, the wealthy and devoted who, it seemed to Red, could not deal with their own demons. Most Gifted worshipped the Vine, but Innrone seemed to have no one deity.

"As I was saying, I suspect you could tell me if this was a safe venture?" Red asked.

"Since when is any thievery safe?"

Red laughed between mouthfuls. "Well said."

They ate in silence from then on and it wasn't until Harper had cleaned her plate that she pushed it aside and brought out her deck. Fascinated, Red put down his fork and watched as she laid out five in a cross pattern and put three others to her right facedown.

"The Lady of Lies. The Deceiver. The Piper." She turned over the five. "The Knot. The Jack. The Prisoner." Harper frowned as she turned over the last three. "Ace of Wands. The Reaper." She looked up. "Who told you about this mask?"

"That rat, Felix."

Her eyes widened. "Really? Now why would he do that?"

"I had a talk with him after that incident. I suppose he figured giving this information would keep me from killing him." At Harper's look, he said, "But I had no plans to."

Harper made no sign of whether she believed him but went back to the cards. "You know what the Reaper means, I assume?"

"I'm going to die?"

"Not necessarily," Harper said. "It can mean a significant change or a new beginning. The Ace of Wands in this position is saying in the simplest terms that you lack direction." She lifted her gaze to him again. "Should I continue?"

"Yes."

"You saw the Lady of Lies and the Deceiver earlier and what they mean," Harper continued. "Everyone knows the story of the Pied Piper and how he led the children away." She tapped the card with the Knot. "This means that you are going to be in a situation that is impossible for you to escape without great cunning."

Red tried hard not to smirk. Great cunning was something he had in droves.

"I wouldn't recommend you go forward with your plans," Harper said.

It was not what Red wanted to hear, but why ask the advice of a diviner if you would not follow it?

Something happened then. Red didn't know what, but Harper's expression went blank, as though she were no longer in the room but somewhere far away. Her pupils grew large, swallowing the deep brown of her eyes.

Then she screamed.

"Harper!" Red lunged across the table and grabbed her by the shoulders. A shudder passed through her body, and she seemed to come back to herself. There was fear in her eyes for a moment as they locked with his, and her mouth moved as though there was something urgent she needed to say.

"Harper!" Marcel rushed into the room with a meat cleaver clutched in his hand. "Get away from her, you bastard!"

"Shite." Red knew there was no way he could explain in time. He released Harper and planted both hands on the table, pushing back. Marcel brought the cleaver down and missed Red's arm by a hairsbreadth. In moments, Red took his second form, came to his feet, and let out a guttural growl.

"Demon!" Marcel cried.

Red crouched into a fighting stance and readied himself for the next attack when Harper's voice halted everything. "Marcel, stop!"

"Harper? What did that freak do to you?"

"Marcel," Harper chided, "you know better than that."

It surprised Red when Marcel's cheeks flushed. The big bad cook was reacting as though Harper were his mother! Red would have laughed if he didn't believe that would reignite Marcel's anger.

"I thought he hurt ye," Marcel said. "Look at him!"

By then, Red had regained his human form.

"I swear, Harper, he was a demon!"

"He's not a demon." Harper's voice was calm. "He's a shape-shifter."

Had Harper seen his second form? Not that it seemed to matter to her. His respect for the woman increased tenfold.

"And I'm not hurt," Harper said. "A vision took me."

Marcel grunted. "Well, as long as you're a'right."

Harper didn't reply, but her expression revealed she was not all right.

Marcel set a malicious gaze on Red and pointed the cleaver at him. "Mind yourself, demon."

When they were alone, Red approached the table. "Are you all right? What did you see?"

Harper drew in and expelled a deep breath. "Darkness. I've seen nothing like it before." She wrapped her arms around her chest. "It was living darkness. It was fear and anger. Anguish and loneliness." She shuddered.

Red wasn't certain if he should ask, "Why do you think you saw it?"

"The cards," Harper said. "They linked my vision to your reading. This thing, whatever it was, entwined with the destiny that will come about if you continue."

Red didn't like that at all. But in his life, he'd never backed down from a challenge. Only cowards did that. And he was no mere human. He refused to be afraid, even if this living darkness was stealing about. He was Red, the greatest thief in all the Riven Isles.

"Thank you for your words, Harper," Red said. "I won't ask you to come with me."

Harper looked at him, her expression unreadable. "I'll come."

Red grinned. "Thank you. I'll up the cut just for you."

"I want nothing."

"What?" His brows furrowed in confusion. "But why?"

"I have my own reasons," she said. "I will tell you if I have another vision or if the situation changes."

"All right then," Red said. "I'll come for you at new morning."

"Fine."

He asked nothing more. He understood having your own reasons for doing something and Red respected Harper enough not to ask for further explanation. It filled him with confidence as he left the den, but somewhere, deep in his soul, there was a bit of something that he could only describe as a seed of doubt.

CHAPTER THREE

Harper lay in the darkness as the first hour of the morning approached. She had a good idea of when Red would arrive. The den was still open, and Harper heard the muted sounds of merriment. Those of the common folk might stay until sunrise, then stumble on home to either an empty, lonely bed or a furious wife waiting with whatever kitchen tool she favored to deliver a vicious crack across his noggin. The more well-to-do would curl up with lovers like a languid cat and return home if they were so inclined. All these thoughts came to her and filled her mind. Anything to forget the darkness.

It was ironic that she was lying in the dark. She supposed she should light a lamp, but her visions seemed more focused without light. But tonight, no visions had come, which disturbed her. Tired of sweating atop the coverlets, Harper got up and dressed. After feeling her way to the door, she exited her room. The sounds of revelry filled the hallway. The light was dim, so her eyes didn't need to adjust. She walked downstairs into the common room.

It was familiar to her, but there was something different. Harper couldn't quite place her finger on it, but—

"Good morning."

"Shite!" Harper drew her knife, turning on her heel and slashing, barely missing Red's chest. He somehow leaped back in time.

"Holy hells!" he said.

"Don't steal upon me like that!" She took in several sharp breaths.

"I'm sorry." His expression was one of shock.

"No, no," Harper said. "It was my fault. I let myself go deep in thought."

"I shouldn't have come up behind you."

She didn't see that anyone had noticed the incident. "Let's step outside."

The night air was oppressive. Not surprising because Innrone was near one of the four lakes that formed the Piper's Keys, and when it was hot, a mist would rise from them, although no one knew how. Some claimed it was supernatural. Harper was certain there was a real-life explanation. Although the north end of the city beyond the forest was Cryssil Lake, where they said the air was always cool and smelled of sea salt, the lake was fresh water. Harper wished she could go there someday, but people seldom ventured into the forest alone.

"What were you thinking about?" Red asked as they walked away from the den.

"I don't know." It was true. She didn't know what was bothering her. She hadn't thought to do a reading before his arrival.

"Have you had visions?"

"No," she said. "Which is strange."

"But not necessarily a terrible thing?"

Harper wasn't amused. "I'll do a read the first chance I get." She eyed the street. "Do you have a horse?"

"No."

She lifted a brow. "You were going to leave the city and walk to the forest?"

"Yes."

She laughed and shook her head. "Do you know how long that will take? Wait here." Harper stepped into the alley alongside the building.

"Wait, where—"

Harper ignored him and continued. Behind the den was a ramshackle shed lit by a single hanging lantern. The scent of new straw and animal musk wafted from within. Harper lifted the lantern off the hook and stepped inside. The old mottled-gray donkey perked her ears up as she recognized her.

"Hey, Jennie-girl."

Pops demanded they take care of and walk her. She was a beast of burden, as was common, but every so often, they used her for travel.

Harper hoped Pops realized she was the one who had taken her. It was likely he would, because if anyone other than she, Pops, or the brothers tried to, the donkey would raise a right good fuss. Harper took the bridle and fitted it over her head. "Come on, Jennie-girl, we're going for a ride."

She led the donkey back out of the alley.

"An ass?"

"A donkey," Harper corrected.

"Oh."

"Here, hold on to this." She handed him the lantern before mounting, but he hesitated.

"Don't worry, she's gentle with me. She won't bite you…unless you annoy her."

Red passed the lantern back and mounted behind her and settled himself. Harper squeezed Jennie-girl's sides with her ankles.

"I'm glad no one can see us."

"Why?" Harper said. "She's a good girl. I figured a thief would know horses are expensive."

"Of course," Red said. "Sorry again."

He was silent as Harper navigated Jennie-girl through the streets, filled with voices and movement. The wealthy seldom came into the city after dark. At night, Innrone belonged to the laborers and servants, the revelers, carousers and, of course, the less-respectable denizens of the city. Harper was a part of it all, so she had no fear.

Even on the sturdy jennet, it would take a quarter hour for them to leave the city behind and arrive in the woods. Harper was fine with the silence between them, but Red was not.

"I meant to say how impressed I am by your power." Harper heard genuine interest in his voice. "Have you had it all of your life?" He amended, "If you don't mind talking about it."

"I don't mind at all." It wasn't like it was a secret. "Yes, I've had this power as long as I can remember."

"Self-taught?"

"Mostly," Harper said. "There was an elderly soothsayer in the city who gave me lessons before she passed away. She also gave me my deck."

"Mm," was Red's response.

"What about you?"

He chuckled. "No, I haven't always been a thief." He was silent, and Harper figured that was all she would get from him.

"I'm self-taught." Was that bitterness she detected in his voice? "I'm surprised I got this far without being hanged."

"You could find some other way?"

His laugh was softer. "This is all I know."

"What about your family?"

"What about your family?" Red's tone was almost accusatory. "Sorry."

Harper figured it was a sore subject, so she let it pass. "Pops is my family. He and his sons are my brothers. I don't remember who my actual parents are, although...."

"Yes?"

"My first memory is of being in a gambling den. There were men around the table playing cards." They had reached the edge of the city. Harper hadn't noticed the time passing. "There was a man closest to me who called me his good luck charm."

"Maybe he was your father or uncle?"

"It's possible. I don't know since someone killed him." She recalled standing on tiptoe, trying to see over the table's edge to watch the group of men move the cards with deft fingers. Lamplight flickered off the piles of gold and jewels. The faces were blank, their voices silent, for although Harper heard the murmuring, their lips didn't move, or at least not until they prayed to some god for a good hand.

"The man beside me won the pot," Harper continued. "A man sitting across from him revealed himself to be one of the Gifted."

Harper recalled the man across the table, raising his hand with his arm extended, his palm out. There was a flash of yellow light and a scream of fear and pain.

The man next to her was on fire.

"Damn to the nether-hells." Red's voice was soft. "I'm sorry."

"Don't be," Harper said. "I don't even remember his face."

They rode in silence.

"I lost my family," Red said finally. "I was very young and had to live by my wits. I had no one to take care of me."

"Now *I'm* sorry."

"Don't be," he said. They didn't speak again after that.

★ ★ ★

The owner of the manor clearly preferred his privacy, as there was a lengthy lane that stretched out before them between the road and the manor house, but also the man stupidly showed his wealth by lining said lane with glowing torches. The light burned soft white within glass orbs, which sat atop ornate brass poles. Harper couldn't identify what made the unearthly glow. It wasn't fire.

"Wil-o-wisp." There was a bitter edge to Red's voice. Harper knew wil-o-wisp were living beings of magic, so it would take a magician of substantial power to seal them within the orbs. It was an unnecessary cruelty.

"Wish I had the power to free them." Harper's eyes didn't leave the glowing orbs. "A sorcerer could shatter the orbs, or a witch whose specialty is the elements." Whatever sympathy she might have had for Red's intended target evaporated.

"Go off the road." Red pointed to the darkness to their right. Harper had seen it too, in the house's corner. When they moved off the road, the wil-o-wisp light followed them for a time.

Harper's cards whispered.

"Wait."

"What is it?"

Harper closed her eyes, breathed, trying to listen—

She'd always been able to hear them, and when many of them spoke, Harper could easily discern what each was saying. This time, it was a cacophony of words and sounds, below her range of hearing. "Something is wrong."

"Maybe you should stay out here?" Red suggested.

"No," Harper said. "I've never heard the cards—" She halted, expecting the scorn of someone who didn't know her.

But all he said was, "All right."

He turned the lamp down to a flicker, and they eased through the trees until they reached the open space where the manor sat. Harper tied Jennie-girl to a nearby tree.

Red was standing still. "I don't smell any horses."

Harper's eyebrow went up in the darkness, but she didn't comment. The cards were filling her head with frantic whispers. Despite that, she followed Red, crossed the clearing to the side of the house. He stopped and laid his hand against the brick. Harper wasn't sure if she should say anything, but when she opened her mouth, Red said, "It's empty."

Did he have the Gift? He'd not said. They continued to follow the wall to the rear of the house.

"Bring the light up," he instructed. "It's all right if it shows."

Harper adjusted the lantern flame as Red produced a pair of lockpicks. She watched him at his work until she heard a click. It was then she realized the cards had gone silent. Red opened the door and stepped inside. "It's likely safe to up the lamp," he said as Harper followed behind him and closed the door.

The lamp revealed a small rectangular table and four chairs. Harper held the lamp higher and turned full circle. Shelves lined with jars of various shapes and sizes. "Are you sure no one is here? Not even servants?"

"I'm sure." He'd found another lantern and lit it.

Harper took out her cards and pulled one chair out to sit at the table. "The cards are no longer speaking to me." She hoped they would show her what their warning had been.

The first card she drew was the Deceiver.

Harper muttered an obscenity under her breath. What was this? The third or fourth time she had drawn the Deceiver with Red involved? But when reversed, it meant someone was using Red's weaknesses against him. She looked up to speak, but he'd left the room. "Red?" As she stood, the Deceiver spoke. "Damn it to the nether-hells." Harper sat back down and drew another card. The Jack reversed, followed by the Jester. "Red?" she called again. The Jack and the Jester were speaking. When Harper drew the Lady of Lies, she'd had enough.

"Red!" Harper shoved back from the table, gathered her cards in a swipe, and strode into the next room.

The darkness was there.

It swallowed the lamplight behind it and moved before her in a wave. As Harper raised the lamp, it did little to chase the darkness away. She saw it crawling like a swarm of insects up the walls, and it bubbled like tar beneath her feet.

Harper couldn't move or speak. She wanted to scream, but when she tried, no sound came out. Where was Red? Harper realized that her arm still held up the lantern, and her muscles stretched taut to protest. Harper fought to hold on to the lamp, knowing if it fell and shattered, she'd be in an inferno.

Then came the visions.

They came, dozens at a time, one bleeding into another. Flashes of evil things that flourished in the darkness, with burning white eyes, peered out from their shadowed hiding places, their gaze like daggers thrust into her soul.

They gathered in a group and stared.

The visions continued around her, scenes of people and places she knew she'd never met or visited. Of a place deep within the earth. Somehow, she knew it was Underneath, where no human dared expect to return unscathed. It was the realm underground, where true creatures of magic dwelled, quite often in the shadows. Her vision pulled her deeper beyond the kingdoms of Underneath to a place that no human eyes witnessed.

Emotions washed over her, not her own. There was anger, grief, sadness, but what caused her to weep was loneliness. It came not from any of the denizens who watched her, but from something at the heart of the darkness.

For a moment she glimpsed its face, and it said its name.

Harper found her voice and screamed.

Then everything vanished. The darkness, the beings, the visions. Harper stood amid an empty room. The entropy gone, Harper crumpled to the floor. The lantern slipped from her nerveless fingers but by the grace of some deity, it didn't shatter.

"Harper!" It was Red. "What happened?"

Still caught up in the flood of emotions, she turned on him. "Where in the nether-hells were you?"

"I found his hiding place," he said. "I thought—"

"It – something – was here!" Harper said. "Didn't you see it?"

"No." He dropped on his haunches next to her. "What do you mean, something was here?"

"Saw it before." Harper shook her head as though she could shake away the memories. All it did was make her skull throb. "No, it was a Rot, and it was alive."

In the dim glow of the lamp, she saw his brow crease. "Stay here. I'm going to get my prize."

He left her, not asking if she was all right. Harper forced herself to move. She turned her body to the side and pulled herself onto her hands and knees. The lantern burned low, but the second one in the kitchen was steady, like nothing was amiss.

Harper stumbled into the kitchen and sat again. She heard the frantic whispers of the cards, which she'd not heard before. Were they going on all this time?

Red returned, carrying a polished wood box. "This is it." His expression was one of longing. "Are you all right?"

"Now you ask me?" It took a moment for Harper to realize she had taken out her cards to lay them in the Celestial Cross pattern.

"I'm sorry," Red muttered, his hands moving over the box in what seemed a caress. He took out his lockpick and went to work.

The Deceiver, the Lady of Lies. The Knot.

He lifted the lid and withdrew a mask. It was beautiful, even Harper had to admit. The artist had made it of fine porcelain, smooth and white as fresh milk. The lamplight gave it a glow much like the wil-o-wisp. Precious gems of different types sparkled like tiny multicolored stars, arranged evenly around the eyes. Someone had taken a brush to it, creating a delicate motif along the edges, of vines entangled.

The Jester. The Prisoner. Ace of Bones reversed.

"Gods," Red whispered, more to himself. "He was right. This must be worth a fortune."

Seven of Wands reversed. Five of Wands reversed. Ten of Grails reversed.

Red held on to the mask and pushed the box aside, turned it around in his hands. "We better go. It's never good to tempt fate, don't you agree?"

Harper laid down the last card.

The Reaper.

CHAPTER FOUR

The mask in his grasp, Red sat behind Harper as they rode into the city. Neither had spoken since leaving the manor. He knew Harper was angry with him. She'd warned him about the cards, including the last one, the Reaper. Red tried to laugh it off in his thoughts, but the card kept appearing there as though it were speaking to him.

If he looked at the mask, he could push the memories to the back of his mind. It was difficult juggling it and the lantern. Red wished he could just toss the lantern aside. Of course, if he did that, he couldn't see his prized treasure.

"Do you think it's worth it?"

He scarcely heard Harper's question. "What?"

Harper snorted.

Red figured they were both eager to get back to the city. Sleep was pulling at him, but there was a fire coursing through his veins. A fever that made his flesh burn.

"We're here."

Red looked up. They were in front of the gambling den. Red slid off the donkey. "Thank you, Harper. I'll bring you your cut—"

"I said I wanted nothing." Red realized how very upset she was. "Especially not now. You need to get rid of it."

"Tonight," Red said.

Harper growled in frustration, and without another word, she led the donkey away.

Red wanted to get to one of his hiding places before daylight, so he ran on the dark street, not paying any mind to anyone he knocked into, their cursing not affecting him at all. As with Harper, he barely heard them.

After the incident with the shopkeepers, he'd gotten a room above an abandoned storefront. The owner lost the business years ago but still made some coins renting rooms above the store with no questions asked. Red slipped into his room and walked to the chest of drawers near his bedside, then lit the lamp he had sitting there. He still held the mask.

Red sat on his bed, swung his legs over, and leaned against the headboard. He turned the mask over in his hands. "You're going to fetch me a pretty penny." He knew who would buy the mask. A wealthy woman who collected unusual artifacts and wasn't choosy about where they came from. And she always paid good money. After this, he would stop and retire, respectably. Leave the Riven Isles. Leave the memories behind in the lands across the Stormbringer Sea. It was those thoughts that were still on his mind when he fell asleep with the mask clutched in his hand.

He dreamed of riches all around him. Of lying in an enormous bed, draped in red silk sheets and soft down pillows. The furniture was just as opulent. Hand-carved pieces in polished wood with decorative cushions. There was paper on the walls, something only the wealthy did, with scenes of birds in flight, ribbons in their beaks, adorning the trees with them. Beautiful maidens danced into his room, one carrying delights on silver trays, fancy little cakes and exotic fruits. Another bought a cask of wine and a gold goblet, followed by a third carrying a small harp. She draped herself over one chair and strummed a haunting melody. Red grinned in his sleep. He wanted this kind of life.

One maiden fed him a cake while the other poured wine and handed the golden goblet to him. He saw his reflection in the dark liquid and grinned again before taking a healthy drink. When he lowered the cup, everything changed.

The maidens were standing still as statues. Their eyes were pools of liquid the color of tar. They cried tears of ink. His head whipped around to the maiden offering the cake, and the ink ran down her cheeks in steady rivulets. Red drew in a sharp breath, twisted his body around to crawl away, only to come face-to-face with the wine-carrying maiden, who smiled at him with jagged teeth.

They were not beautiful. They were malformed and hideous. Something out of a nightmare. They drew his attention to the door as others piled into the room, fighting or leaping over their compatriots. They were goblins, Duine Shee, basilisks, Red Caps, boggarts, grymlins, and a host of others Red didn't recognize. How they filled the room was a mystery.

At first, fear had him shrinking back against the pillows, but over the years, he had trained himself to make his dreams his own, so he pushed the fear back and crawled to the head of the bed on his hands and knees, "So you want a fight, do you?" He called to that feral side of him to come forth. He'd tear them to bloody pieces— Nothing.

The creatures laughed, some tittering, others giving great guffaws. "What's happening?" Red sat up on his haunches, looked at his hands – his normal human hands. His eyes darted around, looking in desperation for a way out. There was nothing beyond the door but the darkness. Red pushed himself off the bed in a clumsy move as taloned hands reached for him, scratching, and clawing at his skin. There was genuine pain as he fought his way through the mass of evil, yet they weren't trying to stop him. Even though his feet moved as if mired in mud, he made it to the door and fell into endless night.

He saw the face and knew it to be the being that frightened Harper in the manor. And like Harper, it battered him with fear, anger, loneliness, all the emotions that made some want to kill and others to die. Red went to his knees, wrapping his arms around his chest. Something burst forth through the blackness and came for him, something – no, someone – familiar who had hated him and bared teeth and claws to tear him apart.

Red jerked awake as it reached him, so real that he felt the fetid breath against his neck. His heart hammered in his chest with his ragged breathing. It was so dark it almost convinced him he was still in the dream. Something continued to be wrong. His face. Why did it feel so strange? Red placed his hands on his cheeks. They caressed the smooth surface and tiny jewels.

Red fumbled for the chest of drawers. He was shaking as he opened the top one, drew out a match, and lit the lamp. The mask narrowed his vision to the eyeholes. How had it gotten on his face? Had he done it in his sleep? Why hadn't it fallen when he'd awoken? He felt behind his head, but there were no straps or ties. He grasped the edge of the mask on either side of his head and pulled.

It refused to come off.

As he tried, pain erupted in his chest. An invisible hand squeezing his heart. He drew his hands away. The pain diminished, but there was still a burning hole left there. Red rubbed the spot in his chest above it, but that only aggravated it. The first seed of panic, sown in the pit of his stomach, blossomed. Pulling again yielded the same results.

All right, I must keep calm. There is magic involved.

Red tried to avoid magicians. He found them too volatile. Except that is, for Harper. But what could she do? He didn't need a diviner. Of course, if he'd listened to Harper in the first place— No time for self-recriminations. He needed to find out what was happening to him. Harper wasn't the only Gifted he knew.

Red pushed himself off the bed and stood. He crossed the room to the small closet and drew out something he hadn't worn in what seemed a lifetime. A hooded cloak, red silk and lined with fur. It would draw attention with the summer heat but not as much as the mask would. He figured he didn't have a choice.

At least he could do one thing with it. "Please," he said aloud. The change came as it always had, and Red used his claws to tear away the fur lining. At least he wouldn't be too uncomfortable. He slipped on the cloak. The thing gripping his heart in his chest pulsed with each beat. He hadn't noticed that before. Red fought not to touch his chest.

He slipped out of his room, down the narrow staircase to the rear door, but as he stepped outside, the world around him was—

There was no morning sun creeping its way into the alley. It hadn't rained in days and the sky had been stark blue, devoid of clouds. The humidity had also gone away, and the air was hot and dry.

But that wasn't what Red saw.

Above him, the sky boiled with clouds an angry green. The closed-in buildings were mere ruins of what they had been, nothing left but jagged pieces of wood, rotted and burn-scarred. It was the bodies, bloodied and mutilated, that caused the bile to rise from his stomach. Faces frozen in fear and shock – those that had faces. Their eyes stared sightlessly at him. Nearby, he heard a malicious chuckle. Red whipped around, but there was no one there. The mask, it had to be.

He clutched the folds of the cloak to his chest. *I will not be afraid.* But even as he thought those words, a chill raced across his skin. When the laugh came again, he resisted the urge to turn. Drawing in a deep, ragged breath, he moved past the carnage, keeping his gaze forward. He continued down what should have been the alley between the storefront and the building next door.

When it opened out into the street, Red halted and stared, drawing in a sharp breath at the scene. Dozens of people, instead of going about their business, having conversations, or haggling with merchants, were but gaunt, pale figures dressed in coarse woolen rags the color of coal dust. They were men, women, and children, who shuffled along with no purpose and cried the ink tears he'd witnessed in his dream.

Red squeezed his eyes shut under the mask. "Please," he said for the second time. Although there was no god, he believed enough to beseech. When he opened his eyes and concentrated hard enough, he saw, beneath the horrid sights, regular people, none the worse, going about their everyday business.

All right, so this is an illusion.

Still, it would not be easy making his way along. Red drew in a deep breath and stepped from the alley, keeping close to the buildings. His movements were slow and deliberate, although he knew such actions would draw attention. Light flashed above him, and he lifted his gaze for a time and saw jagged bolts of red lightning. Where the sun should have been, there was nothing but a sickly gray orb, barely giving light. His head ached the more he stared upwards and tried to see the actual sky.

It was difficult to keep moving. It was by happenstance and the fact that Red knew this city like his own heart that he could continue along. Again, concentrating for too long made his head hurt, so he had to stop after a time. It was slow going, and for the first time in his life, Red wanted to just crawl away somewhere and hide. Several times, he was certain someone was following him, but who among the wraiths?

In a desperate move, he ducked into another alley, forced his vision to clear, and relief filled him when he recognized where he was. Rooming houses like his own but better kept—that is, when he was seeing them. One on the top floor had a flight of stairs leading to the entrance. Red ran up, drew his claws, latched on to the low-hanging eaves, and pulled himself up on the roof.

Now at least no one could sneak up on him. Then again, one wrong step and he would plummet to his death. But he figured he had no choice. He only saw a few of the wraiths on other rooftops, but they paid him no mind. A few times, he had to jump between gaps in the buildings and muttered a prayer each time, deciding that if he had to pray to something, it would be the Celestial Vine. Although, he wondered, could you consider a massive plant a god? He managed to laugh at that thought.

Relief flooded his being when he arrived at his destination. He found a safe place to climb down. He knocked at the door nestled within a small garden wall. When it opened, The sight of a normal little boy left Red grateful. He was about ten, with big brown eyes full of curiosity. "Please, is Madam Dahilde in?" Red asked.

The boy nodded once and stood aside. Everything about the room was normal, despite the strange items in jars hanging from the ceiling and tacked to the walls, the mismatched, yet comfortable-looking chairs in no order around the room, and the shelves filled with books. Red breathed a deep sigh.

"May I help you?"

He knew her only as Madam Dahilde. At an impressive nine feet tall, her frame was draped in colorful robes despite the heat. Descended from the long-vanished race of giants, or not a descendant at all, for giants were long-lived. Contrary to the stories of giants being stupid and savage monsters, they were quite peaceful and intelligent. Nor were they hundreds of feet tall, going around stomping out villages and tearing up the countryside. They lived in a city in the clouds long ago, built by their own scholars, and only came down for need and information. But the greed of man forced them to flee to skies unknown. However there were rumors of giants trapped in the Riven Isles, unable to join their people.

Red pushed back the hood of the cloak. "Please, Madam Dahilde—"

"What in the nether-hells!" She strode forward until she towered over him. "What did you get yourself into, boy?"

There it was. He didn't have to say any more. "I don't know," Red said. "I was hoping you could tell me."

Dahilde shook her head and turned with a flourish. "Come with me."

Red followed her through the doorway from where she'd entered. There were even weirder things there, but it was a long table against the left wall that she approached. Atop it were various boxes and chests. She opened a rectangular box with no decorations or symbols and took out a handful of polished engraved bones. It reminded him of Harper and her cards. Necromancy was another form of divination.

"Sit." She pointed to the floor, and for the first time, Red noticed the rune circle etched there. He obeyed.

Dahilde settled herself across from him and, without preamble, tossed the bones in the middle of the circle, examined them for a time, and shook her head again. "Where did you get that mask?"

Red was loath to tell her.

"Speak, boy!"

"From a manor house out in the woods."

"Take it off, now!"

"I can't!" Red clenched his fists. "Don't you think I tried that?"

Dahilde made a gesture with both hands, joining her middle fingers and thumbs. The hole in Red's chest pulsed. He growled, doubled over, crossing his arms across his body as the pain continued, until it mortified him when tears welled. It only stopped when Dahilde separated her fingers.

"Stupid child," she said. "Tell me, outside of these walls, what do you see out of the eyes of the mask?"

"Nightmares," Red replied. "I can see what is real if I examine things hard enough, but then my head aches." He looked around. "Does your Gift keep me from seeing those horrors?"

"Yes," she said, "the mask is showing you a nether world, not like the nether-hells, but close to it. Just a veil away from one, and that anchor inside of you—"

"Anchor?"

"A more specific name for it is an etheri." Dahilde inclined her head towards him. "Through the mask, they placed it inside of you, linking you to that other world. You are quite fortunate."

"How in the—" Red worked to change his voice. "How am I fortunate?"

"Someone did this to trap you," Dahilde said. "That person wanted you to suffer but not to kill you. Had they wanted that, the mask would have taken you straight to the nearest hell and you could never come back."

Red couldn't believe what he was hearing. "But who? Why?"

Dahilde gathered up the bones again, rolled them between her palms, and threw. "That I cannot answer. They are in the living world. But whoever it is, they have a great hatred for you."

Who could it be? Someone he had stolen from? Then something else occurred to him. "Wait, I stole—" For the first time in his work as a thief, his cheeks flushed with embarrassment. "This was a random thing. The mask was there for the taking."

"No, it wasn't," Dahilde said. "But again, this is within the realm of the living."

"There was a man, Felix, who told me about it, but I've never met him before yesterday," Red said. "How could he have known to set me up?"

"He didn't," she said. "Someone else, someone more powerful than he, pulled the puppet strings. The person who hates you knew you could never resist this mask. Look into your past, thief. That is where you will find your enemy." She gathered up the bones. "I cannot look into the past. Only a witch, or specifically a diviner, is capable of that."

"Harper."

"Who?"

"Harper, she tried to warn me."

"Is she a diviner?"

"Yes, a tarotmancer."

"And you didn't take heed?" She rolled her eyes. Of course, she must think he was a complete ass and perhaps— No, he *was* an ass. Harper had warned him, and he let his pride and greed lead him right into a trap. And his enemy had known him well enough to see that was what he would do.

"Can you remove the mask?"

"No," Dahilde said. "Only the one who created and cast the spell can do that." She smiled with white, even rows of teeth. "I would suggest visiting your diviner friend again and asking her for a reading."

Did he need to ask for another reading? "The last card," Red muttered.

The necromancer raised her eyebrow.

"The last card in her reading. It was the Reaper."

"The Reaper doesn't mean you're going to die." Dahilde climbed to her feet and stretched. She was truly an imposing figure now. "I told you, if that person wanted you dead, you'd be a corpse by now. See your friend again. There is nothing more I can do."

But there were things *he* could do. Find Felix and wrest the truth from him, and if he didn't know, he would find the owner of the manor and make him suffer. Either way, someone would pay for this assault.

CHAPTER FIVE

It was impossible not to stare at the entourage of foreign soldiers that marched through the middle of the square and continued towards the royal manor. Harper watched them from the doorway of the den and pulled out her deck, shuffled, cut it twice, and drew three cards. This worked just as well on a table. The first card – the Celestial Vine reversed. The second, the Witch, and the third, Ten of Coins reversed. As Harper was pondering the three, she looked up again at the entourage and stared into the eyes of one rider.

She wasn't a soldier, although dressed in a similar style in a smart but functional trouser suit, in like colors. The woman was beautiful and dark-skinned, although not as deeply so as Harper. She did her hair up in hundreds of small braids. There was a wood staff secured across her back. The woman smiled at her. Harper didn't know why, but she smiled back, feeling her cheeks warm.

Then the woman was past her, continuing in the procession.

It piqued Harper's curiosity. It was too early in the morning for anyone to be visiting the den and she hadn't gone to sleep after the incident in the manor with that damnable thief. Harper crossed her arms over her chest and gave an annoyed huff. She was furious that the thief had dismissed her warning with such disrespect. Especially after the vicious attack she'd endured. Just thinking about it now— No, she couldn't think about it. She'd stayed awake last night, being fearful of sleep. Since she was used to late nights, it didn't bother her much. Yet she couldn't help but go over it in her mind, trying to figure what that thing was and why it revealed itself to her.

Now, seeing the strangers, she had something else to focus on, so Harper moved down the street, following in their wake. Since the crowds of people made way for them, they were easy to trace. Besides, their presence was the most noticeable thing to happen in months.

Magdalen Brigette, Duchess of Innrone, ruled on behalf of her aunt, the queen, who preferred to stay in the capital of Piper's Keys. Since she'd lost her husband, Duke Lars, in a supposed hunting accident – but no one believed that – she seldom, if ever, came out among the rabble. Except for every holiday or celebration, when she would come to one balcony of the manor, smile, and wave, basking in the adoration, which Harper thought was undeserved. She looked like she would rather not bother.

They arrived at the gates and the guards hustled the entourage inside. Now that she thought about it, Harper couldn't recall the last time the duchess appeared, even on the balcony. The manor hadn't received callers for weeks. Rumors abounded, of course, some saying she was ill, or worse yet, dead, and the high chamberlain or some low-level vassal was ruling Innrone. Not that it mattered to Harper. If they didn't raise taxes and the guards let them be, she wasn't all that concerned with who sat in the fancy chair.

Still....

When the gates closed behind them, Harper turned left down Crown Way, which ran parallel to the manor. At the corner of the next cross street sat a reputable gambling den. Unlike Pops', this den catered to the wealthier clients, who could enjoy good food and drink, expensive cigars, and willing women. Most laborers didn't visit because they found it too pompous. But no gambling den turned someone away if they had money to fill the coffers.

So, when Harper walked in, she looked around for an empty spot at one of the card tables. The air was thick with sweet smoke, raucous laughter, and fried meat, and Harper realized she hadn't eaten yet. She wasn't rich, but she could afford a good meal every now and again.

Harper noticed someone she knew at a table in the far corner of the room, a chambermaid named Helene, so she made her way over. As luck would have it, one unfortunate player was taken for everything by the others. He pushed back from the table like a petulant child and stormed off, the laughter of the other players following him. Harper greeted her friend, bought into the game of Red Dog, and slipped into the empty chair.

The server approached, and Harper gave her order. Three people were at the table. Helene introduced Harper, and the others introduced themselves as well. Upon finding out Harper was a diviner, they all clamored for readings after the game. She didn't have long to wait before the subject turned to the foreign soldiers.

"Helene," a young man named Peter, who was a blacksmith, said to her friend, "what's all this about foreign soldiers visiting the manor?"

"They arrived in town last night. They sent a messenger to the high chamberlain to request an audience."

"What for?"

Helene leaned closer, although there was too much noise in the room for anyone to overhear. "You hear of the war in Rhyvirand."

"War?" Peter said. "It was a minor skirmish, I'm told!"

Harper had learned the opposite. It was an all-out war. Wilhelm of Rhyvirand had used some type of magical artifact to conquer Tamrath and Avynne. Refugees escaping both kingdoms had carried with them rumors of Wilhelm using dark magics to keep himself young and virile. She'd also been told about the king of Avynne abandoning his people. If the man was smart, he'd keep himself well hidden because, if anyone found him, they would put him to death in the most horrid way imaginable.

"But there was a coup, and we received news that they ousted Wilhelm Stark," Helene continued.

"Who rules there now?" Peter asked.

"The Arch-bishop of Tamrath." Helene leaned forward again. "There is a witch by his side."

"What's so awful about that?" Peter said, "Miss Harper, you're a witch, aren't you?"

Harper shrugged because she wanted to get back to the subject. "So why are they here in Innrone?"

"Not sure," Helene said.

"Perhaps the trouble down south is coming here?" Peter said.

"Who would want to conquer Innrone? It's not the largest of the Keys," Helene said. "They'd do better with Damarnyr or Bale."

"Who said anything about conquering?" The man who spoke introduced himself as Yagami, a clothing merchant from Jack-In-Irons.

"The soldiers," Helene said.

"So, who's doing the conquering?" Peter asked.

"All I know is it started in Underneath."

Now Helene had their undivided attention.

"One of the stable hands heard the soldiers talking about convincing the duchess to ally with them and some queen in Underneath because the Vine was in danger."

"Did he hear anything else?" Harper asked.

"No, they escorted them into the manor," Helene said. "Then one of the kitchen boys who laid out the sideboard in the audience chamber said one woman, a dark-skinned lady carrying a staff, said she felt some influence there."

"Influence?"

Helene shrugged. "Hell if I know."

Harper remembered the beautiful woman with the staff. What had she meant about influences?

"So did the duchess speak to them?" Harper asked when Helene fell silent.

"Yes, according to the kitchen boy, but they cleared the room before she arrived, so that's all we know."

Harper wanted to make sure there was nothing left out. "Did anyone see her?"

"No one has in weeks," she said.

"That makes little sense!" Peter said.

Yagami said, "The young man is correct. Someone is bringing her food, attending to her, drawing her bath?"

Again, Helene shrugged. "I'm not privy to that information."

"Helene, can you find out?" Harper asked.

"Why?"

"Just curious," Harper said. The smiling woman was still on her mind. "I just think it's important. Shouldn't we all want to know what's amiss?"

"I'll see what I can find out," Helene said. "You can ask for me at the postern gate as usual."

"Thank you." Harper was more than curious. "Why don't we finish this game, and I can start your readings?"

There was only one way to get to Underneath from Innrone.

There weren't many green areas around the city. If the citizens wanted anything like parks or fountains, the local leaders handled such things. Someone had thought to build a park on a steep mound of earth at the easternmost part. It had never come to fruition. Or at least that was the consensus. The only thing left of such an idea was a crumbling old well, dried up for years. Offshoots of the Vine now covered the opening and snaked down the collapsing sides.

As a child, Harper and the other street children had often placed bets on who had the courage to climb the hill, clear away the offshoots, and peer down into its depths. Harper had taken the bet, climbed the hill, eased aside the greenery, but it was too dark to see anything. She shrugged to herself and walked back down, and her friends crowded around her, eager to hear what horrors she had viewed, but since there were none, their disappointment was obvious.

An older boy and his sister – Harper had forgotten their names – convinced she had seen something and was just too afraid or too prideful to tell, both climbed the hill to see for themselves. Harper had no concern for what they thought of her and was ready to go home when a vision halted her in her tracks.

She was peering down into the depths of the well, but through the eyes of the boy, when a pod the color and texture of ink erupted from within, striking the boy in the face. He stumbled back, his arms windmilling and causing him to grab on to his sister to steady himself, pulling her down with him. For a while, the world was upending and rolling from sky to earth and by the time Harper came out of the vision, both the boy and his sister lay in a heap at the bottom of the hill.

Even though the boy and his sister suffered only minor injuries, after that, no one dared go near the well again. Not that it mattered because the city officials cordoned it off and threatened anyone who got near it with heavy fines.

Harper forgot all about the incident until the conversation in the high-end gambling den. She wondered if the darkness from the well and the darkness she'd seen in the manor that night with Red....

Red.

She'd almost forgotten about him and now found herself angry all over again. Playing cards had taken her mind off things and given her the drive to stay awake longer, but by the time she returned to the den, her feet were dragging. Instead of going through the front entrance, she went down the alley and slipped in through the kitchen door. She didn't want to have to speak to anyone just then. Marcel was sitting, reading the paper and smoking a cigar, and only grunted a greeting to Harper so she could get up to her room. Nothing much she could do now but try to get some sleep and hope she didn't have nightmares.

The cards started their whispering.

"Damn it to the nether-hells!" Harper dropped onto the bed with one leg tucked under her rear, the other hanging over the edge of the bed, and took them out. She'd never gotten angry at the cards before, knowing how important they were and what they had to say, but she just needed sleep right now. She had to rub her eyes to keep her vision from blurring.

The Prisoner.

The Deceiver reversed.

The Celestial Vine reversed. The Jester.

The Jack reversed.

The Knot.

Harper groaned in frustration and fell back onto the pillow, stretching her legs out down the bed.

It's none of your concern, Harper, just leave it be. How can you be sure the cards are even speaking about Red?

But of course, they were, and Harper knew. Then again, Red hadn't listened to her before. What made her think he'd listen to her now?

Never mind, no, never mind.

Harper couldn't say when she fell asleep, but she knew when she dreamed. Her Gift gave her a keen sense of lucidity. After much practice, she'd learned to separate herself from the happenings and observe like an audience member, watching a stage play, or just wake herself up. This was especially useful if a dream was going down a dark or frightening path.

However, with this dream, there was something wrong with her vision. It seemed…narrow, like something was covering her face.

Harper's brows knit as she tried to figure out what was happening. She lifted her hands to move them over her cheeks and drew in a breath at the unnatural smoothness until her fingers found tiny bumps that lay in a pattern.

Realization came. The mask. It had to be. The mask that Red had stolen. Now she was confused. She'd never worn the mask or even touched it. So why—?

When she moved, and it was without her willing it, Harper knew it was not her dream. This experience, so new, had her forgetting to concentrate, and when she did, she sensed someone, a living being, there with her behind the eyes. So instead of stepping aside, she allowed the dreamer to lead her. If it was the mask she was wearing, then unless Red had sold it like he'd said, this was Red's dream.

The problem with continuing meant she would experience Red's fear. Harper realized a steady thumping of a heartbeat in her ears, along with labored breathing. There was a pain in her chest that she couldn't quite describe, like there was something missing, a part of her pulled into a hole that sat dark and still.

Harper examined their surroundings as they walked. It was Innrone, but it appeared as though a war had raged through the streets, catching the innocent people in its wake. Bodies lay bloody and broken, some with their faces frozen by whatever horrors they had seen.

Harper shivered as Red did. His fear was a cold stone at the bottom of his stomach. This was no dream; it was a nightmare. Something else occurred to Harper. Why would the dream have him wearing the mask unless Red had put it on? Was he sleeping with it on right now?

When Red stepped out into the open street, Harper saw at the same moment. Wraiths shambled about, dressed in rags of tattered gray wool that hung on their rawboned bodies, not even fit for a scullery maid or shite tender. Ink tears fell from black, eyeless sockets and streamed down sallow cheeks. They not only seemed starved for food, but for meaning in their miserable lives.

Red was moving, creeping along the side of the road. His movements were deliberate. For a moment, Harper's fear dissolved into confusion. He wasn't moving like he was in a dream. The wraiths were not coming for him, and Harper had no feeling of the change that often comes when a dream slides into a nightmare. That anxious sensation that causes your whole body to tense, and your breath to be painful in your chest.

The longer she stayed, the more bewildered she became. Red dashed over the rooftops and came down to a door. He knocked, and it opened and there stood a little boy.

With the boy was a giantess, her expression both serious and fearful. And Harper realized this was no dream. This was a memory. All this had happened. This knowledge shocked her into wakefulness. Harper lay there for a while, frowning into the dusky light. She could smell food in the air and hear the voices of their first customers. She'd slept the day away.

"Red," Harper said aloud, "what in the nether-hells have you gotten yourself into now?"

Harper gathered up her deck. She would have to find the stupid ass and...and what? He'd ignored her reading, and whatever the mask had done to him, she doubted she could do anything about it. Well, she wasn't the only Gifted in the city. Somebody had to know how to...what? Red had boasted about selling the mask on the black market. Maybe it wasn't even in his possession anymore. But why the memory, then?

Harper needed to find him, but where to look? Simple. The black market. The one place where Harper did not want to go. But what choice did she have? She knew the places and people involved. Before she could change her mind, Harper left her room. She went through the kitchen again. Marcel was busy at the stove and didn't even notice her leave.

When Harper stepped out of the alley, she saw for the second time that day something that had the citizenry gathered. Dozens of men, laborers by their dress of drab trousers and shirts, made from burlap sacks, were pulling several wagons filled with dirt and rocks. Muscles corded and glistening with sweat in the sun as they struggled to move forward.

Young women gathered, calling and giggling at the men as though they would forsake their work and give them a good time, but of course, if you didn't work, you didn't get paid, and men like that made a pittance. Still, Harper moved to the front of the crowd and called out, "What is this about?"

It surprised Harper when one man, tall and bronze-skinned with hair flowing down his back, answered, "We're going to fill in the old well."

CHAPTER SIX

Red wasn't certain why he expected Felix to still be there. Likely, he'd fled right after Red had confronted him. He approached the proprietor, gathering the hood close in a vain attempt to hide his face. He knew it was likely fruitless and expected her to have all manner of questions. Instead, she went on a tirade about how that filthy thief had left her with two months of rent due. He'd left in the middle of it, making her go on a new rant about what a bastard Red was being.

And Red somehow realized his anger fed the darkness in his heart. It made him giddy, like he sipped on the best brandy, and focused on his goal. He imagined how the owner of the manor would cower before him. He'd lost his chance with Felix, and thinking some stupid son of a bitch had fooled him made the want of satisfaction sharpen to a knifepoint.

As Red strode back onto the primary avenue, the gathering crowd, which caused the knife blade to push deeper, halted him. No longer did he fear the wraiths, for they were merely hindrances to his purpose. He growled from between his teeth and pushed his way through, and when he stepped out in front, he noticed the group of men trotting down the street, pulling carts of dirt and rocks. Red walked, but not of his own volition. Like a man drawn to a lover, a need arose in him to follow the darkness. His goals forgotten, he found himself first jogging, then breaking into a run to keep up.

Where were they going? Red did not have to wait long. They got to the mound of dirt, where the old well stood at its summit. Red had never bothered going near it, especially not since the city forbade the citizenry to approach. He watched as the men pulled the carts up the slope.

Closer, closer, he silently urged. Something was waiting, and it wanted Red to see it. The men worked, some with pickaxes, chopping the last of the crumbling stones; others shoveled dirt, while the rest dumped whole wheelbarrows full of stones and bricks of various sizes and shapes. Red snorted in derision. Did they think they could shut them out?

Red didn't know if he was the first to feel it. A rumbling started light like the tremor one feels when faced with the unexpected. But it rapidly increased in volume, like a giant of legend brought back from his death sleep. A great roar filled the air. Perhaps it was the giant coming to life after these arrogant children disturbed his resting place. Red watched with glee as the earth around the well cracked. Great fissures opened, which spewed dust into the air.

Red was barely aware of the surrounding people. They screamed louder than whatever struggled to rise from underneath. The crowd fled as one, but Red stood firm, watching. Laughter bubbled up from his chest as people pushed and shoved and stumbled to get away, trampling and breaking their fellow man. Red continued to watch.

The hill collapsed, catching the workers who couldn't escape in time. They fell, their cries drowning out the rumbling. Red strode up the hill as the last of the frantic people pushed past him. He moved to the edge, peered over, and laughed again.

It entangled them in the dark, feeding the thing that now lived in Red. Their eyes bulged with fear, their expressions agony and their mouths gaping without sound. When the ground gave beneath him, his own fear suddenly filled that place in his chest. It protested, trying to force him to stay, to give himself up to the dark, but something, perhaps the animal side of him, refused. That wily fox that never gave a quarter. Red shook himself as though caught in sleep paralysis, turned, and ran back down the hill.

He saw nothing around him. The scenes moved by in a blur as he ran. He didn't consider where he was running to. He wanted to be away from the thing. All the while, the knife in his heart twisted to where his stomach roiled, and his head ached. Despite that, he forced himself to keep moving. When he couldn't take another step, Red collapsed and curled himself up in a ball.

He heard laughter coming from somewhere, malicious and taunting. *Here you are, the talented thief Red, the faint of heart, the fool!*

Red screamed to drown out the voice, and he continued to scream until his voice was hoarse and the one who taunted him became silent.

* * *

Nightmares brought him to abrupt wakefulness. His mind clouded and his body shivering, Red tried to make sense of where he was. He squinted in the gathering dusk. He was in the woods. How had he gotten there? He had to return to the city by nightfall. When he became more aware, Red realized he'd fallen underneath a tree when he reached up and felt the rough bark. Pushing against it, Red climbed to his feet. He assessed his legs and almost collapsed again. *Just take care of how you step, Red.*

He was deep in the woods and would have a hell of a time finding his way out, but to his shock, the trees thinned quickly, and he came out on the road. Next, the sense of familiarity. He was on the road he and Harper had taken....

Red tried to run but his legs wouldn't allow it, so he moved in a half run, half-stumbled gait until he got to the avenue lighted with the wil-o-wisp torches. But they were no longer there. Each glass bulb was smashed, the poles covered in rust, some with holes eaten through, to the point where they'd snapped in half.

He tightly closed his eyes again, although he knew the sight wouldn't change. What had happened? Red continued to walk until he came to the manor itself, not bothering to hide his approach this time. It was in ruins. By all evidence, no one had lived there in decades, with the shattered windows, overgrown grass, and sagging roof. Red figured it was much worse inside.

Harper's reading abruptly made sense to him.

He'd not only fallen into a trap, but an elaborately planned one, which would likely take a magician more powerful than Harper or anyone familiar to him. Movement within one of the window frames drew Red's attention. He squinted into the waning light. A face was gazing out at him, grinning with pointed teeth. It placed gnarled hands on the sill and hoisted itself up and over.

It was a squat, stunted thing. Its head seemed too large for its body. Its ears, wide and pointed, twitched as though to shoo away an annoying insect. It was naked and by its low-hung parts, it was male. Red saw what it was right away. A second crawled out of another window, while a third peeked around the doorframe.

Goblins.

What in all the nether-hells were goblins doing Above Ground? Red dared not move, uncertain he could outrun them in his human form. They made no move to approach him further. They seemed to wait, but for what?

Something else was coming from within the crumbling manor. A viscous fluid poured from every place open to the night air. It surrounded and flowed around the goblins, who danced and cheered in unbridled joy. And the darkness in his chest, which Red had found relief from for a brief time, came alive again, as tendrils reached out from the black mass, crawling towards him, curling like black worms disturbed in the dirt. The knowledge came to him. Harper had seen it that night. Again, she'd tried to tell him. Gods be damned, why hadn't he listened? He almost wept at his stupidity.

Come home, Reynard.

That name! How could it know? Of course it did. A part of it was inside him. With access to all his secrets. And as it spoke Red's name, it whispered the name it had taken for itself.

Rot.

He needed to get away. Red forced his legs to move, to turn and flee through the woods and down the lane.

Run, run, run, little fox. Soon you will come home.

★ ★ ★

Somehow, he made it back to the city. No small feat since he'd expected the Rot would simply ensnare him and drag him back, or the goblins would overcome him and tear him to pieces. And the part of the Rot entrenched in him? It had been mercifully still.

The city, however, was not. In fact, it was more active than usual. Most people went about their business despite guards. Some even taunted the guards, while others merely stayed out of their way. Red chose the latter.

The rumor mill was going strong. There were reports of the dead laborers crying out for help, so loud you could hear them throughout the city. He'd reached out to them, and their suffering nearly stopped him dead. The darkness was transforming them into creatures of evil. A witch conjured a ring of fire around the sinkhole. Red sensed the heat and the light, and the Rot shrank away from it.

Red's vision had not changed. There were shadows, but they moved independently of everything. And the impression they were watching his every step. He wanted – needed a place to hide.

But where could he go? None of his usual hideaways felt safe anymore. Besides, whoever trapped him likely knew everything about him. It made him want to shout into the night, *Here I am. Face me, you bastard! Or kill me and get it over with!*

Red came to Pops' Den without even realizing it. Dahilde sent him to Harper. Yes, he recalled now. She could tell him who it was by looking...into his past. He didn't want Harper looking into his past. What would she think of him? Red gave a harsh bark of laughter. Same thing she probably thought now, considering how much of an idiot he'd been.

When he peered into the window, he drew in a deep breath. Everything looked normal. But how? Harper? Was she more powerful than even his enemy? Then again, Dahilde's home had looked normal as well. Maybe you just had to be Gifted? Well, standing here pondering it wouldn't do him any good. Hoping he wouldn't cause too much of an uproar, Red pulled his hood up and held the sides closed as he entered.

Nobody paid him any mind. They were so into their gambling,

drinking, and wenching that they didn't even spare Red a glance. And he found he wasn't all that concerned. He was glad things looked ordinary.

"Can I help—"

Red turned at the voice. The serving wench drew in a sharp breath and pressed the back of her hand against her mouth.

"I need to see Miss Harper, please. It's an emergency."

"Oh—" The girl took two steps back, "Excuse me for a moment."

She left him standing there. Annoyed, Red moved to the bar and sat. He kept his head down and his mouth shut.

"Help you?" Red noticed the big man who stood in front of him, who was the size of an oak tree, if you were to ask. Salt-and-pepper hair bound in a ponytail, somewhat neatly trimmed beard. A scar ran down his face, barely missing his left eye, and, of course, the perquisite broken nose that came with being in this business. This had to be Pops.

"Harper, please."

"What you want with her?"

Red took a full breath and let it out. "I need her help. Could you tell her Red is here?"

The man narrowed his eyes, and a vein in his temple bulged. "So, you're Red, eh? Got my Harper into a mess of trouble."

Red looked into his eyes. "She's in trouble?"

"Well, she must be." His face reddened. "The city guard came looking for her today."

"Oh, gods—"

"Gods indeed," the man spat. "Anyhow, she had the good sense to make herself scarce."

"Where could she be?"

"Anywhere." The man balled his fists. "I just hope she's all right and comes back soon, but if she ain't—" he jabbed a meaty finger into Red's shoulder, "—I'll have yer ass, you son of a whore."

Red didn't know what to say. *I'm sorry? I never meant to get her into trouble.* Red thought, *Just kill me now.* Instead, he said, "Please, may I stay here and wait for her?"

Red thought Pops would refuse but he said, "Yeah, yer gonna stay here, all right. I don't want you sneaking off like the lying scum you are."

"Thank you." He'd never been so humbled. Pops put a glass in front of him and poured in an amber liquid. Red wasn't much of a drinker, but he figured the situation called for it. He had a few coins, which he placed on the bar before swallowing the whiskey and waving for another.

CHAPTER SEVEN

The cards warned. *Get away!*

Harper had to warn them, but how? Shout *run*? Would anyone listen? "Everyone, get away, now!" No one moved. Some glanced at her, but the rest remained entranced by what was going on.

"Listen to me! It's not safe here!"

"Quiet!"

"What insanity are you spewing?"

"You go away!"

Harper saw some had their children with them. "At least get the children away, let them go home!" Still, no one heeded her warnings.

The cards were screaming now. Their voices filled her ears and her mind, making her head feel like it was going to burst. She could only do one thing. She ran.

Please protect them. Don't let any innocents die.

Harper felt the tremors as she reached the bottom of the mound. She turned around and saw the ground collapse and the laborers disappear into the depths. Harper pressed the back of her fist to her mouth to stifle a scream. The onlookers closest to the edge turned to flee and collided with those behind them, who continued to stand, not quite aware of the danger. This caused chaos within the crowd, as people were still moving up the hill while others shoved them out of the way. When the danger became clear, the crowd fled as one, paying no heed to anyone who stumbled and fell. They were like a herd, trampling the weak, escaping in their panic.

After running off to the side, Harper pressed her back to the wall. It took a few moments for her to notice the Match Girl was speaking to her. Harper pulled her deck from her inside jacket pocket and drew the first card.

The Match Girl was alive.

She knelt on the hard cold earth, in her rags and bare feet, her dark hair dusted with snow. She guarded the sack that held the precious Matches. The Girl drew one out and lit it against the flint and lost herself in the flickering light and the visions of everything she wanted. It reflected in her dark eyes, making them dance. An expression of peace brightened her sallow cheeks. And she smiled at the visions in the fire.

The crowd slowed, and people were being helped. Children who'd been separated from their parents were now back in their arms. The sound of weeping eased. Harper, still entranced by the Match Girl, felt a tickle at her ankles. Looking down, she saw offshoots, green and supple, coming up from the ground, were making a slow journey up her legs. Her first reaction was to pull away, but a thought coming from nowhere warned her not to.

The Match Girl always saddened Harper when she drew it because of what had happened to her, but she was a symbol of happiness, warmth, and a sense of belonging. The Match Girl stilled when the last person came down from the mound. Harper looked up. What had just happened?

Then Harper saw the witch.

Even though the witch didn't catch her attention that time, Harper saw the fierce determination in her stride. She held the staff grasped in her hand as she made her way up the mound. Harper called a warning to her. When the witch reached the edge of the hole, where she stood without fear, she drove the staff into the moist earth. The sound of the chant reached Harper's ears and without warning, a fire blazed before the witch and expanded to encircle the hole.

The witch appeared to be conversing with her staff? Harper had heard of magical artifacts with life trapped within them. She thought of her cards and wondered, were these the spirits of cursed people? The cards were a big part of her life and always had been.

The witch strode back down the hill. Harper wanted to pursue and ask her, *What about the laborers? You've trapped them!* Harper thought the witch might look her way again, but the royal guards were waiting for them. There was a heated argument between the witch and the guards, which ended with the guards escorting – more like forcing – the witch and her companions to go with them.

Harper wished to speak with the witch. Maybe her fellow Gifted would have some idea how Harper – or more accurately, the Match Girl – had calmed the fleeing citizens. She had never done it before. As Harper started for home, she wondered, could she do it again?

For now, she wanted to get home and tell her family what had happened. No one was going near the hole now, although a few curious souls were sitting on the grass a safe distance from the ring of fire. "Vine, protect them," Harper whispered the prayer. She went to take a step, then halted and looked down. The offshoots were returning to Underneath.

* * *

It turned out Pops was already aware of what happened. It wasn't too surprising. He gave her a talking-to for being there in harm's way and sent her to her room. Something he hadn't done in years. Considering Harper was a young woman now, it was pretty much just his way of showing how worried he was. Harper was all too happy to go. She lit the lantern before sitting down on her bed with her legs drawn under her, and removed her coat, taking out her cards.

"What do you have to tell me?" Harper laid the cards in the simple Three Card Spread.

The Harlot reversed.

"What in the nether-hells...."

Ace of Wands.

The Celestial Vine reversed.

"Shite." She dropped back on the bed and closed her eyes.

She noticed a strangeness in the air. It was quiet. Harper had grown accustomed to the noises of the den and had no trouble sleeping through them. But the raucous sounds were missing now. Harper sat up, scooped up her cards, and grabbed her jacket. Her first impulse was to run downstairs, but her instincts took hold and she trod carefully until she reached the landing.

She heard Pops, clear as day, ask, "What you want? This a raid?"

"No." It was a woman's voice. "We're looking for the diviner, Harper."

"She ain't done nothing!"

"She has done nothing," the female voice corrected him. Harper had to admire her lady parts, taking a chance like that. "What makes you think she's done anything?"

Harper risked peeking around the doorframe, hoping not to be seen. There were two city guards. Harper stepped back. "Shite." That was the second time she'd said that tonight. Nothing good ever came of the city guard coming for you. She thought to just step forward and turn herself in, but she recalled the portents of her readings.

Likely, both exits had guards, so she took the stairs back up, thankful she knew where to step to avoid the creaks, and slipped back into her room. Harper tore the coverlets off, reached underneath the mattress, and pulled out a billfold filled with all the money she had in the realm. She stuffed it into her bodice. She'd hung her dagger and sheath in the closet. She retrieved them and fastened them to her waist.

There was a window in her washroom just large enough for her to fit through, and it gave her access to the den roof. She'd become good at climbing out, as she had done it dozens of times before. It was rough. After all, she wasn't twelve anymore, but she hoisted herself up.

She lay on the roof for a few precious moments, watching the stars. Why were there tears filling her eyes? She'd be back. After all, Pops was right, she hadn't done— "Damn it all!" It was a whisper forced between her teeth. "That shite-eating mask!"

How had they known? Had they captured Red, and he gave her up? Thinking of Red and the mask brought back the memory of that thing made of pure hate. Harper shuddered.

She forced herself to stand, and braced her legs, hoping she gauged the distance correctly. The city was always filled with light, but not the alley separating the den and the other building. Harper took a deep breath, got a running start, and launched herself across the space, landing correctly and not spraining anything. She didn't stop there; following a path by heart, Harper put as much distance between herself and the den as possible. It was easier once she got back into it. She was much stronger now and kept her body in good shape. One never knew when they would have to run.

When she stopped to rest, she realized she had a bird's-eye view of the mound and the ring of fire which continued to burn. She wondered if the witch was still in the city and if the flames would go out when she left.

Harper drew her legs up against her chest and thought about her next move. She couldn't return to the den for…how long? If it was serious, they'd likely wait her out until the Vine itself shriveled and died. She tapped her forehead with two fingers, trying to release some idea of why else they'd want her. It wasn't her license because it was the one thing she'd gotten legally. Pops handled the guards when they came snooping around the den. But this wasn't about the den. They had no interest in Pops. They wanted *her.*

The theft of the mask was the only thing she'd done, and she'd regretted it every day since. Now it was coming back to bite her on the arse. If Red had given her up, and the guards had him in custody, he wouldn't last one day in lockup. Nobody likes a snitch. It's assumed that they would snitch on everybody. To keep that from happening, you get rid of them.

If Red was out, there were people that Pops knew – she snorted – people *she* knew who would make him disappear. A smile came to her lips at that thought, and she didn't feel the least bit guilty. Harper blew a breath and straightened her legs out, balancing with her palms flat on the roof behind her. She hadn't had to go with him, but all the same, she'd kept his secret, but he'd not returned the favor.

Enough with Red. It was getting late, and the air was chill. Unless she wandered the city until daylight, she needed a place to bunk. Maybe one of their customers would put her up for the night. That gave her at least some type of plan.

As Harper stood and pulled down her jacket, a warm puff of air, like a breath, tickled the back of her neck. "Shite," she said for the third time tonight. Harper drew her dagger and brought the blade around. Whoever had come up behind her was not only stealthy but quite the acrobat. Her strike hit nothing but air.

The figure moved with incredible speed. There was no way a human moved that fast. The figure dashed to her left, came at Harper again. Harper turned her dagger blade, holding it while her arm was bent, and plunged it forward, to hit only the air again.

"Who the fuck are you?" Harper dropped into a stance, waiting for the next attack. Her opponent would be mistaken if she thought Harper was some soft maiden who'd never been in a fight. The next attack came right for her. Harper sidestepped but wasn't fast enough. Her assailant slammed what Harper thought was an elbow into her ribs with such force that it sent Harper careening backwards as the air exploded from her lungs.

Harper fought to regain her balance and realized there was nothing to gain it on. The hit had knocked her to the edge of the roof. Her arms windmilled back, and her dagger flew from her grasp. She thought she heard it clatter far below onto the stones. Harper screamed as she followed her dagger over the side.

So, I'm going to die now. Damn you to the nether hells, whoever you are.

A hand closed around her forearm and pulled her against a warm body. An arm encircled her lower back.

"Hang on." It was a woman's voice. Something about her body seemed wrong to Harper. Also, hang on to what? Unless she was a sorceress and a master of levitation, they were both about to die. And a sorceress wouldn't need to engage in physical violence.

The beating of wings filled the air.

Her fall slowed. Harper didn't know what was happening, so she did as the voice commanded and hung on. Then her feet were touching the ground. As soon as her assailant's – now her rescuer's – grip loosened, Harper shoved away. She'd lost her dagger, but that didn't mean she wouldn't at least try to defend herself, and her brothers had taught her every dirty trick in the book for fistfighting.

The woman didn't move.

"Who in the nether-hells are you?"

A light sparked to life, although Harper couldn't quite see how. It didn't matter when she got her first good look at the *woman*.

"Dear Vine."

Harper realized why her body had felt wrong. The person standing before her was amazing. Tall and regal. What Harper had first thought was an unruly cloud of hair was dusky-gray feathers. They crested at the crown of her head and flowed down her back. Her wings, the outer layer of feathers of the same dusk color in front with black and white stripes on their underside, were large enough that when opened, they spanned the length of the alley. But her eyes were her most striking feature. A piercing burnt umber. She dressed in a billowy long-sleeved blouse, under what appeared to be a leather bustier and loose-fitting pants, but no shoes.

"I am Aislinn of the Kingdom of Vale," she said.

"Why did you attack me?" Harper said.

"I was trying to subdue you," Aislinn said. "I was unaware of what a threat you would be."

"You some highfalutin' lady beast, aren't you?" Harper wished she had her dagger. "You were gonna subdue me, were ya? What for?"

"I am looking for someone who is said to be in your company."

"If you mean somebody I hang with from the den—"

"No," Aislinn said. Her wings opened and closed in a leisurely motion, as though she was aware Harper couldn't escape her. "I am under orders from His Royal Majesty King Leonine Noble the Third to bring the criminal Reynard the Fox back to Vale to answer for his many crimes."

"I don't know any Reynard," Harper said. "Sounds like—" Then she realized. "Sounds like you need to carry your pretty arse to the royal manor and speak to the duchess. I'm sure you and she got a lot in common."

Aislinn didn't respond, her eyes glittering in the light as she stared.

"Now are you gonna let me by, or am I gonna have ta' tear those feathers out of yer skull?" Harper balled her fists.

"Stop speaking like that," Aislinn said. "You are too well-educated. Calm yourself."

Well, wasn't that a backhanded compliment? "I said, are you gonna let me by?"

"Yes," Aislinn said. She nodded off to Harper's right. "Your dagger is over there."

Never talking her eyes off Aislinn, Harper moved to the side and bent to retrieve her dagger.

"It is safe for you to return to your den." Aislinn inclined her head. "My traveling companion caused quite the diversion. It's likely they won't return tonight."

"I suppose you know why they wanted me?"

"Yes," Aislinn said, "for Reynard."

"I told you I don't know no Reynard." Harper sheathed her dagger, then inclined her head to the right. Aislinn moved out of her path. Harper strode past her.

"I shall visit you again."

Harper turned back. "Not if you know what's good for you, bird lady."

CHAPTER EIGHT

Harper hugged her arms around her chest as she hurried down the sidewalk, her steps leading her towards the den. It was hot, but a shiver ran across her skin, the effect of almost dying taking hold of her senses. It was the force of habit that had her heading for home. She was almost there, mere steps away when she halted. Was she going back to the den? Harper figured the guards that came looking for her were likely hired by Aislinn. It was easy to find corrupt guards.

She didn't want Pops to worry and there were nights she'd stayed out until dawn. But this was rare. With much effort, Harper changed her course, turning left and crossing the street. She couldn't help but look over her shoulder. Even though Aislinn allowed her to leave, Harper figured she wouldn't allow her freedom for long.

Her cards had been silent as to the fact of the matter – why hadn't they warned her about Aislinn? Their presence took the form of whispers. Harper reached into her inside jacket pocket. Although she already guessed the truth, she went to check them.

She'd lost her precious deck.

"Oh dear Vine." Her heart dropped to her stomach and a chill pervaded every bone. There was nothing to focus her power, nothing to warn her of danger or protect her. She might as well be naked.

"Calm yourself." Harper always walked the streets with an air of confidence. Now a piece of it was gone. Had she ever had it? Harper breathed in and out. She drew herself up, trying not to convey her genuine sense of emptiness.

Harper only noticed she'd reached the streets of the black market when the smell of grease and sweet smoke filled the air. Raucous laughter rose above the enticements of the whores, who hung out of their windows, calling to prospective customers. Merchants, if you could call them that, hawked their wares that they claimed were from countries from across the sea. These ranged from fine clothing and jewelry and exotic foods, to substances that rotted your insides and made you crave more at the same time.

The black market resembled market square only in that they both currently took up two cross streets that each ran for only about a half mile or so. But unlike the market square, it didn't stay in the same place. One moment it could occupy abandoned buildings in a derelict part of the city; other times, it took over a rotting warehouse. Once it landed at an abandoned mansion until the guard came for it. They always had forewarning, so they were gone by the time the guards arrived.

They'd been in their current space for almost a year now. The guards never bothered with them except for the staged raids to keep their superiors happy. And now with that trouble at the well....

Harper came to a tavern she was familiar with; the owner was a customer of Pops. She slipped inside. A few people called to her. She somehow returned the greetings, although she thought she might vomit at any moment.

The owner was tending bar, and when she heard Harper's name, she turned to face her with a confused expression. "Harper? I don't believe I owe Pops."

"You don't," Harper said, managing a wan smile as she slid onto one stool. No one knew the owner's real name, so they called her Kae. Spelled with an *e*, figuring it set her apart.

"You don't look so good."

"I'm not."

"You want a drink? Got some good stuff. Just come in from home."

Any Gifted with a grain of sense never consumed alcohol. It was the worst thing you could do. Harper had seen for herself when a wizard, drunk out of his mind, caused an entire building to come crashing down.

But tonight was different. Harper needed something to fill the emptiness. "Anything." Harper lowered her gaze.

Kae nodded and stepped away.

Harper knew there was only one place she could have lost her deck. In the alley after her fall. Would it still be there? She doubted anyone would pick up a tarot deck. All right, so there was hope. She would stay put until the morning.

Kae placed a cup in front of her. Harper nodded her thanks. She didn't notice what it was and didn't much care until she took a healthy swallow and shrieked as it burned a path down her throat into her – she realized – empty stomach. A rush of heat followed, traveling up through her body, spreading to a flush in her face.

"Good?" Kae asked.

Was it? Along with the fire, there was a distinct taste of cinnamon and another unidentifiable spice. It was likely she would not finish it. "Yes."

Kae grinned and strode away.

That was the last thing Harper recalled. She woke up in an unfamiliar bed with the sun sneaking its way through the slats of the blinds. She was alone, which was a major relief, and still dressed, except for her shoes. She tried to sit up, and a throbbing began at her right temple. Harper swore never to drink again.

Someone knocked. "Yes?" Harper said.

It was Kae. She carried a tray with some biscuits, a tiny jar containing what turned out to be honey, a cup of – thank the Vine – strong coffee, and a headache powder.

"You not a drinker, huh?"

"No." Her cheeks flushed again, but not from liquor.

Kae chuckled. "Try to eat."

"Thank you," Harper said. "What do I owe?"

"No, no, no." She waved Harper's attempt at payment away. "I see you next time, I bet."

This time, Harper smiled. "Of course."

Once Kae left, Harper had a sip of the coffee, savoring the aroma and warmth going down her throat. She ate the biscuits with a dribbling of honey with just a minor protest from her stomach. The headache remedy she gulped down.

Harper slipped on her shoes. Maybe her Gift— She remembered her deck. Now she moved with an urgency as she carried the tray downstairs, left it in the kitchen, and said goodbye to Kae. Despite still not feeling well, Harper broke into a run while she beseeched the Vine that the deck was still there.

When she came to the alley, she had to step over several bodies sprawled in the filth. It would have been nice to sleep all day and let the liquor leave her system. Harper tried to figure out where she had stood while Aislinn confronted her.

After the first few minutes of searching, her hope dwindled. There was no sign of the deck. She thought to find maybe even one card, perhaps grimy or wet, but at least she would have something. She poked the sleepers until they turned over or she did it herself if they were small enough, which took a lot of time.

Not one was there. Harper wanted to curl up into a ball and weep. This was her last hope. She'd had that deck since her teen years. Yes, she could buy another, but it would be like starting all over again. And she *loved* her deck. For a moment, her sadness overwhelmed her. She dropped to her knees in the alley and stared at her empty hands.

A spark of anger burned away the sadness, filling her with a heat not unlike the liquor. She stood and balled her fist, her teeth clenched and her jaw tight. First thing, stop by the den and let Pops know she was all right. And second – Red. He was the key to all of this. Harper didn't run, but her pace quickened the closer she got to the den. The door was wide open when she got there, which might not be odd for some, but for Pops, it was as good as telling the guards to come snooping around. Harper hesitated. Had the guards come back? It wasn't until she heard a scream and what sounded like furniture being smashed that she rushed inside.

What she saw made her blood run cold.

Harper took in everything at once. The huge grizzly standing on its hind legs with all its viciousness and bristling brown fur, baring pointed teeth. Aislinn was on the other side of the room, to her right, standing with her arms folded, looking as serene as if she'd stopped by for brunch.

And Pops facing the bear down, a meat cleaver clutched in his fist. Marcel lay atop the remains of the table. His brother was nowhere to be found.

"Come at me, ye demonic bastard!" Pops waved the cleaver back and forth. He'd taken on his share of unruly customers, but this was different. The bear accepted the challenge by roaring from deep in its lungs, spraying spit from its mouth.

No one had noticed Harper yet, or so it seemed.

She drew her dagger with a scream of rage, rushed forward, leaping between the bear and Pops.

"Get back, gods-be-damned you!" Harper grasped the hilt backwards, holding it near her chest. She might die today, but she was going to get some hits in.

"Harper!" Pops screamed.

Harper dropped into a fighting stance, something she had trained for in case her cards failed her. *The eyes, I must go for its eyes! I won't let it hurt my family anymore!*

The bear stood on its hind legs again and gave another roar. Harper lunged forward.

"Stop!"

The bear raised its paw, ready to take Harper's flesh right off her skull.

"Bruin, stand down!"

The bear obeyed, dropped back on all fours, turned around and lumbered away, but as it took its first steps, something Harper didn't expect occurred; the bear shifted its form, and even though she'd seen such before it still left her in awe. The man was just as formidable as the bear, keeping his height and muscular build. If it weren't for the bristling hair that covered him, he would be naked. Not that he wasn't.

Aislinn walked past him and approached. Harper kept her stance. "I am sorry."

"Are you?" Harper kept her attention focused on Bruin, although she figured Aislinn could do with a good guilting.

"I thought your father was lying to us when he said you weren't here."

"So, you would have killed my family if I hadn't returned?"

"Of course not, we're not murderers."

"Where is Osvald?"

"If you mean the other man—"

"My brother!"

"He is unconscious in the kitchen. There was no serious harm done to him."

"What the fuck do you want from me?" Harper already knew.

Aislinn moved around Harper's right and addressed Pops. "You will tell Reynard we were here, and that Harper is coming with us."

"Ye ain't takin' her—"

"Pops." Harper straightened her stance and sheathed her dagger. She moved closer to him and flung her arms around his midsection. He returned the embrace. "Don't worry, I'll be fine. I'll be back as soon as I can, I promise."

Tears welled in the old man's eyes. Harper had never seen that happen before. "Ye will come back." Then his face hardened. "Ye, demoness." He pointed a single finger at Aislinn. "Hurt her and I'll see ye dead. I know people who hunt bitches like ye and like it."

"You have my word no harm will come to her. Just make sure Reynard knows we were here."

"Just who the fuck—"

"She means Red," Harper said.

"So, they're his demon kin," Pops said between clenched teeth. "A'right, I'll tell him."

"Go see to Marcel and Osvald," Harper said. She hugged him again. "I'll see you soon, Father."

Harper didn't want to stay any longer. She approached Aislinn. "Where will we go?"

"Well...." Aislinn hesitated.

Bruin spoke for the first time since regaining his human form. "I'm hungry, Aislinn."

She smiled. "Come to think of it, so am I."

She turned and walked out the door. Harper and Bruin followed.

"But," Aislinn continued, "I need for you to wait for Reynard, so..." Aislinn reached into her vest and pulled out a pouch, "...visit any street vendor you like as long as you monitor the den and I promise when we get home, I'll treat you to your favorite."

Bruin's eyes lit up like a child getting a birthday present. "All righty, Miss Aislinn," he said with a grin, his teeth still sharp. It was a terrifying sight.

"Now, would you suggest a place for us, Lady Harper?"

"I ain't no lady," Harper grunted. "I like the Mellow Vine." For more than obvious reasons. "Most highfalutin ladies like you eat there."

Aislinn's lips quirked upwards. "Then I will like it. Please lead the way, Lady Harper."

They were just in time for tea. That wasn't why Harper liked it. Their baker was a very talented woman. She made a sweet baked custard that was worth going to lockup. And she was more than generous with the fruit compote on top. It was a nice place, not like the dives Harper visited. Although the dives were safer than places like this.

They sat, and Aislinn waited while Harper ordered the custard. She preferred coffee but figured Aislinn would want tea. Neither spoke until after their meal arrived and once their server left them alone, Aislinn took a sip of her tea. "May I ask you something, Lady Harper?"

"Just Harper."

"Harper." It was strange how she'd said Harper's name. Like she felt sorrow for her. "You've heard the tale of Reynard the Fox? I'm willing to wager you haven't heard it all."

"I suppose you'll tell me." Harper sipped her own tea.

"It's all truth," Aislinn said. "Reynard was – is – as cunning and vile as the stories say. After leaving Vale in an uproar—"

"Vale?"

"Our kingdom," Aislinn said, "our home."

"Where is it?"

"In what you call Underneath."

Harper stopped with her fork poised over her custard. "You made the well collapse."

"No, we didn't." Aislinn's expression went blank for a moment. "We didn't even come to Above Ground that way. A new entrance formed several weeks ago outside of the city."

"And you have been chasing Red – Reynard – for how long?" Harper took a bite of the custard, enjoying the smooth sweetness despite her current situation.

Aislinn said, "We have been pursuing him for almost a century."

"Red is one hundred years old?" Harper widened her eyes. Then another thought occurred. "The Riven Isles are small. What took so long?"

Aislinn inclined her head to the left. "We thought he was dead until we discovered he'd gone to the lands across the Stormbringer Sea. We'd find some traces of him, but he always eluded us." She took another sip. "There was a lot of ground to cover."

"So now you have him," Harper said. "What does that have to do with me?"

"You were there the night he stole the mask."

Harper's throat closed, choking on her tea. "How did you know that?"

"The mask," Aislinn said. "We arranged for Reynard to steal it, and the spell cast upon it would compel him to put it on. Only the sorcerer who did so will remove it." Aislinn gazed intensely at her. "As to what it has to do with you, your presence will ensure that Reynard will return to Vale."

"So, I'm to be used as a pawn." Harper didn't hide the bitterness in her tone. "You're so certain Reynard is that concerned with my well-being?"

"Absolutely."

Harper wasn't as certain. Who was she to Red? "Reynard was a thief and trickster."

"He was much more than that," Aislinn said. "You know of how he deceived King Noble with his wily ways and persuasive speech."

Everyone knew the story of Reynard, although it depended on where you lived and who told it. To some, he was a folk hero. To others, he was a deceitful son of a whore who played cruel tricks on friends and enemies alike.

"Bruin the Bear," Harper said. "Reynard tricked him, and they caught him, wedged in a tree where there was a bees' nest."

"Yes," Aislinn said, "after Reynard invited him to feast on the honey. The king summoned Reynard to his palace to answer for his crimes, but whenever he stood before Noble, his silver tongue would play on his failings. I should not say this, but Noble the Second did not deserve the name or title. He was greedy and paranoid. His vanity and Reynard's ability to play on it is why the fox could continue his activities."

Harper shook her head. "And you are so intent on punishing him for tricks that happened a century ago? What ails you people?"

"Tricks," Aislinn said, "are not the only thing he is guilty of. Many of the Above Ground believe they know the entire story, but they don't."

"What is the entire story?"

"Reynard is not only a trickster." Aislinn's expression hardened, and her eyes glittered with malice. It was the first sign of anger Harper had seen. "He is a murderer of children."

CHAPTER NINE

Red woke up in filth.

He recalled a little about last night. He'd waited, and he drank, and the more he thought about Harper, the drunker he tried to get. He recalled when his coin purse was empty, and Pops had one of his sons – Red forgot which one – pick him up and throw him outside into the cold. He must have crawled somewhere to shelter. Red took stock of his surroundings.

He was curled up in a small space that smelled of piss and moldy cabbage. Someone had piled crates up around him. Had he done it? He recognized them as produce crates. Well, that explained the cabbage. He chuckled, and a pain like an ax being driven in his skull had him cringing.

Red, you have never been so low.

He sat up with his back against the wall and waited for his vision to clear. Harper. She hadn't come back last night, at least not while he was in his drunken stupor. Red ground his teeth and forced himself to stand, using the wall as leverage. He recalled some patrons taunting him when his hood slipped off and exposed the mask. He recalled them being impressed that he could drink with it on.

He was still wearing the cloak, although it had twisted all around his limbs. He straightened it and replaced the hood. The mask did nøt protect his eyes from the torture of the sunlight. Red made his way across the street, avoiding being run over by a cart. Even when he reached the entrance to the den, Red went to lean his forehead against the stone, but realized he couldn't. Gods, was he growing accustomed to this accursed thing? He grasped the latch and pushed the door open.

The place was in shambles.

Red's hand dropped from the latch as he stared, immobile, at the scene. It wasn't uncommon for tavern brawls to erupt in a place like this, but the bouncers would escort the brawlers out, much like they'd done to Red last night. This damage couldn't have been from a simple brawl.

Tables and chairs were smashed into splinters. Broken glass was strewn over the bar and crushed into the stone floor. Shattered dishes and old food were also a part of the mess at his feet. When Red stepped into the room, he noticed Pops standing to his left and his sons resting on the floor. It was hard to see, but they appeared to be injured. Red took a step back and his foot came down on something with a crunch.

Pops whirled on him. "You!"

Red thought to run but seeing Pops barreling at him rooted him to the spot with an icy lance of fear piercing his chest. The Rot reacted to his fear and Red collapsed with the pain.

"Don't try no games with me, you son of a whore!" Pops grabbed the front of his cloak, hauled him up, and shook him until the pounding in Red's head became unbearable. "Where did they take Harper?"

"What?" It was tough to concentrate through the pain. To his horror, his stomach roiled. Pops must have known because he shoved away from him just as he vomited, but the mask trapped most of it within, while some trickled out of the openings.

"Look at his sorry arse." It was Marcel. "If he don't tell where Harper is, I say we skin him and serve him up."

Red was caught in a fit of coughing with tears burning his eyes. The stench of his vomit threatened his stomach again. "Harper—" he got out. "What happened?"

Instead of answering his question, Pops said, "Marcel told us ya were a demon in disguise." Pops approached him again, his expression filled with disgust. He pulled Red up, shoved him across the room. Red wasn't on his feet for long.

"Please." Red wanted to die. "What happened to Harper?"

Pops eyed him, gauging whether he was lying. "Ya don't know? Two of your demon kin came and took her away."

"They were here after you," Marcel chimed in. "They tore up the place, and Harper got betwixt them and us." His voice cracked on the last words. They were worried about Harper's safety.

"Kin? I have no kin."

"I tell you they were like you!" Pops said. "One was a woman, said her name was Aislinn. The other—"

"He came in like something outta the nether-hells," Marcel said. "Did all this." He motioned with his arm in a wide arc. "A big ole grizzly bear."

"A bear?" Red pushed himself up. "She had command of the beast?"

"Command?" Pops spoke again. "She said, 'Come Bruin', and the bear followed her out."

"Bruin." Red's heart began hammering, and a cold sweat broke out on his skin. "You're certain she said Bruin?"

"What I just say?" Pops said. "You know them!"

Red didn't respond. He closed his eyes, hoping this would all go away. That he was anywhere else but sitting here in a gambling den, with vomit on his chin and struggling with the realization that his past had caught up with him.

The Rot was telling him to flee. To save himself. What did a woman matter? He'd just have to take a chance that they wouldn't hurt her.

"What you gonna do, just sit there like an ass?" Pops' voice broke through these thoughts.

Red climbed to his feet. "I'll...." What? What would he do? Tell Bruin and this Aislinn that over the decades he'd changed? That he wasn't the same person? They would never believe it and Red realized he didn't either. "I'll go to her."

"You better do more than that!" Pops warned.

Red stepped outside where everything still looked murky, and the people ghostly, but he no longer cared. He walked without knowing where he was going. His head hurt, his stomach was still churning, and he wished for death.

"I got you, you scheming bastard!" The big man – the bear of a man – stepped from behind him and, like Pops, grabbed him by the neck of his cloak. "Aislinn said you'd be back!"

He looked much like Red remembered, hair bristling from all over him to end in a shaggy top of brown that fell down his back. He had deeply tanned skin like that of the laborers who spent their days under the sun. His nose was bulbous, and his thick lips split into a smile of pointed teeth.

"Bruin," Red said, "where's Harper?"

"She's at a place...." He halted and frowned, his nostrils flaring. "What in the nether-hells is that smell?"

"You don't like it? Let me go." Already he was slipping back to his old self. Bruin was stupid, all brawn and no brains. "I know where you can get some—"

Bruin cracked him so hard at the side of his head that the entire world started spinning.

"Aislinn said to do that if you started up." Then, like Red was nothing more than a sack of grain, Bruin dragged him down the street.

No one tried to stop him, and Red didn't expect anyone to. A hairy man over eight feet tall? No, thank you. And he couldn't escape, considering the condition he was in. They hadn't gone far when Bruin stopped and pulled Red to his feet. "Get yourself together."

They were standing before one of the many eateries for the common folk in the market square. The smells of frying food and warm ale did nothing for his sour stomach. Which was ironic because he was hungry and thirsty. Bruin opened the door and pushed him through. Here, everything looked normal. Red was both relieved and apprehensive. People looked up at them, then got back to their meals. Bruin guided him to the rear of the eatery, then pushed him to the right.

Harper sat at the last table near the window and across from her was who Red assumed was Aislinn.

"Here he is, Aislinn," Bruin announced. He placed both hands on Red's shoulders and forced him to kneel.

"Harper, are you well? Gods be damned, woman, if you hurt her—" Red directed those next words at Aislinn. He didn't care about himself, he wanted to ensure her safety. He had to get her away from this—

Harper looked at him, her expression one of mild disdain. "I'm fine."

"Oh gods," Red said aloud. They had told her.

"Oh gods indeed," Aislinn said. There was a tea service on the table and the remains of desserts. They were having tea. Aislinn lifted her cup to her lips and took a sip. Harper looked none the worse for wear. "It took a long time to find you, didn't it?" Aislinn said. Her nose wrinkled. "Bruin, what is that vile stench?"

"Don't know," Bruin said.

"Vomit." Red didn't know why he'd said it. Maybe to see a crack in that cool façade of hers. He spat droplets as he spoke.

Aislinn didn't blink. "You are disgusting."

"The mask," Red said. "Take it off."

Aislinn raised a delicate eyebrow. "I can't."

"You bitch."

Bruin cracked him across the head again. Well, he should have expected that.

"I can't take it off because I am not the one who bespelled it."

"Harper." Red's voice held a plea. "Please let her go."

"Now you have manners?" Aislinn dabbed at her lips with a napkin.

"I've changed."

"Perhaps you have." Aislinn lifted the teapot. "More, Lady Diviner?"

"Please."

They spoke like they were old friends, or maybe Harper knew better than to antagonize Aislinn. "You were correct, Lady Harper. Those sweets were divine."

"I'm glad you approve."

"I knew you were well-educated." Aislinn seemed happy at that knowledge. She slid off the stool on which she sat. "By order of King Leonine Noble the Third, I place you under arrest for crimes against the people of Vale."

King Noble. It was a century past since he'd heard that name, but if this monarch was the third, that meant that *his* Noble had passed on. Not that it mattered.

"Are you ready, Lady Harper?"

"Yes."

"Wait." Red reached out to her. "You can't take her."

"I'm afraid we are," Aislinn said.

"This is not the business of humans."

"Then you should not have included her in your schemes," Aislinn said. "Besides, anyone with eyes in their head can see you're fond of her."

"Harper, stay here." Red kept his eyes on Aislinn. "She can't force you to go with these witnesses present."

"Don't presume to guess what I will or won't do," Aislinn said. "My liege gave strict orders to bring you back." Aislinn leaned near. "I will injure any human who stands in our way, including your precious Harper.

"You may as well come along." Aislinn stood, straightening her vest. "It's the only way to get the mask off."

Bruin hauled him up again and stepped back to allow Harper to stand. Then Bruin, keeping a tight hold on his shoulders, guided Red to follow. Why didn't Harper cry for help? She was being abducted in broad daylight. The answer came to him. Pops and his sons. Pops said Bruin threatened them, and Harper threw herself in between them. She was going along for their safety. Red could only hope someone would run and tell Pops what was happening.

Once outside, they turned to the south and continued. "The well is the other way." Red tried again to stall.

"We're not going that way, especially not with the witch-fire surrounding it," Aislinn said.

So that rumor was true. "Then how?"

"A new entrance opened up several miles outside of the city."

"So, how did you travel here?" Red wondered if he could distract Bruin and give Harper an opportunity to run. "Surely you didn't—"

"Your attempts at distraction grow tiresome," Aislinn said. "I have said that the mask will stay on until the person who cast the spell removes it. Isn't that what you want?"

It was, right now, more than his own freedom. But he had to know. "Who was it?"

Aislinn laughed. "You will find out soon enough."

Bruin laughed as though Aislinn had said something funny. Red wanted to tell him to shut his big mouth, but he realized that would end in him being cuffed again. "And who are you, Lady Aislinn?"

"Who am I?"

"I don't believe I recall you or your family," Red added. "I would recall someone as beautiful as you."

"Oh, for Vine's sake," she responded, "my cousin was right about you."

"Your cousin?"

"No more talk!" Bruin piped up and shook Red by his shoulders.

"Thank you, Bruin." Red heard the relief in Aislinn's voice.

His pounding head returned. He tried to keep track of the route they were taking, but it was impossible. At this rate, they wouldn't make it beyond the city limits before nightfall, let alone several miles. He thought to make that known but figured that Aislinn was quite aware and had a plan.

They walked until they reached the homes of affluent citizens. The dirt street gave way to cobbles. When anyone crossed their path, their expression was a mixture of disgust or amusement. They continued to the next area of unsavory businesses and people, where the buildings were ramshackle, unpainted, or abandoned.

It was here that Aislinn turned left off the main road and led them down a narrow street. The stench of the stable hit them long before it came into view. It surprised Red that Aislinn would frequent such a place. She commanded them to stay outside and walked into the office. When she came out, she was being followed by a squat, plump man.

When they were close enough, he said, "So ya got yer thief, eh?"

"Yes." Aislinn reached into the inside pocket of her vest, brought out a small bag, and dropped it into the stable master's waiting hand.

"I'll have yer horses ready inna bit."

"You have the other item I asked for?"

"Ya, milady."

The stable master led out two horses, gorgeous animals, one a dappled gray and the other a solid smoke. They looked well-fed and cared for. There were no saddles or tack of any kind, although the stable master handed a length of coiled rope to Aislinn.

"Thank you. You gave them the special treatment?"

"Aye milady, they got the best."

"Thank you."

"Tell me, wot," the stable master said as Aislinn turned away, "how ye git them to folla ya?"

Aislinn didn't respond, but Red knew right away. They walked away from the stable and before returning to the main road, Aislinn turned to Bruin. "Bind him."

The rope was for him? Red tensed as Bruin took the rope from Aislinn. When the bear got close enough, Red dropped to his knees and rammed a fist between Bruin's legs. The bear howled and Red dashed off, wishing he could shift into his fox shape, but escaping from being bound was enough. He'd never let anyone do that to him again.

If he could just get lost in the crowd....

The hole in his chest constricted. Red had almost forgotten about it and now it squeezed his chest tight until he couldn't draw a breath. He dropped, and the world around him faded. Before he lost consciousness, he saw Aislinn standing over him, a look of disgust in her expression before the darkness took him.

CHAPTER TEN

Red hadn't wept since he was a kit clinging to his mother's skirts, so when he did now, silently, for once he was glad of the mask as it hid his shame. And when he had wept, his mother had scolded him.

"You are Fox," she said. "Always remember cunning and guile are our strengths. Weeping is for sniveling cowards. Is that what you are? What you aspire to be?"

Red wiped the tears from his face. "No, Mama."

"Never let me see you weep again."

And he hadn't, even in physical pain, even when the homesickness threatened to overwhelm him. He easily set it aside because he knew that if he returned home, it would be the end of him.

Now he had no choice.

A rough shaking underneath him jarred him awake. The smell within the mask assaulted his senses, but he had nothing more to vomit since he hadn't eaten since…when did he last eat? Not that he could with the mask on. Drinking, however, came easy to him. Red wondered if he would die before they arrived. He wished.

"Hey," Bruin said, "you awake?"

Any other time, he would have said no just to be contrary. Now he didn't have the energy to respond. With another painful jarring, Red realized he must be in a wagon bed. He heard the wheels rolling now, and every time they hit a pothole or bump, it sent pain through his body.

"Wake up, ya lazy bastard! We're here and I ain't carryin' ya."

Red gathered what little strength he had and pushed himself to sit. They'd stopped beside the road. Bruin had climbed down when he noticed Red was awake. "Come on, ya fucker, help me with Dagmar and Camilla."

Red went to hop down, but his brain and his body still weren't working together, and he ended up falling on his face in the dirt. Bruin gave a guffaw.

Try again. This time, Red kept his balance. Bruin was removing the tack from the smoke gray, and he supposed they expected him to unloose the dappled one, but when Red reached for her, she lurched back, bumping into the other horse, who looked put out.

"Guess she doesn't want ya touching her." Bruin walked around to the dappled gray. "Not that I blame her."

Since neither horse wanted Red near them, he joined Aislinn and Harper. They stood several steps from the road beneath the trees.

There rose a great oak, as old as the Riven Isles themselves. Its trunk was so wide it would take five grown men to encircle it with their arms. Red would have appreciated the sight of it were it not for the rip straight down the center, which opened into darkness. Offshoots twisted around the entrance in such a manner that it seemed they were holding the gash open. Aislinn and Harper were speaking, or at least their lips were moving, but Red couldn't make out a sound.

Looking into that dark entrance, Red experienced a sense of…not fear, but familiarity. The dark was a living creature. The Rot.

"No," Red whispered. Then louder, "No!"

They turned slowly, as though they were dolls being directed by an invisible hand. The darkness filled their eyes.

"Get out of her!" Red tried to rush to her but again, with his body still in its state, it became more like a series of stumbling. "Bruin, help!" He hated to call for the grizzly man, but he knew even as he reached for Harper, he'd not be able to help. His hand closed around her upper arm, and she looked at him. A smile. It was a gruesome thing, but it wasn't Harper; it was the Rot.

"Get out!"

Bruin lumbered up, followed by two newcomers. "Here now, what you at?"

"Bruin," Red said, "You've got to—"

"Let go of me!" Harper snatched her arm away. Hearing her voice surprised him, for she hadn't spoken to him since...well, the last time he'd seen her.

"Harper—" Her eyes were normal. Red ached to reach for her again. When he tried, Bruin was behind him, circling his arms in a death grip around Red's midsection.

"You OK?" Bruin said, although not addressing anyone specifically.

Aislinn replied, "We are." Her eyes were normal again. "How dare you put your hands on the diviner?"

Red thought of protesting, to tell them what he'd seen, but now in the aftermath he was no longer certain himself. The entrance had the faint glow from the mushrooms that filled the dark cavernous places Underneath. A few wil-o-wisp peeked around the edges of the opening. Had he imagined it? Was this ordeal driving him to insanity?

He knew the face of the Rot. It pulsed in his chest, reacting no doubt to the familiar. The thing that had him by the balls had set its sights on Harper.

What about it? You need to figure out a way to escape.

Well, the time certainly wasn't now, with Bruin still holding on to him. Didn't that brute ever get tired? Aislinn conversed with the two newcomers. After a few moments, they both slipped through the entrance. Aislinn approached.

"They will go ahead of us and announce our arrival." A smile quirked her lips. "You can put him down now, Bruin."

Red only realized that his feet dangled several inches off the ground when Bruin released him, causing him to drop painfully onto his feet and then on his knees. Bruin's laughing was bad enough, but Harper's chuckle and her attempt to smother it made Red feel lower than he thought possible.

She's merely a stupid girl. What do you care if she shows her ignorance?

Shut up! Red shouted inwardly at the voice. It laughed.

Bruin hauled him to his feet. "You go first." And then he shoved Red so hard, he tumbled into the opening, but didn't expect what came next. Red figured he would land on rough ground or in loam but fell through open space. He couldn't help the cry, convinced he was the victim of a cruel prank and would fall to his death.

His shoulder came down painfully on something solid and rough, which he recognized in some dim part of his mind as a root. The next few minutes he continued to tumble, arse over end, tender body parts being bruised with every strike. When he finally came to rest on solid and flat earth, he was never more grateful. Now sore on every part of his body, Red lay there until he noticed his surroundings.

They stood in a wide-open space – a cavern lit by a flickering blue light from an immense pool. The surface glowed with a luminescence that Red realized came from the hundreds of fungi growing around and under its surface. Red reached out, recognizing for the first time how parched he was, his throat and mouth dryer than the deserts across the sea.

"What you up to now?" Bruin said.

"Water, please?"

Bruin laughed. "You hear that, Aislinn? He said please."

"I did indeed," Aislinn said. "I suppose it's near impossible to eat and drink in that thing. Help him, Bruin."

"Here." Bruin's idea of help was tossing a waterskin next to him.

Red grabbed it desperately, shoved the spout through the mouth hole, and guzzled. Memories of his life here resurfaced with every swallow. The water was sweet and cold, just as he remembered.

"When did you last have solid food?" Aislinn stood over him.

"I don't know." His stomach clenched unexpectedly. He'd likely drunk too fast.

"Well, that won't do," Aislinn said. "I wanted to continue on, but let's rest here a bit."

"Fine by me," Bruin said.

"Are you hungry, diviner?"

"Yes."

Harper's voice soothed his rattled nerves somewhat. Red wished he'd never drawn Harper into this mess. He should have thanked her for saving him and left her be. He could only…what? Pray to the Vine? Maybe that was in order.

He must have dozed off because the next thing he knew, a pleasant earthy scent reached his nostrils. He felt a hand on his shoulder and opened his eyes to find Harper kneeling beside him. Red drew in a sharp breath. He wanted to apologize to her. He didn't want to show any overt emotions, lest Aislinn latch on to it. She held a heavily veined leaf laid across both upturned palms. When she lowered it to his eye level, there was a pale golden paste spread on top, which was the source of the scent.

Red pushed himself to sit up and took it from her, their hands briefly touching as he accepted it. There was no emotion or spark from her. Her eyes remained cool and assessing. "Thank you."

When she climbed to her feet without speaking, an explosion of anger made his face burn and his throat tighten. Tendrils of the Rot spread out from his chest, expanding and seeming to follow the flow of blood in his veins. Red nearly crushed the leaf in his grip. What did the bitch expect of him? *I'm the one suffering with this damnable mask.* And what of the mistreatment of him by his kin? Isn't that what Pops had said?

Kill them. First chance you get, kill them.

A shudder passed across his flesh. Not because the voice had demanded it, but because he entertained the thought.

Dear Vine, what is happening to me?

Red realized he'd crushed the leaf. In his anger, however misplaced, Red allowed the Rot to spread like a plague through his body, threatening to overwhelm him.

How long would it be before he completely lost control?

Red released his grip and concentrated on scraping a bit of the paste on his little finger and sticking it into his mouth. He remembered it too. The cantharus mushroom. A flavor both spicy and sweet and another memory that made his heart ache for home despite everything.

He was just able to get his tongue out of the mouth hole enough to lick the leaf clean. His stomach rumbled slightly but minded itself. He'd been careful this time. Movement drew his attention to where the others sat. Aislinn had risen to her feet and brushed the wrinkles down her trousers.

"It's time to go."

Red decided he'd had enough of Bruin manhandling him, so he climbed shakily to his feet. It didn't stop Bruin from glaring at him. Both he and Aislinn had backpacks, which Red hadn't noticed before. They must have stored them on their way to Above Ground.

Red didn't know if they realized he didn't have the strength or the wherewithal to escape as they allowed him to walk by himself. He didn't know how much time had passed before things looked familiar. Finally, they came to the Grand Entrance, or at least that's what King Noble called it. Two doors that stood together formed the shape of an arch, even taller than Bruin. In fact, taller than two Bruins. The artist had carved offshoots at the top of the arch, meeting at the center. Below this was the wooden visage of a lion with its mouth opened in a perpetual roar. One of Noble's ancestors. The so-called lesser animals knelt and paid their respects to their king.

There were no knobs or handles to grasp, and the doors were so well-fitted that there was barely a seam. The spell to open them was a heavily guarded secret, and very few people outside of the royal family knew it. So, it shocked Red when Aislinn walked forward and laid her hand in the center where the edges met and closed her eyes, her mouth moving without words. Who was this woman?

The seam appeared, starting at the top and traveling to the earthen floor before the ponderous groan of old wood in motion as the doors opened inward. Light spilled through the opening, the shaft ever expanding the wider out the doors moved. A scent of the coming rain and spring flowers poured forth along with the sound of myriad birdsong, and from his right Harper drew in an astonished breath. Red raised his arm to shield his eyes, although he shouldn't have to. It proved how very long he'd been away.

They stepped through. Aislinn turned back with a sweeping motion of her hand and the doors closed. On the Vale side, the door settled into the cliff face. Red recalled within was the aviary where the flying denizens of Vale gathered for entertainment or conversation. The way Aislinn looked up with longing confirmed that it was still there.

"How is there sunshine?" Harper asked.

It was the first time Red saw Aislinn smile fully. "You are in another place entirely. Underneath and yet Above Ground."

At Harper's perplexed look, Aislinn said, "My apologies. I wish I had a better explanation."

"I'm sure I'll understand soon."

"Oh, you will, Lady Harper," Bruin said eagerly, like they were long-lost friends. "And you'll fall in love with our home right good!"

Harper turned and leveled Bruin with the same sharp look that she'd given Red. *Serves him right.*

"Bruin," Aislinn said as she continued to walk, "aren't you forgetting something?"

"Hmm?" He looked at Aislinn and then at Harper. "Sorry for what I did, Miz Harper."

"Don't expect forgiveness from me." Harper looked straight ahead. "For either of you."

Red felt a modicum of satisfaction at her words. He wasn't the only one who had earned her ire. With the mask on, it was difficult for Red to see everything around him, unless he turned his head fully to each side, which was irritating after a while. And when he looked forward, the solidly packed dirt road wound far ahead of them, disappearing with hills and dips.

Someone had farmed the land, as the farther they went, they saw neat rows of everything from corn to fruit trees, staves with netting where sweet melons and beans grew and mammoth sunflowers, their florets heavy with seeds. He wondered if he might convince Aislinn to stop and partake. Maybe he could slip away unnoticed? He was about to speak when the sounds of a cart approaching drew his attention away from his plans.

They saw the wagon as it crested the small hill, being pulled by two oxen. Two figures were seated, one a young man with silver hair, and the other...

"Grymbart?" Red smiled underneath the mask as the wagon rolled to a halt before them, forgetting Grymbart wouldn't see and glad he didn't. His best friend. How much trouble had they gotten into as kit and cub? Grymbart had always loved his pranks and after they ran away and escaped from whoever chased them, they would find one of their many hiding places and laugh until their sides ached.

Red ignored the wagon's second occupant, choosing instead to walk around the magnificent beasts – who didn't shy away from him – and approached his friend, his grin widening, until he saw Grymbart's expression. It was the same as Harper's – cool and distant.

"I was never unkind to you, Grymbart."

"Weren't you?" Grymbart said. "Do you know what happened to me after you left?"

"I asked you to come with me."

"And leave my family? Just like you left yours?"

It was like a punch in the gut. What could he say to that?

"Aren't you even interested in where she is?"

"She's still with him."

"Not anymore."

"What do you mean?"

Grymbart's grip tightened on the reins. "Did you have to bring him back?" he asked Aislinn.

"You know our king demanded it," Aislinn replied.

"What happened?" Red's voice rose in pitch. "Where is Hermeline?"

For the first time, the other occupant of the seat spoke.

"My mother," he said, "is dead and you are to blame."

CHAPTER ELEVEN

Hypocrites!

The sudden niceties they tried to pile upon her did not impress Harper. The fact of the matter was, they'd hurt her family and now caused her to lose her deck. So, as they made their way through the caves of Underneath, Harper concentrated on walking and keeping her mind clear. Yet it was impossible.

He is a murderer of children.

She couldn't look at him. When she'd first met him, she'd figured him for a happy-go-lucky thief and nothing more. But Aislinn was telling her differently.

"You know the story of Reynard and Chanticleer?"

"Yes," Harper said, "and how he killed Chanticleer's daughters."

"Reynard is cruelty and deceit. I've been told that he has been since childhood. The stories known by man are but a taste of his treacherous nature."

Harper waited, knowing that Aislinn would continue.

"Bruin was one of his victims," Aislinn said. "You've noticed his scars and his lack of ears?"

Harper recalled that part of the tale. Not that his appearance made Bruin any less terrifying.

"The fur ripped from his paws –" Harper shuddered at that, "– grew back but never his self-worth. Oh, he acts with bravado, but he is empty inside."

Harper couldn't eat anymore of the custard as her throat closed. She set her fork down and tried to swallow some of her tea to relieve the ache. It did little good.

"Reynard trapped three of Chanticleer's daughters and devoured them," Aislinn said. "And Chanticleer cried for justice and Noble, as vain as he was, allowed Reynard to sway him yet again."

"And what about Isengrim?"

Aislinn shook her head. "Reynard tried to say some of his crimes were the fault of his uncle, but of course, no one believed him."

The boy who cried wolf. Or in this case, the fox who cried wolf.

"Of course, he never admits to anything," Aislinn continued. "He blames others, or he flees."

"But he always returned after winning the king's favor."

"True."

"What made Noble decide to pursue him?"

"He didn't." Aislinn took another forkful of the custard. "The Noble who knew Reynard died not too long ago. It is his son, Noble the Third."

"And he is nothing like his father?"

"Not one bit."

"But he was witness to Red's – Reynard's – crimes?"

"Oh yes." Aislinn laid down her fork. "He and I grew up together. He told me one day when he became king, he would right all the wrongs visited on our people." The last words were a touch wistful.

"You're fond of him."

"What?" Aislinn's eyes widened, and her face flushed. "He is a friend. We couldn't, even if...."

She trailed off. "When I came of age, he asked me to come home and lead the search for Reynard."

"Come home?"

"I spent my time being trained as a tracker in the town of Belltide."

"Belltide?"

"Of course, you wouldn't be familiar with it. It is one of man's towns," Aislinn said. "Both my cousin and I spent time there." She grinned. "In fact, my cousin is a diviner too. She will be happy to meet you and...talk shop?"

The ache in Harper's heart returned. She stared at the people going about their business, knowing who they were and what their lives were about. "I'm not a diviner anymore."

"Your pardon?"

Harper turned her glare at her. "The night you attacked me, and I fell, I lost my cards. I could not find them."

"Oh dear."

"You have no idea what this feels like, do you?"

Now Aislinn looked out the window. "No, I don't, but –" she drew in a deep breath and released it, "– I did not know what a formidable opponent you would be. Please accept my apologies for both your loss and for underestimating you."

Harper looked at her, not trusting herself to speak, so she changed the subject. "Aren't you going to ask me? Can't I use anything else?"

"No." Aislinn seemed confused. "Why would I do that?"

Harper raised her brows and widened her eyes. "Everyone does. They're under the mistaken notion we can just change our method as easily as we change clothes."

"Well, that's ridiculous. I asked my cousin about it once." Aislinn poured more tea into her cup. "She said the Vine chooses the method. It's up to the Gifted to determine what that may be."

"The cards spoke to me."

Aislinn nodded, "That sounds about right."

"What is your cousin's name?"

"Her name is Eica," Aislinn said. "You'll meet her soon enough."

Even though she was a prisoner, Harper wanted to meet her fellow diviner. Only she would understand Harper's feelings. It was then the bell at the door tinkled. Harper looked up to see Bruin with Red by the scruff of his neck, like an errant puppy. She had nothing to say to him.

★ ★ ★

Harper stood next to Aislinn, listening to the conversation between Red and Grymbart. Although in his full human form, Grymbart was hairy all over, like the badger that he was. But Harper's attention was now on the young man sitting next to Grymbart. Was he Red's—?

The young man looked nothing like Red. His silver hair and ice-blue eyes were in direct contrast to Red's fire. And the steely gaze he set on Red might as well have been daggers to pierce his flesh.

"Dead?" The word was whispered in disbelief.

The boy said, "As if you care."

"She was married, she seemed happy—"

"She was until we found out you were still alive." Now that gaze fell on Aislinn. "You could have lied. Told the king—"

"I would do no such thing," Aislinn said, matching his haughty tone, "and such words are treasonous. Would your dear mother wish you to speak them?"

The young man shrank back as the flush turned his entire face scarlet. "Of course, forgive me, Lady Aislinn."

Harper had enough. "What is all of this? What is this about?"

Now all eyes were on her.

"Who is this unintelligent human girl child—" the boy began.

He never finished the sentence. Harper, in one fluid motion, unsheathed her dagger and threw. It stuck right between the boy's legs. Harper figured he'd have the same parts and wouldn't appreciate them being threatened.

"Say something again." Harper forced the words through her teeth. "I dare you."

The air crackled with tense static.

Then the boy laughed, not knowing, or caring that the sound infuriated Harper. She would take great delight in dragging him down from the wagon seat to pummel him. But before she could do it, he said between his chortles, "My apologies, milady." The boy pulled the dagger out and hopped down himself. "I was not aware I spoke with a true warrior." He handed Harper her dagger.

As she sheathed her weapon, Harper thought, *Why does everyone think I'm a warrior?* She was just someone who didn't take shite from anyone. "I ain't no milady," Harper growled, "and who in your nether-hells are you?"

His expression sobered. "I am Finnick."

"Doesn't anyone else in this world have true surnames?" Harper arched a brow.

"We do," Finnick said, "but we prefer not to say. Unless, of course, we are close to that person and wish to tell them."

"So, you are Reynard's son."

"Nether-hells, no." Finnick's expression hardened. "My father is called Jean-Pierre."

"You're Jean's boy." Red had come up behind them.

Finnick turned to him. "I am not a boy." He pointed at Reynard for emphasis. "And my father turned us out."

"What?" Reynard turned to Aislinn. "Why didn't you tell me?"

"You never once inquired about your former wife," Aislinn said.

"I am not surprised," Finnick said. "Mother...." He struggled for his next words. "Her grief and humiliation consumed her." He turned away from Red, and when he faced Harper, his eyes glistened with tears. "She went into the woods one day and disappeared for several days." The tears fell. "We came upon her by chance one day, dead at the feet of a hunter. He did not know, of course. He said a fox had killed several of his chickens."

The mask hid Red's expression, but the pain in his voice was clear. "She regressed."

"Of course she did," Finnick said.

Harper had heard many tales of shape-shifters remaining in their animal forms for too long and losing their humanity. A perfect escape for someone who couldn't stand their pain. Perhaps Hermeline realized she would end up dead, without taking her own life.

"I'm sorry," Red said, "I know that doesn't make it better—"

"You're right, it doesn't." Finnick turned his attention back to Aislinn. "May we leave now?"

"Of course," Aislinn said.

"Hop in the bed then." Grymbart motioned with his thumb.

Fresh hay was strewn across the wagon bed. Aislinn climbed in first, with a hand from Bruin. When the bear held out his hand to Harper, she grudgingly accepted it and allowed Bruin to help her too. Finnick returned to his place. Red stood there with his shoulders slumped and his head bowed. His body shook. Harper could see it even from where she sat. He might have stood there forever, but Bruin walked up behind him, grabbed him by the scruff and dragged him to the wagon bed.

So, Harper thought, *he has a conscience.*

★ ★ ★

The wagon continued down the road. They must have made good time. Finnick explained the king had sent them to escort Aislinn and her party to the royal manor. Harper suspected that including Finnick was the king's idea of breaking Red's spirit before his proper punishment began.

Other than that, no one said anything else once Finnick stopped speaking and that suited Harper fine. The tumult of emotions made her blood boil.

Gods be damned, I wish I had my cards.

It took a few moments before Harper noticed that the road had changed from dirt to paving stones. The farms gave way to well-kept houses, similar in shape and size. Each of them had a flower bed. Whenever they passed a gardener working at it, they would look up and wave. Harper wasn't certain if they realized why they were traveling. It wasn't long before the houses turned into town houses, lined in neat rows down a crisscrossing of streets. Again, they received waves and friendly calls. Once they passed the houses, then came the shops. There was a giant fountain in the center of their market square where a massive lion spat a stream of shimmering water to shower over five lionesses. The one thing Harper did not see were the ones who struggled to survive day by day. The servants and the laborers. The *poor*, although Harper hated that word. Harper guessed there wasn't a black market here either. Had this King Noble solved the problem of poverty? Harper doubted it. No monarch in the realm's history had ever created a perfect realm.

"Something troubling you, diviner?" Harper jumped at Aislinn's words.

"Besides being held prisoner and being used as a pawn?" Harper muttered. "No."

Aislinn didn't respond, and Harper was grateful. How could this highborn lady understand? However, the streets were bustling like the market square. People shopped and bantered and traded, trying to get the best bargain. "Where are the laborers?" Harper asked. "The poor?"

Harper expected Aislinn to look confused, but she said, "There is no poor. If you mean stewards and servants, they are here." She made an expansive gesture with her arm.

"I mean the poor. The laborers and workers that make life so easy for you nobles."

"You wonder why there is no poverty or filth? No black market and illegal businesses? There is no need for such things. Noble made sweeping changes when he took the throne. Now everyone makes a wage they can live on, even the servants and laborers."

"How is that possible?" Harper asked.

"You will soon see."

Harper was unbelieving but eager to meet this king and see for herself. It seemed the more she looked, Aislinn was telling the truth, and Harper became impressed. As the wagon moved on, people noticed them. Some waved and called greetings to their fellow citizens in the wagon until some spotted Red.

As the old saying goes, Red's reputation preceded him. A crowd of citizens was following the wagon down the avenue. Some cheered for Aislinn and Bruin, while others mocked Red, shouting vulgar oaths at him. Harper grasped the hilt of her dagger. She'd seen crowds like this after the guards had caught some notorious figure and, in their bloodlust, took the law into their own hands and ended up not only killing the felon but the guards who'd captured them as well.

She was about to see how civil they were. Bruin was too busy basking in the adoration and Red…well, it was impossible to know what he was thinking behind the mask. The way his muscles tensed had Harper thinking they were of the same mind.

Of course, that didn't resolve the matter of his crimes, specifically Chanticleer's daughters. If Harper recalled the story, they weren't children at the time, although she figured their father would have disagreed. She would have never considered it before she knew his identity that he was capable of such. It didn't matter, he had committed murder.

Harper pondered their relationship. In the short time she'd known him, she'd asked about Red's past once and because it seemed to upset him, she didn't ask again. It seemed now he'd not trusted her enough, but Harper supposed she couldn't blame him for not telling her.

For everything else, the blame rested on Red's shoulders.

Harper came out of her musing when she noticed the people had not attacked the wagon. Although they were still quite vocal, the crowd kept a respectful distance. Now she was interested in this King Noble.

Harper would soon have her curiosity satisfied, it seemed, as they were approaching a rather modest-looking manor. Not as large as the nobles of Innrone used. In fact, Harper wouldn't even call it a manor, more like a country home.

The ornate iron gates stood open in welcome. The white brick lane stretched out before them to the steps of the manor, made of black-veined marble. On either side of them were neat flower beds, which were being tended by several young women. They laughed and gossiped. Some were singing. They seemed happy.

Some artisan had crafted the manor front from the same white marble. Heavy wood doors, unfinished and arched like the doors leading to Vale, stood open in further welcome. Two guards in their half-human forms – the animal part of them covered in red and black scales – stood motionless until long tongues flicked out to catch whatever insect flew by.

As they came to a stop at the foot of the stairs, a tall, lithe figure strode with purpose from within the manor and down the stairs. In her half form and armed with sword and dagger, the catlike female stopped before their wagon and bowed at the waist.

"Lady Aislinn, you've returned," she said.

"I'm happy to see you, Princess Asta."

Princess? Was this Noble's daughter?

"Oh, don't you dare." Asta smiled, however, until her gaze fell on Red. "And I see you've brought the vermin home." She nodded, her eyes and voice filled with hate.

"As our lord commanded."

"Lady Aislinn, Our Majesty wishes you to attend in the throne room. He is eager to greet you and your companion." Asta's gaze on Harper was one of mild interest. Someone in the crowd must have run ahead and let Noble know they were coming.

"Bruin, would you assist the princess, please?"

Bruin heaved himself off the rear of the wagon. Asta approached him and caught him in a hug. "I'm so pleased to see you."

"I'm glad to see you, little princess." Bruin hauled Red from the back of the wagon.

Asta reached into her uniform jacket and pulled out a pair of ratchet cuffs. "We made these specially for him."

It was the first time Red tried to struggle, which ceased when Bruin slammed his head against the side of the wagon. Asta had no trouble putting the cuffs on, and Bruin dragged Red away. Asta followed. Behind her, she heard Finnick laughing.

Harper climbed from the wagon before anyone offered help and found herself uncomfortable at the center of attention, which she did not like one bit.

"Miss Harper?" Finnick was beside her. "May I?"

He was so blasted polite that Harper allowed him to take her elbow. She noticed Grymbart turning the wagon, maneuvering it with some skill through the crowd. "Grymbart isn't coming with us?"

"I believe Master Grymbart has had enough of Reynard."

The crowd parted as they walked, and their cheers of welcome continued. No one was paying attention as Asta and Bruin took Red away. They forgot the fox.

CHAPTER TWELVE

Red didn't dare move as the wagon continued down the avenue. For once he was glad he wore the mask, so the mob – and however civil they remained, they were a mob – couldn't react to his expression.

The Rot filled the muscles on his face, contorting them into something Red knew looked as ugly as the cause. The Rot gave him the curse of being able to see himself from the outside. There he wasn't wearing a mask, his face twisted, his eyes narrowed with murderous intent, and all the while, the Rot goaded him to act. What the blasted demon expected him to do with the mask still dampening his shape-shifting was anyone's guess.

I am not hampered by the mask! I will give you the strength to break their bones, to gouge their eyes out—

It made no sense. The few times Red had tried to escape or hurt someone, the hole in his chest had reacted, keeping him from doing so. Now it was saying the mask wasn't a deterrent. Red almost forgot that he was trying not to move and stopped himself from raising his hand to scratch his head.

You are a fox. You are the craftiest of all in the Kingdom of Vale. Figure this out!

No matter what the Rot was about, he would not throw what little he had of his life away.

Red found himself on the grounds of the royal manor. Though the crowd remained gathered around, Red noticed the she-cat approaching. She looked familiar although he couldn't quite place her, but she wore the uniform of a high-ranking officer. Vale had no military; there was no reason. Red was even more confused when Aislinn addressed her as a princess. Was she one of Noble's daughters?

He had no more time to ponder when Bruin grabbed him by the front of the shirt and dragged him out of the wagon bed. As the she-cat approached, that feeling of familiarity was overwhelming. Then it became a lesser worry when she drew the cuffs out of her jacket.

Red needed no goading from the Rot or anyone. He would not allow himself to be shackled like—

Bruin grabbed him by the hair and slammed his face against the side of the wagon, and then came the sickening crack and the wave of pain. The mask had supplied no protection, yet as far as Red was aware, it was solid.

"Careful!" Asta said. "Noble wants him whole."

Bruin had him by the collar again, and Red allowed himself to be pushed forward. It was difficult to concentrate between the pain and the taste of his own blood, but he somehow kept walking. The crowd no longer focused on him. There was no dungeon in the manor, so Red guessed he was likely being taken to some storeroom or stables.

Bruin goaded him to walk, at the same time answering Asta's many questions. Red hadn't the strength to even try to trick Bruin into letting him go. He still needed to get the mask off.

Bruin continued to press forward, leading him past the neat gardens and down a narrow lane to one of the postern gates. They kept going away from the grounds and out into a wooded area.

"We got a special place for ya." Bruin spoke to him for the first time.

That special place turned out to be a structure, nothing more than a shack of rough-hewn stone, pale, likely left over from the manor's construction. A single door seemed the only way in, and there were no windows. If you didn't consider the single rectangular opening, no bigger than a sheet of paper, in said door, which was barred.

It was unlocked, for Bruin pulled open the door. There was nothing inside.

"Wait—" Where was he supposed to attend to his toilet?

Bruin didn't respond to his protest and shoved Red inside, closing the door. Bruin must have had the key on his person, because the lock clicked. With nothing to do, Red moved to sit against the back wall.

"So now what, Reynard?" Red said aloud. "Just wait for them to execute you?"

Well, one thing he was going to do was to ensure Harper's safety, even if it meant sacrificing himself.

Time passed. There were no voices, no movement, and even the Rot was silent. It seemed forever and only a few minutes at the same time. It was impossible to tell despite the wan light filtering through the barred window.

Movement outside of the door awoke him from a doze. Again, the lock clicked. Red pushed himself up. Whatever was coming, he'd face it standing. The door came open and a tall, muscular figure filled the doorway.

"Oh gods." Genuine fear was bitter in Red's mouth and burned in the pit of his stomach.

"Well, I'll be damned." Isengrim the wolf grinned with his pointed teeth. "I didn't dare to hope."

Red swallowed around the tightness in his throat. "Uncle."

Isengrim gave a harsh bark of laughter. "Nephew."

He stepped across the threshold. "How much time do I have, Asta?"

Asta stepped into the doorframe beside him. "As long as you want, Master Isengrim. No one will come for him soon."

"And I can count on your silence?"

She laughed. "I'm going to go home and tell Father we have caught him. He will be very pleased."

That's when Red knew. "You're Tybert's kit." Aislinn's calling her princess made sense. Tybert, although a citizen of Vale, was also the Prince of Cats.

"Besides," Asta continued as though Red hadn't spoken, "no one will care." She turned and waved. "I'll see you at dinner."

When they were alone, Isengrim threaded his fingers and cracked his knuckles. "I can't imagine fucking being more pleasurable than this."

"So, this is how it ends? With you killing me?"

"Who said anything about killing you? Noble wants you alive,"

Isengrim said, "but he didn't say what condition you had to be in. Either way, I'm more than willing to face his wrath."

The door closed behind him, and the lock clicked in place.

Had he his power, Red would have given as well as he got, but now, there was no way to fight Isengrim. But he'd be damned if he let his uncle just beat on him. *Now where are you with your talk of filling me with your strength,* he challenged the Rot.

"I'll not even shift," Isengrim was saying. Red backed up until Isengrim had forced him into the corner. Even without his power, instincts took hold and Red crouched, ready to attack.

Isengrim laughed again.

"Can't help yourself," he said. "You'll have a fair chance since I'll have to hold back, and it isn't easy."

For a split second, Red thought to just give up. Just allow Isengrim to rip his throat out. But as Isengrim attacked, Red leaped to meet him.

★ ★ ★

"Ya didn't kill him, did ya?" It was Bruin.

"No, no, he's still alive," Isengrim responded.

"Don't look it." Even the slight nudge against Red's side sent a wave of searing pain through him.

"What is this?" There was an unfamiliar voice now, female. "What have you done? Noble wants him alive!"

"He *is* alive."

The female voice growled in frustration, "Well, you can damn well carry him inside!"

Red tried to open his eyes, but everything was a haze of scarlet. When someone, he guessed it was both Isengrim and Bruin, lifted him, he groaned in agony from deep in his throat.

"See, I told you he was alive."

"Bah!" This knowledge didn't please her.

Red figured he'd lost consciousness because the next thing he knew, he was in the water. The wounds on him burned, but when he opened his mouth to scream, water filled it, going down his throat and causing a fit of painful coughing. Then he was breathing air again. He couldn't help it. Tears flowed. He wanted to say sorry to his mother, but she was dead, wasn't she?

Red tried to open his swollen eyes without success. Yes, after giving his all – which turned out to be nothing – against Isengrim, his uncle had taken great pleasure in hammering him in the face. *So you won't be as pretty*. The mask itself had no padding and offered little protection, nor had it shattered as Red hoped it would and each blow cut into his flesh.

"Damn it." It was the woman again. "Where is Shahir?"

"I am here, Mistress Agnes," answered another male voice, deep and commanding.

Red was floating, whether in water or air he didn't know. Maybe he'd died and had left his body. He hoped.

"Can you get him at least presentable?"

"He's badly injured," Shahir said. "What happened?"

"Never mind that," Agnes said. "Get to work."

A coolness settled over his skin, spreading along his arms and legs as the pain lessened. And after came warmth, pleasant and soothing, relaxing tense muscles.

"Can we get this damnable mask off now?"

Yes, please! I'll do anything....

"Not yet," Shahir said. "Could you work around it, Mistress Agnes?"

Agnes huffed, "For now."

Get this gods-be-damned thing off me!

"Our Majesty wants me to remove it before him."

Red knew when the healer finished. The pain was tolerable now, and he found he could move his limbs somewhat. But his eyes....

"I am finished," Shahir said, "but I cannot guarantee his right eye will heal. Likely, he'll be blind."

"No," Red moaned.

"Looks like he heard you," Agnes said.

Red opened his one good eye. There was a buxom older woman leaning over him. Her face was round, and she did her dark hair up in a bun. She wore a plain brown dress and a splotched white apron. With little effort, she reached down, grabbed his arm, and pulled him up.

"Damn it to the nether-hells!" He was stark naked.

Agnes smirked. "At least they left something alone." Agnes stepped out of his line of sight, then came back with a large towel, which she threw at him. "Dry yourself off. There are some clothes over there." Agnes motioned to her left.

Red didn't hide his nakedness. He dried himself and picked up the shirt and trousers, thrown over the back of a nearby chair, and dressed. He turned back to Agnes. "No shoes?"

There was a snort and Red had to turn full around to face the one called Shahir. He was impressive. Tall and dark-skinned, his muscular body clad in loose-fitting trousers and leather vest. His hair was curly, his eyes deep, set under thick lashes, the color almost black. He wore a neat beard that surrounded his full lips, underneath a broad flat nose. "You will go before the king barefoot," Shahir said.

"I don't remember you," Red said.

"You wouldn't," Shahir said. "I have lived for many years in what the humans call Morwynne." That explained his dress.

"And you put this accursed mask on me." Red balled his fists.

Shahir laughed without mirth. "You put it on yourself."

"You knew I would."

"Of course," Shahir said. "I've studied and watched you for many years."

"You?"

"And you never knew," Shahir said. "You went on your merry way as I helped my cousin trap you. It was my pleasure."

Red wanted to kill him, and he would the moment the mask came off. No matter what the consequences. If he could get him before he shifted—

"You will come with me now." Shahir turned without waiting for a response. Since there was no reason not to, Red moved to follow him.

"Thank you, Mistress Agnes," Red muttered as he moved past her. A snort was her response.

It was impossible to see his surroundings, so he concentrated on Shahir's back and trying to keep up with the man. He seemed unconcerned that Red was having difficulty. Most people were ignoring him, although others whispered and chuckled behind their hands. Red didn't care. Shahir came to a stop before a small door.

"You will treat the king with the respect he is due," Shahir said.

It wasn't until now that Red realized how terrified he was. He couldn't think around the pain and the mask, which was likely how they wanted him, so he couldn't use his wits to get out of this dire situation.

The door opened and light spilled in. Shahir stepped aside and motioned with his head for Red to go first. There was a murmur from the citizens and courtiers gathered, which went silent as Red stepped into the receiving hall. Unlike most royal enclaves, the receiving hall wasn't some grand thing. True, the furnishings were of fine quality, but they had a comfortable look about them. It wasn't as he recalled. The new king had it redone.

And the new king, Noble the Third, sat on the throne, with his queen next to him, both in their half-shifted form, while everyone else had on their human personas. It was a sign of his power. Now Noble's gaze fell on him.

"Shahir, bring him forward."

Much like Bruin, Shahir took him by the collar and pushed him to stand before the thrones, then forced him down on his knees.

"Remove the mask," Noble said. "I want to see his face."

Red didn't care what happened next. Shahir began a magical incantation. Noble continued to speak.

"Even though the mask is being removed, you are still beholden to it. Shahir will keep the mask and punish you if you try to escape."

Red swallowed when he felt Shahir grip the edges of the mask. He had a ridiculous notion that the thing wouldn't come off, but it did with a nasty sucking.

The moment it came off, Red breathed in, his only concern taking in as much air as possible. The skin on his face itched and despite his makeshift bath, he still smelled like his vomit.

"That mask was on for a long time, wasn't it?" The female voice caused Red to look towards its source. Noble's queen was looking at him with a mixture of curiosity and disgust. She was golden, with a mane of silky blond hair. She was petite, almost childlike in stature and appearance, with a round face and eyes like two shimmering gold coins.

"Indeed, the lack of sunlight does that to skin," Noble said. "How did his eye get that way?"

"I'm uncertain, sire," Shahir said. "I assume someone took out their aggressions beforehand."

"Hmm," was Noble's response as he rubbed his hair on his chin.

Red didn't know what to do or what was going to happen next, so he spoke. "My king, your most glorious—"

"Silence!" Noble came off his throne. "How dare you, vermin!"

Red couldn't help but shrink back under his gaze.

"I am not my father, who fell for your lies and flattery," Noble said. "I will tell you what is about to happen to you.

My father did one good thing, and that was to allow the citizens who had grievances against you to come forward, so tomorrow morning at sunrise all those in the kingdom may come forward to air their grievances. After which you may speak on your own behalf, but I warn you, if you so much as utter a word that I believe is deceitful or meant to twist the words of others, I will order your immediate execution."

For the second time, Red felt like he'd been gut-punched. It came to him that he might die at sunrise. This Noble was nothing like the one he knew. He would have done anything to have *his* Noble sitting on the throne again.

Noble waved his hand in a dismissive gesture. "Take him back to wherever you're keeping him."

Red thought to talk his way out of it as he used to. He even entertained begging for his life, but he was too exhausted, too hungry and trembling, much to his embarrassment. He didn't resist when someone grabbed his arm. It turned out to be Isengrim, who jerked him to his feet.

"See him," Noble said as though Red were no longer in the room, "to be brought so low."

CHAPTER THIRTEEN

Harper was relieved when they reached the doors until the group followed them inside. People came from every door and hallway. Perhaps it was just the almost crush of bodies and the mixtures of scents that made Harper shudder, but she wasn't certain. If she had her cards....

It came to her as they entered what she assumed was the Great Hall, how much she depended on her cards. How many people did she know who followed their instincts when deciding? For her, it was always the cards. Was she so helpless? Incapable of following her own instinctive responses. If she had any to begin with?

All thoughts fled when the crowd parted again, and Harper found herself in the middle of the cavernous room and facing the king and queen of Vale.

They were.... Beautiful didn't describe them. What word came to mind? Godlike? Well, she'd never seen a god or goddess, but if Harper had to guess, the royal couple were the closest thing to them.

It was the king that drew Harper's gaze. His eyes held hers. They were a glittering amber, with coal-black irises that said, *I am ruler here.* The tawny fur of his mane surrounded his sculpted cheekbones, tapering down to his firm chin. The pristine white shirt he wore, opened to his waist, showed lean muscle covered in a fine golden fur. Harper had to fight not to allow her gaze to continue...downward.

Harper's fingers moved, itched to place a hand against that chest to feel if the fur was as soft as it looked. Then she drew in a sharp breath. *What's wrong with me?*

The king was looking right at her.

Dear Vine, had he heard—? No, mind reading was an old wives' tale and anyone who claimed to do such was a liar, but Harper would swear that the king's lips quirked up as he held her eyes.

Harper noticed the others kneeling until she felt a tug at her sleeve. It was Finnick, guiding her to do the same, or at least trying to. Harper had never bowed to anyone, and she'd be damned if she started now. So, she gathered herself up and locked eyes with the king again. Damn it all if the bastard didn't look amused! Meanwhile, the gathered people, scandalized by Harper's behavior, were whispering behind their hands or glaring at Harper with outright hostility.

"Welcome back, my loyal citizens," the king said. "Please rise."

He stood, holding out his hand to his queen, who grasped it, and they both descended from their thrones.

"Aislinn, my dear, so good to see you."

They hugged her at the same time. It was a shock to Harper.

"And Finnick, you're looking well." They grasped hands, and the queen mimed kisses to his cheeks.

"Please forgive my intrusion," Finnick said.

"Nonsense! You're always welcome here." Then that gaze returned to Harper. "And you must be the diviner. Lady Harper, welcome to my kingdom. As you well know, I am King Leonine Noble the Third."

"Thank you," Harper said, "but let's not pretend I'm an honored guest. I'm a prisoner."

"There are no prisoners," Leonine said, "except for Reynard, of course." The crowd chuckled. "But I understand why you say that you are not here by choice. I would blame Reynard for that."

"I do."

"Then I take it you will want to attend his trial tomorrow?"

She wanted to get the nether-hells out of Underneath. "Yes."

"Done," Leonine said. "Lucea?"

A young girl separated herself from the crowd, approached, and knelt before the king. "Yes, Your Majesty?" She wore a dark blue uniform of jacket and ankle-dress, which pooled out around her legs. It had red threading on the front and at the shoulders.

"Lady Harper is to be given our most comfortable of rooms. She is to be treated as an honored guest," Leonine said. "You will see to her every comfort and report any displeasure to me, understood?"

"Yes, Your Majesty."

Lucea climbed to her feet and approached Harper, curtseying, "Please follow me, milady."

Harper wanted to say she was no *milady* and to just call her Harper but decided it might embarrass the girl, so she just nodded and followed.

Most servants she knew didn't speak to guests because they risked punishment. Harper figured if Lucea was to see to her every need, they should at least be able to converse.

"So, what do you know about Reynard?"

Harper must have guessed right because Lucea responded, "Only what I've been told by my great-aunt and uncle."

"And they are?"

"Prince Tybert and his wife, Felicity."

"So, you're a princess?"

"Oh no." Lucea flushed. "I suppose I'm more a duchess. Although I serve our king."

"The duchess rules my city of Innrone."

"Does she serve your king?"

"In a sense," Harper said, "but she doesn't—

Lucea turned and grinned at her. "Escort guests?"

Too late to turn back now. "No."

"What does she do?"

Besides sitting in a big chair and wave from a balcony? "I couldn't venture a guess."

Lucea giggled and stopped before a door. Harper supposed they'd arrived, for Lucea pulled a tiny gold chain from within her bodice. On the chain were a group of gold keys. Harper counted seven. What was it she'd heard about keys and locks being in sevens?

Although the key seemed too small for the lock, it fit. Lucea turned it with a click. Grasping the latch, she pushed the door inward. And although Harper didn't see how she'd done it, Lucea removed the key and handed it to Harper. Was she imagining the slight tingle when it lay in her palm?

"This will be your room during your stay."

Before she saw the room, she had asked how long that would be. She expected lavish and gaudy furnishings, but in fact, the room had a homey feel to it. There *were* fine furnishings made of polished wood and a four-poster bed large enough to sleep a whole family from market square. Harper let her gaze travel around the room. Glass doors opened out on a small balcony to her left, next to a desk and writing implements. One cabinet, shaped like a woman, was to the right. Next to the washroom was a dressing table.

Lucea was pushing her towards that door. "Now, I have a nice bath all set up for you."

"You do? How did you…." Lucea hadn't lied. A claw-foot tub filled with steaming water topped with a fluffy cloud of foam, which Harper was certain hadn't been there before. There was another open-front cabinet filled with folded towels to her left, and on a small cart were what Harper assumed were cakes of soaps and colognes.

"Now, get cleaned up and I'll lay some nice dresses out for you."

Dresses?

"And if you need anything, just ring." She nodded to the pull ring hanging from the ceiling near the doorway. Harper had seen them before when she was doing readings in the homes of more prominent merchants. Thinking of that made Harper think of the one thing she'd tried to push into the back of her mind – her precious deck.

Lucea was still speaking, but Harper had missed pretty much everything else she had said.

"Just call when you finish," Lucea said. "Dinner should be ready by then." And she bustled out as fast as she'd gotten Harper in.

"Well, now what in the nether-hells am I supposed to do?" Harper asked. The nearest they'd had to a bath in the den was a large round wooden tub and you had to boil the water and carry it up to the room, or at least *she* had to as bathing in the kitchen suited Pops and her brothers.

Seeing no reason not to, Harper hurried and stripped down and removed her dagger and sheath, wondering for a bit why they hadn't taken it. She approached the tub, dipped one toe in, finding it hot. She lifted her other leg in and sank into the heat and silk. She let her dagger drop to the floor. Harper sighed in pleasure. If this wasn't Up Above, it was close. After enjoying just lying in the water, Harper reached for a large sponge and went to work on every part of her body, scrubbing it raw. Next, she reached for what she hoped was shampoo, worked up a lather, and took care of her hair.

The water was tepid and a lot dirtier than she would have liked. She wondered if she could have another tub sent up. Wouldn't hurt to ask. Harper rose from the tub and wiped off the excess water from her body. She stepped out and approached the towel cabinet. She chose the largest and wrapped it around herself. Then she walked over to the pull cord and gave it a yank. She heard bells in the distance, yet it seemed like no time before Lucea appeared.

"Would it be possible to get a clean bath?" Harper asked.

Lucea's eyes lit up. "I'll take care of it for you right now." She moved toward the tub and knelt, dipping one hand into the water. She swirled it around like some dirt soup. Harper watched, fascinated. The water bubbled, and the murkiness vanished, the froth rising from clean, steaming water.

"There you are!" Lucea said and rubbed her dry palms together. "Please enjoy."

"Wait," Harper said, "you're a witch?"

"Yes," she said, "that is, I mean to say, I'm a chronomancer."

"You jest!" Harper's jaw dropped. She'd never met a real chronomancer. In fact, the power was so rare that only kings and queens could obtain their services. Which made sense why she served Leonine. "How wonderful."

"Thank you." She curtsied. "Enjoy."

Harper did. When she finished again, she picked up her dagger and returned to the bedroom after finding a thick robe to wrap herself in. As she approached the bed, she saw them – dresses. Four to be exact, of various colors and designs, bejeweled in such a way that Harper knew would make the wearer a moving target in market square night or day.

Harper hated dresses. Since she was a toddler and a customer of the den had sewn her one in hopes Pops would give her more time to pay her debts. It had been a struggle to get Harper into it, and Pops had stood off to the side, laughing at the woman's struggles. Meanwhile, Harper kicked and punched her way into it, and the moment the woman let her go, she made a beeline outside and had it dirty and torn before an hour had passed.

Pops had felt so bad about it he forgave the woman's debt, and they did not make Harper wear a dress again.

Now here were four of them. She thought about asking for her trousers. Another tug on the rope and Lucea arrived.

"Yes, milady?" Her eyes darted to the dagger and back to Harper.

"Please call me Harper. We are sisters." Harper stuck out her hand at the same time Lucea curtsied. She straightened and stood to grasp Harper's hand.

"I hope you don't mind me calling you again."

"Not at all," Lucea said. "The king is busy dealing with…." Lucea drew her hands down her skirt. "What can I do for you?"

"These." Harper motioned with her hand towards the dresses. "Can you find me something else to wear?"

Lucea looked hurt. "Are these not good enough?"

Oh, dear Vine. "No, no, not that," Harper said. "I'm sure they are for the ladies of the court, but I prefer a good pair of trousers."

"Oh!" Lucea's expression was first thoughtful, then resolute. "You can't go before the king in trousers."

"Why not?" Harper said. "If he doesn't like it, he can—"

"No, no, it just won't do." Lucea shook her head and laid a finger on her chin, then she brightened. "I know, here, let me choose."

Lucea approached the bed and then turned back to Harper. "We must work on your hair and makeup." Before Harper could protest, Lucea took her dagger and tossed it onto the bed. "You won't be needing this right now."

You mean I'll be needing it later?

"Your skin is so dark it glows. You're beautiful, are you from Morwynne?"

"I don't know," Harper said, flattered.

Lucea approached her and took Harper by the elbow. She led her across the room to the dressing table, pulled back the chair and guided Harper to sit. "We'll start with your hair first." Lucea picked up a pink comb veined with white and began her work.

"Ow!"

"Sorry," Lucea said, "you've got a lot of tangles here, but once I'm done, you won't have to worry about them again. Just be certain you comb your hair out every day."

Harper opened her mouth to retort, then closed it again. Why was she allowing this girl to make her up like some harlot? She couldn't guess. It turned out that wasn't what Lucea was trying to do. In fact, the girl applied the cosmetics with a light touch, choosing her colors. When she turned Harper back to the mirror, she couldn't help but draw in a breath. Her looks had always satisfied her and to hell with anyone who thought she didn't meet their standards, but even she had to admit to liking what Lucea did.

"Thank you," Harper said. "You're very talented."

"You look even more beautiful!" Lucea clapped her hands together. "And you're welcome. Now for the dress, I think it will look nice."

She picked up a ruby-encrusted monstrosity with a flared skirt. "No, not this one."

"Lucea." A thought occurred to Harper. "Do you have a split skirt?

"Oh yes, that I can do." Lucea selected one in blue. The shirt flared, and the cloth of the skirt wrapped around from left to right with the jeweled button to secure it. And it didn't have the opulence that the others did.

"Perfect," Harper said. She didn't protest as Lucea helped her into the dress. She needed it. But the young witch remained silent as Harper strapped on her dagger. Harper looked up to meet Lucea's eyes, seeing the sadness there.

"You won't need that here."

"Lucea, despite what King Noble said, I am a prisoner. A pawn to use against Reynard."

"Reynard cares for you?" Lucea asked.

"I have no idea," Harper said.

Lucea didn't press the issue and instead touched Harper on the elbow. "Come over here."

There was a full-length mirror on the other side of the room. "Well, am I talented?"

Unlike other women, Harper wasn't some dainty little thing. Years of working had left her well-defined and muscular. Still, Lucea's choice of attire fitted her well, molding to her form and stressing her curves. Harper smiled.

"I'll take that as a yes." Lucea turned and walked back across the room, "One more thing." She returned with a pair of boots dyed dark blue. "These should fit."

She had Harper sit again and slipped the boots on, and they fit her perfectly.

"Perfect!" Lucea motioned Harper to the door. "Come along now, the king is waiting."

Harper moved forward and tripped on the fine cloth.

"Goodness –" Lucea reached out and caught her, "– haven't you ever walked in a dress before?"

"No." Harper couldn't hide her annoyance.

"Grasp the material and raise the skirt slightly and take your steps." Lucea showed by lifting her own skirt.

"I'd still like a pair of trousers."

There were a few false starts and near misses, but Harper felt she was getting the hang of it as they continued through the halls of the manor, where Harper got many an admiring look from both men and women they passed by. Harper tried not to glare at them.

They came to a room, where there were arched doors of white wood and carvings across their face painted gold. Two guards stood, one a man and the other a woman. They smiled as they approached them.

"Hello, Miss Lucea," the woman said, reaching for the door latch, "the king is running a bit late, but he asked me to tell you he would be with our guest as quickly as possible."

"Thank you." Lucea again motioned Harper forward.

"You're not coming in?"

"You'll see me again soon," Lucea assured her. "Make yourself at home. You'll find a nice repast prepared."

Then she was off. Harper stepped farther into the room, noticing on her right a table set, covered with every type of food imaginable and some she'd never seen before. It was enough for twenty people. Harper turned when she heard movement behind her.

"Greetings, Lady Harper." Leonine was even more magnificent, if such a thing were possible. "I've been looking forward to speaking with you." He motioned her towards the food-laden table. "Shall we?"

CHAPTER FOURTEEN

Harper realized she was hungry, and she wasn't one of those women who ate like a bird. She filled her plate with many familiar things. Others were unfamiliar but looked good, anyway.

Leonine didn't skimp either, which made sense. Afterwards, they walked over to the nearest couch and sat, laying their plates on a low table. Leonine asked, "Would you like to drink? Nothing strong, I assume?"

"Yes, thank you."

Leonine approached a sideboard near the table, chose two goblets. Into one he poured a dark liquid and an amber-colored one into the other. "We have many Gifted here and I've known not one of them who drink."

"Don't you agree it would be dangerous?"

"Absolutely." Leonine set the goblet down. "Apple juice?"

Harper figured it should be safe. She took a sip. It was nectar.

Leonine said. "The dress becomes you."

"Thank you—"

"You are quite a woman," Leonine continued. "I can see why Reynard is fond of you."

"I don't know that," Harper said.

"Speaking of Reynard." Leonine leaned forward, "I will ask again, when I judge him, do you wish to be there?"

That intense gaze of glittering gold caught her again. His scent was masculine, smelling of an earthy musk that Harper tried not to breathe in too deeply. There was that desire to touch him. Leonine had edged closer to her.

"If you don't, I can arrange for other pursuits to occupy your time."

He draped an arm across the couch back. “Aislinn told you about her cousin Eica?”

“Yes.”

“She’s eager to meet you.”

“And I, her.”

“I’m sure she would appreciate you taking some of her clients.” Leonine grinned. “Her days are quite full.”

“There are no other diviners here?”

“There are, but Eica is our greatest,” Leonine said.

“The answer is yes, I want to be there.”

“Very well,” Leonine said. “It will be unpleasant.”

“I am not some swooning maiden,” Harper said. “I’ve seen much worse.”

“I admire your courage.” He was close to her now, too close.

“Sire—”

“Leonine.”

“I am no one’s mistress.”

“Pardon?”

Harper edged back. “You have a queen who I am sure loves you.”

He looked confused. “Of course, I love her too. Why does that—?” His eyes widened with realization. “Oh dear, I’d forgotten.”

“That you had a wife?”

He chuckled, which infuriated Harper. “No, you don’t understand. Please don’t look as if you want to throttle me! I have four wives.”

“What?”

“The lioness you saw beside me is my first, High Queen Elsabe,” Leonine said. “As king, it is natural for me to have many wives. In the human world, they are called a pride.”

“And you show them equal love and attention?”

“When I am able,” Leonine said, “which is no easy feat.”

“I’m sure.”

He laughed again and, although she was not as angry, it annoyed her still. “I know most humans believe in having only one mate, but tell me, aren’t there humans in Above Ground that take more than one wife? My cousin lived in Morwynne and the Dhar has anywhere from two to twenty."

"Twenty wives?"

"I wondered how does he keep that many satisfied?" Leonine said. "And they are not all women. I have seen men be a part of their pride."

"Who they fuck is their business." If her use of profanity shocked Leonine, it didn't show. "But I'll admit that's a damn good question!"

He laughed again, and it was infectious. Harper joined him. When the laughter faded, he asked, "I am preparing a feast tonight for my people. Would you go with me?"

Harper raised a brow.

"For dinner and then perhaps dancing, nothing more." He grinned. "Unless you wish it."

Harper didn't respond. "We'll see."

* * *

"You still haven't answered my question."

They were both full and satisfied and despite herself, Harper relaxed against the comfortable couch cushions.

"You mean what happens to you?" Leonine smiled, his position comfortable, like Harper's. His legs stretched out, his goblet in one hand, and his arm still draped across the couch back. He resembled the cat he was. If he started purring, it wouldn't surprise her. "I suppose that depends on what you want to do."

"I didn't want to come here."

"Now that you're here, what do you think?"

"There is something too perfect about this place, I think."

"You have limited belief in perfect places."

"My belief is nonexistent."

Leonine leaned forward from his relaxed stance. He grasped his goblet in both hands and stared into its depths. "Vale is far from perfect. I just wanted it to be better."

He seemed sincere, although Harper knew many a person who could act that way and wasn't.

"And capturing Reynard was one of your ways to make it better?"

"Yes," Leonine said. "You know the stories. Well, they don't even touch on what Reynard has done. Pain like that doesn't go away. I was so angry with my father, but I thought anger did no good. I'll do better when I'm king." He tensed, again like the cat, ready to pounce, and trembled slightly.

Harper moved closer and laid a hand on his shoulder. "You are doing more than most human kings do."

He relaxed and smiled at her. "Stay here in Vale." He embraced her, pulling her close, and he kissed her before she could protest. Did she even want to? She relaxed against him and allowed herself to run her hands across his chest. The fur was as soft as she imagined.

It wasn't until liquid heat pooled in the bottom of her stomach that she pulled away from his kiss.

"I'm sorry," Leonine said, "I thought—"

"You thought right," Harper said.

He sighed with relief. "I didn't want you to think— I'd never force a woman."

Harper's lips quirked. "It wouldn't have been that easy."

Leonine chuckled. "I can imagine."

"I can't stay here," she said. "I have life Above Ground."

"I know," he said. "So stay here a little while. I'd like to convince you. I can have Aislinn send a message to your family."

"But to what end?"

"Exploring this more." He kissed her again. "I would make you my queen."

"I don't want to be queen."

"It's not what you know from the human world," Leonine said. "Let's not get ahead of ourselves. I still must convince you."

He straightened. Harper followed suit. "But the hour is getting late, and I have business to attend to you. Would you like to return to your rooms?"

"I would rather meet with Eica."

He brightened. "She will be upset that I kept you this long."

Leonine stood and extended his hands to her. "Come with me."

Harper took his hands, and he pulled her to stand, releasing one and drawing her to stride behind him. He was like a boy, eager to show her a favored toy, nothing like a king. She managed to keep up and grasp the edge of her dress at the same time. First thing she would ask for would be a pair of trousers.

When they came to their destination, a carved wood door, the king knocked. Minutes passed. The door opened. "What in the nether-hells—" The person standing at the door reminded her of Aislinn, so of course, this was Eica, except her feathers were a light blue with streaks of black. Her hair was short, with the same white and blue streaks decorated in a tuft.

When she saw who it was, she said, "Oh, it's you." Then her gaze turned to Harper. "Is this her? The diviner? You kept her to yourself long enough."

Harper couldn't believe how Eica had spoken to her king. These shifters acted nothing like most noble houses she'd heard of.

"Always a pleasure, Lady Eica," Leonine said. "Yes, this is Lady Harper."

Her eyes lit up. "Come in!" Like the king, Eica reached for her with a childlike enthusiasm. "Shoo, Leo!"

Shoo, Leo?

"Very well." Leonine grinned, waving his hands in a motion of surrender. "Take care of our guest."

"Yes, of course." Eica was already closing the door. "Are you comfortable with that?" She motioned to Harper's dress with a nod.

"No."

"You're about my size. I have a trouser suit you can wear."

"Thank you."

"So," Eica said once Harper was in the suit and they settled, "may I see your deck?"

"I…." Harper swallowed.

"What?" Eica said. She listened as Harper told of her encounter with Aislinn and losing her deck.

"Why didn't you say so sooner?" Eica said. "Aislinn knows better." Eica rose and ran across the room to a cupboard. She opened it and withdrew several sheets of stiff paper and a set of what turned out to be paints. She carried them over and set them on the low table before them.

"You are going to make new vessels."

"Vessels?"

"For the spirits that live in the ethers."

"The what?"

"Gods, don't you know anything?"

"What the actual fuck—"

Eica cut her off. "These are pieces of paper. They are vessels for the spirits of your deck. They are the same, yet different for every diviner. Can't you see them all around you?"

"No," Harper said.

"You have received no formal training, have you?"

"No."

"Then I will be your teacher," Eica said without preamble. "But first we must make the vessels and you must call your spirits back. Then you will hear their voices again."

"It's possible to hear the same voices?" Harper said.

"Yes," Eica said, "would you like me to teach you? To help you be a diviner?"

"Yes," Harper said, "please help me get back my voices."

CHAPTER FIFTEEN

"You can't tell me how to hear the cards," Harper said matter-of-factly.

"No," Eica said as she arranged the paints and the card stock, as she called it.

"Tell me what I need to do."

"You need to listen for their voices," Eica said. "You must learn to distinguish each one and you must follow their instructions on how to create their cards."

"I don't know how—"

"To what? Well, you'd better learn. You have heard them all your life, so don't tell me you can't do anything."

There was such conviction in Eica's tone that it filled Harper with her own confidence. "All right."

"Take the shears and cut the papers into the correct size," Eica said.

Harper stopped herself from saying, *But how will I know?* She picked up a sheet. It was sturdy, with a smooth surface and sheen. She held it for a moment, enjoying the feel. Imagining how her old cards looked. She took the shears and cut. Once finished, she saw it was wrong. The shape and size were off.

"No," Eica said. "What were you thinking?"

"My old deck—"

"No!" Eica slammed one hand down on the table. "Don't think of your old cards. They are gone!" Eica snatched the ruined paper from Harper's grasp. "Try it again."

Harper's ire rose a bit, but she fought to tamp it down.

"Think of your spirits." Eica's voice was soft while still being commanding. "They are there in the places between the veils."

Harper was familiar with the veils. She was decent with manipulating them.

"Remember their voices, how distinct they were," Eica continued. "You learned them each and they haven't changed."

Harper lifted the sheet and shears and closed her eyes. She thought of the first of the Major Arcana, the Celestial Vine. It wasn't a voice, but a sensation. The kind you noticed when standing in a field with the sun high over your head and a soft breeze caressing your face. There was the smell of warm earth and wildflowers.

There came another sensation, of the supple new vines like the one from the offshoot in market square, reaching for her out of the ether, entwining themselves around Harper's fingers and wrists and guiding her movements. Warmth spread throughout her as she raised her face to that sun overhead, and it made her smile.

"Perfect," Eica said from far away.

Harper looked down and saw neat stacks of cut squares. The Vine continued to guide her hands as she chose the colors of paint and a tiny brush. The Vine brushed off the idea that she wouldn't do the pictures justice.

And Harper painted.

Each voice returned, and as Eica said, Harper recognized every one of them. They were a part of her, being her Gift. It thrilled them to be heard. Next came the Lady of Lies, the Piper, where its voice was the sound of a fife playing a merry tune. The Knot, like the Vine, was more sensation. The Deceiver, the Match Girl, the Reaper—

Then Harper was done, and she thought the Vine would retreat, but it continued to climb up her right arm. There was a tickle on her cheek that had Harper laughing, and she was certain it was moving in a pattern. Then it withdrew, releasing her arms and fingers.

Harper opened her eyes, then drew in a sharp breath. Placed in neat rows on the low table was a brand-new deck. Her deck. This was hers, not just the one given *to* her.

It took a few moments for Harper to notice that Eica was no longer present. Where had she gone? Next, she noticed the smell of food.

It surprised Harper when her stomach growled. Now, how was she hungry again?

"Ah, I see you've finished." Eica appeared, carrying a tray. "You can gather them up. The paint won't smear."

She was right. The paint was dry.

Eica set the tray down. "How do you feel?"

Harper smiled in gratitude to her. "Whole."

Eica grinned in return. "I'm glad."

On the tray was a plate of small triangle sandwiches. There was also a carafe of lemonade. "I can't believe I'm hungry again. You knew?"

"Yes," Eica said, "you may not have felt it, but this takes an immense amount of quintessence."

"I've learned that word," Harper said.

"Thank the gods for small favors."

"Oh, shut up."

Eica laughed, and Harper was glad she'd guessed right, that Eica wouldn't be upset.

"Many of our citizens don't eat meat," Eica said, "but humans enjoy such."

"Thank you," Harper said. "Eica, do your people have a name?"

She frowned in confusion. "What do you mean?"

"You call my people humans," Harper said between mouthfuls of what tasted like venison, "but what would I call you?"

"Oh, I see." Eica rolled her eyes. "You humans must always have names for everything. We go by many, but the humans of this world refer to us as animalia, although that isn't accurate."

"Why not?"

"Humans are also animalia."

"I've never heard of it either way," Harper said, "although it sounds like an animal. How can humans be animals too?"

Eica frowned, her face one of sudden concentration. "Well, the human definition of animalia is *to live and breathe and be of a lower form than humans with lesser intelligence.*"

"That's insulting."

"Agreed." Eica rose and disappeared into another room and came back with an enormous book that she was flipping through. "Here, look at this." She handed it to Harper.

Harper laid the book on her lap, leaning her head to the side like a confused puppy. "What in the nether-hells…."

It was strange, yet fascinating. Harper began turning pages, learning that some scholars considered humans animals – more accurately, mammals. "So, humans aren't special? Separate?"

"You think humans are special and animals are not?"

"No-no, that's not—" She saw the expression on Eica's face, one of amusement. "You jest."

Eica chuckled. "Keep reading."

Harper continued, learning about primates and how they had a subgroup, apes. They weren't something found in the Isles. "Are there apes here?"

"Yes," Eica said, "we have many primates. Most notably, Rukenawe the She-Ape. The oldest of all our people."

"You don't call yourselves anything?"

"We are the people of Vale. That is what we have always been."

Eica sat across from her. "You may want to look in a mirror."

Harper creased her brow. "Why?"

Eica was smiling at her as though she had a great secret. She rested her head on her palm. "There's one over there."

Harper wiped her mouth with her napkin and stood. She walked to the other side of the room where a round mirror hung on the wall. As Harper approached it, she saw what Eica had seen. Where she'd noticed the tickle earlier there was now the— Was it a tattoo? Of three vines and leaves entwined. Harper drew her fingers across it, and she felt the warmth against her skin. "What is this?"

"It is from the Vine," Eica said. "You are a Beholden to it."

"What does that mean?" Harper asked.

"The Vine helped you," Eica said, "and now, when the Vine needs you, you must answer the call."

Harper wasn't certain she liked that. "The Vine never asked for anything in return for my Gift." She turned back to the mirror, rubbed at the tattoo, hoping it would disappear. "Why now?"

"To be honest, I'm uncertain," Eica said. "You could have made your cards yourself, but perhaps the Vine felt it important to lend its help."

"I thought the Vine freely gave Gifts."

"It does." Eica stood and approached. "I don't pretend to know why the Vine chooses someone, but there are reasons unknown to us."

Eica went back to the couch. "Now come back and finish your meal before it gets cold."

Harper obeyed, but she couldn't help but continue to touch the tattooed skin.

"Stop picking at it, it won't come off. Come sit down."

Harper expelled a breath and joined Eica at the table again.

"Now, tell me how you use the spirits."

Harper wasn't sure she understood. "Mainly for divination. They also warn me of danger and, depending on what I draw, I can glean up an idea of what that may be."

"That's all?"

Harper's brow creased. "What else is there?"

Eica rolled her eyes. "Vine, love a duck."

"Now what?"

"So, you've never called on the spirits to manifest themselves?"

"Until several days ago, I didn't know that was possible."

"What happened?" Eica poured herself some lemonade.

Harper told her of the incident at the well and how the Match Girl had appeared to her.

"Her presence calmed the crowd."

"She couldn't come without your summons, even indirectly." Eica reached across the table and picked up the newly painted Match Girl. "Try it now."

Harper was unsure of what she should do. She looked at Eica.

"Draw on your power," Eica said. "As you do when you divine. It will come to you."

The Match Girl was speaking, and Harper smiled. She imagined the Girl coming out again, with her handful of Matches, caught in the beauty of her daydreams.

When Harper opened her eyes, she was there, sitting at the table, her form corporeal as before. Harper drew in a delighted breath.

"There, you see!" Eica said. "So now when they warn you of danger, they, whichever is best equipped to deal with the problem, will come forth."

They spent the next few hours with Harper practicing and calling the various spirits until she could do it without a thought.

"There is one more thing." Eica's voice was oddly quiet. "I wonder if I should tell you."

"What?"

"I hope that you never have to do this," Eica said. "But I feel you must know."

Eica straightened and placed her hands on her knees. "The spirits can do more than appear. They can lend you their strength."

"Truly?" This was a new power. Harper was eager to learn.

"Don't be so ambitious," Eica said. "It is a very dangerous thing. For this to work, they must possess you."

Her enthusiasm dimmed. "I...." Harper hesitated. A part of her wanted to experience it. Yet another feared the results. She had never seen a possessed person, but some of the stories around the den would terrify the stoutest of heart.

"If you choose this path, prepare yourself for the consequences."

"This is not a path I will travel," Harper said.

"Still, I will tell you how you may," Eica said. "You must open yourself to the spirits, but not so much as they completely take hold."

Eica went on to tell her other things. Of the dangers and what she must do if she found herself being overwhelmed by the spirits.

"Remember, they are not your servants," Eica said. "To them, quintessence is like the finest wine."

"I will take care," Harper said. By never doing it. Hopefully she would never have the need.

⋆ ⋆ ⋆

Eica gave her a vest with inner pockets and a velvet drawstring bag to place her deck in. Harper couldn't help but pat it a few times to be certain it was there. Even though she knew it was. Eica walked back to the king's parlor with her, where the two guards greeted them both. They talked for a while, as though they were all friends. And for the first time, Harper relaxed.

"I'll run down Leonine for you and tell him you're waiting for him."

"Thank you, Eica, for everything."

"You're welcome."

⋆ ⋆ ⋆

"Hold still!" Lucea demanded as she forced Harper into another dress, this one white, inlaid with tiny pearls and with a low scooped neck. And Lucea had accommodated for her dagger. Harper again strapped it to her thigh and her cards she secreted in her bodice. They were silent, which was fine because, for the first time, Harper could sense their presence. Lucea placed a spray of tiny white flowers in her hair and chose a pearl choker. The young witch stepped back and looked at her, admiring.

"You will be the prettiest of all!" Lucea said.

Harper became a bit more talented at walking with the blasted dress on, so she had no trouble following Lucea to the dining hall. Like many other rooms in the manor, it had a homey feel. Fine wood paneling lined the walls, where pictures hung of various Noble lines. The table was made of the same dark wood and the place settings were of fine porcelain and silver utensils. The servants waited at the sideboards, ready to serve.

There were a few people already seated. Leonine and the beautiful Elsabe were at each end of the long table. Aislinn and Eica were on the queen's left and right, with Bruin on the king's left and a tall, muscular man that Harper didn't recognize on his right. When Harper approached, he looked at her with eyes that reminded her of one thing: *wolf*.

He grinned, his teeth as sharp and white as the king's, but somehow the look was fiercer, hungry. If this wolf thought Harper was one of those simpering females who couldn't give as good as she got, he was mistaken. Harper kept his gaze, letting the indifference show in her expression. It was the wolf who turned away first, speaking with Leonine, who ignored him as he rose to meet Harper.

"Welcome, Lady Harper." He moved around the table to grasp both her hands. "The ladies have been eager to speak with you."

If she didn't have to sit near the wolf, that would suit her just fine.

"Harper, please sit." The queen motioned with a delicate hand to the seat next to Eica.

"It's good to see you again, Aislinn," Harper said as she made herself comfortable.

"And you as well," Aislinn said. "Eica has been singing your praises since we sat down."

"Really?"

"I'm glad she could assist you in replacing your deck," the queen said. "Would you mind doing a read for some of our other guests? I know it's a lot to ask—"

"It isn't." Harper was eager to try out her new deck. "I'm glad to."

Elsabe beamed. "Excellent!"

Others joined them, whom Harper recognized, Grymbart, and to her surprise Finnick; he was welcome in the manor. She wondered if his father was welcome. If the king was like his namesake, he'd already exiled him.

After dinner, they filed into the next room, where they had pushed chairs and couches against the walls. Decorated in the same wood paneling with more portraits of various outdoor scenes. Seated in an alcove, back by four tall windows, was a string quartet. She'd often seen them playing during celebrations. The king and queen sat in the largest chairs and signaled to the band, who played. Couples paired off.

Harper wasn't certain what she was supposed to do. When she

saw the wolf coming for her, she tensed, but right as he reached her, Finnick stepped before her. "May I have this dance, Lady Harper?"

Harper doubted Finnick could take on the wolf if he decided he wanted to dance with her more. "Yes." Harper also knew the fancier dances the nobles were fond of, thanks again to some of the wealthier patrons of the den who either gave her lessons or invited her to parties for readings where she watched.

"You look lovely," Finnick said.

"Thank you." One thing they hadn't taught her was how to make banal small talk. Not that it had ever mattered.

"They are treating you well." It wasn't a question.

"Better than expected."

"No one will punish you for Reynard's transgressions."

It was the first time someone had mentioned Red since the king in the sitting room. "If they had, I wouldn't have let them."

Finnick grinned. "I believe that."

He continued to lead her around the room while the music continued, and couples danced in all their finery.

When the song ended, Leonine approached. "May I, Master Finnick?"

"If you don't mind, Lady Harper?"

"It's fine," Harper said. She watched as Finnick approached Aislinn and bowed to her.

"He's quite the young man," Leonine said.

"I'm glad you took him in."

"It was a tragedy," Leonine said, his tone bitter. "Did he tell you the story?"

The music started again. "That his stepfather turned him and his mother out?"

"Yes," Leonine said, "I saw Jean-Pierre suffer a fitting punishment. Somewhere in the forest, a fox will meet his due."

"Good," Harper said.

The ballad ended and a bell sounded.

"Ah, the entertainment has arrived!" Leonine said.

The couples were clearing the dance floor. From outside the room came more bells, whistles, and drums, and in danced a troupe of colorful performers, ten in all. The obvious ringmaster came first, introducing the members of his troupe one by one as they entered behind him. First came two jugglers, miniature versions of adults, their pixyish faces and ears that stood tall and yet folded inwards like a rabbit. They were fae.

Next, a tall dark-skinned man, who tossed several sticks, which flamed at the tips, in the air. A Gifted fire-eater. Two dancers followed him in revealing outfits, their beauty mesmerizing, and their skin milk-white. Trailing behind were the musicians with their instruments. The crowd began showing their appreciation, laughing and applauding their antics.

An enormous woman was the last to enter, draped in voluminous robes and made up like a clown. Harper could only stare. Not because of her size – she'd seen circus fat ladies before – but because collared on the end of the leash she grasped in her hand was a sickly fox with one eye swollen shut.

Her cards whispered.

Harper was on her guard, but her eyes couldn't leave the fox. She recalled Eica's words about how to relax to hear the cards, but their words made no sense.

The laughter began, all eyes on the poor injured fox. Harper stared in horror and disgust at the rest of the troupe. And it was all very wrong.

Then came a voice she didn't expect. The Martyr. *Lament, lament!*

The room was growing dark, the bodies and faces of the people contorted, flowing between their human and animal sides. Blackness filled their eyes. And something was drowning out the voices. What did it mean? She tried reaching for her deck, but she couldn't move.

The fox was looking at her with its one baleful eye.

"Reynard?" Harper's voice sounded strange to her own ears. Something was filling her head, a sharp pounding behind her eyes, and a laugh escaped from her lips by its own volition. Harper knew what it was. She'd felt its influence back in the manor so long ago and now it was permeating the room with the stench of rotted corpses. It spread and grabbed hold of people, flowing up their legs, down their arms, and black tears fell. Another laugh burst from her lips, and she couldn't stop it.

Help me!

The Match Girl was kneeling before her, ghostlike as always, but the Match she struck flared bright as the light spread across the room, burning the Rot wherever it touched.

Harper noticed movement in the light of the Match Girl; something leaped forward but it could get no farther until, with one mighty heave, it broke free of its captor.

Reynard came for Harper with his teeth bared and sank them into Harper's right hand.

She screamed an obscenity, and the entire world around them seemed to shatter. Laughter turned to screams and hollered oaths. Harper ripped her dagger from its sheath and plunged it into Reynard's shoulder. The darkness retreated and the next Harper knew she was on the floor, holding her injured hand. Patrons tackled Reynard, smothering him in a heap. She heard Leonine screaming for the guards and for help. Then he was there, lifting her in his arms and carrying her out of the room.

Reynard had disappeared under the mass of bodies.

CHAPTER SIXTEEN

It was the sound of malicious laughter that woke Red from his fitful sleep. Not that it mattered. He didn't move as the door came open. Isengrim stepped inside. Gods, didn't that wolf have anything better to do than torment him?

Isengrim clenched something in his fist. He threw it across the small space. "Take your fox form."

Something was wrong. There was a strange echo in Isengrim's voice, like someone or something was speaking through him while it stood in his shadow. Red pushed himself onto his hands and knees and crawled to where the item had landed. In the dim light of the shed, Red saw it was some sort of costume, much too small for him. Was that why his uncle wanted him to take fox form?

Someone moved into view from behind Isengrim. It was a kitchen girl by her dress. She stood there wringing her small hands and looking as though she'd rather be anywhere else.

"Don't be afraid." Isengrim nodded. "He won't dare hurt you."

She approached and picked up the costume, "I-I'm sorry—"

"Don't apologize to him!" The shadow voice was more prominent. He saw the expression of pity turn to fear. She'd heard it too.

"It's all right." Red tried to be reassuring. It was more difficult to change than it used to be and since his beating; it was painful.

"Maybe we should shave him and cover his body in oil." Bruin's form filled the doorway. "He seems to enjoy doing that."

It was a painful reminder of how Red had used wits to defeat Isengrim in a judicial duel. One of the many times, Isengrim had demanded satisfaction, Red had thought of a way where Isengrim couldn't keep a good grip on him until finally his energy had run out. Red was proud of that one. A look of fury and then embarrassment flashed across his uncle's face. Red couldn't help but smirk.

"What are you sneering at, you rat bastard?" Isengrim took a threatening step but only scared the kitchen maid. "Get that thing on him. We're late enough as it is."

Late for what?

Isengrim turned and strode from the shed.

"We'll be back for ya later," Bruin said with a wink. As he closed the door, Red heard Bruin call out, "Hey, Isengrim, why ya so mad?"

Red thought to ask the girl what was happening. She seemed calmer and happy to dress Red up like he was a pet. She was human, he could tell by her scent. A girl from one of the human villages. When she was done, she said, "You're so cute!" He thought, *Now I have been brought so low.* It only got worse when Isengrim and Bruin returned and both guffawed.

"Come on out here!" Isengrim motioned with his arm.

Red trotted out, the light as always making his eyes tear up, to find a small troupe gathered a few steps away. He was so enthralled by the sight that he didn't consider escaping. One of them turned and approached him, a tall skinny man wearing the suit of a ringmaster. "That him?"

"That's him, all right," Isengrim said.

The man put two fingers in his mouth and whistled. An enormous woman detached herself from the group. She carried something. Red couldn't tell what it was at first, but when she got close enough, he saw—

"Gods be damned!" Although in his fox form, it came out with a feral snarl. If they put that on him, someone was getting their throat torn out. The fat woman must have understood him, even as a beast, because she hesitated.

"Don't be afraid," Isengrim said, "he can't hurt you."

Still, she wavered.

"He does and he'll be worse for it, and he knows it," Isengrim said. "Here."

He reached for the collar and leash and approached. Red's hackles rose, and he bared his teeth snarling – then every muscle in his body seized in pain and he toppled over.

"Told you!" Isengrim laughed as he shoved the collar over Red's ears and onto his throat.

Then Red recalled Noble's words: *he was still beholden to the mask.*

The fat woman took the leash with relish, jerking it and pulling Red across the grass. This kept on for several moments before Red regained control of his body. Still, it took him some time to follow the woman as she yanked him along. Unlike before, they entered the manor through the front doors.

Red heard music coming from somewhere nearby. He recalled where they were going, and they came to the dining hall where servants were cleaning up the remains of a meal. They threw leftovers out, but Red overheard the servants speaking of partaking. This Noble differed from his father.

The next room was the ballroom, not as large as many, but the music stopped when the troubadours entered, and the people made room for them. Red's fur stood on end and a chill passed over his flesh. He halted, his hackles rising again as he sensed the Rot filling the room. The part in his chest, however, had no reaction. He would have pondered it longer had not the lavishly dressed people laughed. And he saw Harper amongst them. She caught him in her beauty; he'd never seen her like that before.

He wished as he looked at her, he could tell her how sorry he was and that they'd met under any circumstances than these. Then he saw the shadow moving across the floor, like a group of venomous serpents, twining around legs and tracing paths up the delicate lacing and trails of jewels. The laughter increased to a fevered hysteria.

No, he couldn't allow that thing to touch Harper again. Did she even notice? Red leaped forward, but the leash caught him, the collar pressing to his throat. He didn't care. He called out, and she looked at him. Recognition came and Red howled, willing her to come back to him. But the Rot only pressed forward, and he saw the blackness fill her eyes.

Red bunched his muscles together and, with a feral growl, launched himself forward. He could only assume that the lady had ceased to pay him any mind, or perhaps she feared him, but he was loose, and he bounded across the floor, his eyes intent on Harper. The Rot didn't impede him, perhaps because Red's own fury fed its hunger.

Red could think of no other way to bring her out of it, so with a silent plea for forgiveness, he sank his teeth into her hand. Harper screamed, and the music and dancing ceased. He tasted her blood and felt sick with himself as he savored it.

There was a flash of silver. Her dagger. Harper had brought her dagger, of all things. He had to admire her for that. Who would keep their guard up, even in such lavish surroundings?

Red was helpless to stop her from plunging the blade into his shoulder.

He howled and let her go just as something struck him across the temple. He didn't know what it was, but he was grateful that he no longer had ahold of Harper.

There was chaos all around him, but Red couldn't comprehend with his skull exploding and his shoulder on fire before someone tackled and pinned him to the floor.

"Smother him!" A cry came up and Red panicked, struggling to throw off the weight that became heavier, which each body added. The light was going out, and he was suffocating, trying to draw in a deep breath of what air remained, filled with a sickening mixture of colognes and sweat. As Red drew in what he figured was his final breath, the weight lifted off him.

Red somehow focused around the agony in his shoulder and the pounding in his head enough to see Finnick standing over him, his eyes burning with hate that had nothing to do with the Rot. He held a walking stick, which belonged to one of the other patrons, Red supposed.

"You will not move," Finnick said.

How could he? He could smell his own blood as it matted his fur.

And every noise or movement caused a stab of pain where Finnick had struck him. "I would beat you to death it if weren't for Noble's order." He graced Red with a fierce grin. "Besides, I don't want to miss my opportunity to see you tried and hanged."

Red almost wished for the time to come. Of course, he might bleed out if someone didn't attend to his wound. *That would fix me.* Dying by Harper's blade.

Harper. "Save her."

"What?" Finnick said.

"Harper…." Red swallowed. "Please protect her."

"As if you care," Finnick said. "You should never have involved a human in your treachery to begin with."

Bruin approached. "Bastard's bleedin' all o'er the place. Noble wants him back in the shed."

"I suppose we should look to him," Reynard recognized the voice as Shahir. "I'll heal him enough, but no more."

As Red lay feeling the healing warmth as it spread all over his body, the room took on a surreal atmosphere. The servants were going about their duties as if nothing had happened. The troupe huddled near the door, comforting the fat lady, and the guests all vacated. No one seemed to pay attention to the foxes, the bear, and the cat.

Bruin hoisted him up and over his shoulder like Reynard was only a sack of grain and carried him out. The fat lady wept as they walked by. How odd it seemed. Had she been that afraid of him?

Bruin carried him all the way back to the shed. No one bothered to remove that humiliating outfit, but at least someone had left him what seemed to be an actual decent meal and waterskin. Maybe the kitchen maid had taken pity on him.

It was a treat, fried fish with roasted mushrooms. His stomach both growled and roiled at the scent. There alone in the dark, he wondered, why hadn't his darkness reacted? He ate every morsel and lay down, hoping to get one last sleep before he met his fate.

Someone was sitting across from him. They were first a shadow that took shape, like an artist bringing a painting to life. And when it was whole, Red saw it was himself. He sat grinning at Red, his expression one of the cunning that Red used to covet.

"You don't look well." It was his voice, laced with the phantom tone he'd heard with Isengrim.

Irrational anger filled him. "Where were you when they were leading me along like a common dog?"

"Tsk, tsk." Phantom-Red wagged his finger. "Some of your kin are dogs."

"Answer me!"

He grinned, his teeth glittering against the night. "We found it quite amusing."

"We?"

The grin faded. "I suppose I've said too much."

"Who are you?"

His eyes narrowed. "I am you. I am Reynard the Fox!"

"You are not!"

"No. *You* are not Reynard," he said. "You were once Reynard the Cunning. Reynard the Trickster. Now look at you!" His tone became bitter. "You are nothing. Say it."

The words wanted to come. He wanted to scream out he was nothing. A failure. The once-glorious Reynard the Fox. He should have known – *he knew* – that someday his past would catch up with him and now—

But something lurked beneath the darkness in his chest. When he closed his eyes, he could see it. It was a mere spark of something, a single red flame. He imagined reaching out for it and it flared bright, but instead of comforting him, it burned him. "Gods be damned!"

His phantom was on him, so quick he had no time to react. Its face contorted and misshapen. "We will snuff out that light! No beast is greater than us!"

The light had burned him, caused him pain. He was glad to snuff it out. His phantom-self stilled, but his hot, fetid breath washed over Red's face. "Then say you are nothing."

"No."

The thing arched its back and howled not in anger but in agony, then the form faded. "No matter," it said, "you are but one."

Then he was alone again with nothing but the wan light of dusk.

"What does any of this mean?" Red didn't expect a response and didn't receive one. "You're going mad. That's it. That's the only explanation for all this chaos."

Somehow, that amused him.

CHAPTER SEVENTEEN

It was the pain that helped her focus.

Why had Red bitten her? It hadn't taken Harper long to figure it out. Unable to warn her in his fox form, he did the only thing possible. She hadn't understood, and her own feelings of betrayal had fueled her actions.

But Red hadn't betrayed her. He'd saved her.

But did that make a difference? She wouldn't be in this danger if it weren't for him. And now—

Her hand. She could still divine, but with one hand? It would make the task harder than it should be. Harper was apart from the chaos and still in shock over her attack. Still, she recalled Leonine ripping the fine shirt he wore off and tearing the delicate silk into makeshift bandages. He wrapped her hand while shouting orders to others who came to their side. His scent and the way his muscles tightened as he carried her from the room – the attraction was there. There was nothing pure about what she was feeling.

When Leonine set her down on a couch, she put aside her thoughts. They were in a library, if the surfeit of books on shelves and piled on tables was any sign.

"Where is Shahir?" Leonine demanded.

"Here, sire." The tall dark-skinned man approached and knelt next to the couch. "May I?"

Harper held out her injured hand. This man Shahir removed the bandages. Harper figured the punctures looked worse than they were. Still, her stomach churned when she saw them. Shahir covered the bite marks and began an invocation.

With the pain lessening, Harper's mind cleared. "Your Majesty?"

"Yes? Did you need something?"

Harper wondered if she should say anything. Two servants were in the room. And servants loved to gossip. Yet perhaps it was a good thing. "I believe…your kingdom is…under attack."

"What?"

Now all the attention was on her.

"What do you mean under attack?" Leonine demanded. "By whom? Does Reynard—?"

"No." Although, how could she be sure Reynard didn't bring the Rot here? "By a…." How to explain it? "A presence. A thing of pure evil."

Leonine and Shahir exchanged a glance. There must have been some unspoken agreement between them because it was Shahir who spoke next. "What type of presence?"

Although Gifted, she wondered if a healer would understand.

"It calls itself the Rot."

Shahir's eyes widened, and he drew in a breath.

"Shahir, you are familiar with this?" Leonine asked.

"I heard rumors of it when I was in Morwynne," Shahir said. "I paid no true heed though because I was into my…studies."

Harper doubted studying was what he was doing, but kept silent.

"But what *is it?*" Leonine pressed.

Apparently tired from being on his haunches, Shahir settled on the floor. "From what I've learned, it's something created in Underneath, which is…the true underground dwellers. Those from Deep Earth."

"I hope you're not saying other denizens of Underneath are trying to take our kingdom?"

"I wish I had a response for you, sire," Shahir said. "Tell us, Lady Harper, what else do you believe?"

Harper didn't want to bring Reynard up, but…. "It was in the manor where Reynard found the mask," she said. "It's like…a living shadow, well, not a shadow…." How could she explain what she'd seen and felt? "I wish I could give you more. It was here when you brought Reynard—"

"Reynard," Leonine growled the name. "Of course."

"No, that's not—"

"He will tell us what this is."

"Listen to me, gods be damned!" Harper supposed this would scandalize the gossips. "Reynard has nothing to do with it. This thing is ancient, that's the sense I got from it."

"And why did you sense this, and I didn't?" Shahir's tone was accusatory.

"What the fuck is that—" Then Harper saw.

Shahir's eyes were black. The color of oil moved within his sockets and then was gone. "That's how it does it," Harper said. "It sneaks in and takes hold. It feeds on hate, cruelty, and suspicion."

Did Shahir not sense the Rot's influence? It didn't matter because she couldn't trust him. Or anybody? She thought of Eica.

"How I sensed it and not you? I don't know."

"You fought it?" Leonine asked.

"No." Harper caught and held his gaze. "In fact, if Reynard hadn't bitten me, it would have taken complete hold." That's all she would do for the wily fox.

"I don't recall any influence either," Leonine muttered. "I am the king. Nothing takes hold of me."

Harper almost said, *You're human.* Not that it mattered. The look on Leonine's face told her he refused to believe it. She knew how dangerous it could be. Any sign of weakness—

Harper refused to coddle him. Wouldn't his people be in greater danger? Again, she spoke. "I can't explain the motives of a beast."

The king was quiet. Then he appeared to decide. He stood, facing the servants. "You." He pointed to the nearest one. "Fetch Eica." To the second he said, "Find Lucea and bring her here. And send for Prince Tybert."

Leonine turned back to Harper. "Eica will do a divination. Harper, you will observe and assist."

Since she wanted to talk to Eica, Harper didn't protest being ordered about.

"Shahir," Leonine said, "I am sorry, but I need to send you away again."

"Don't apologize, Your Majesty," Shahir said, "I will be happy to return to my studies, but, and please forgive my forwardness, but what of the mask and Reynard?"

"The spell won't hold?"

"Oh, it will," Shahir said, "that is, if no one damages it. Right now, it's locked up, but if I stay away too long, its influence over Reynard will fade."

"He doesn't know that," Leonine said. "Things will progress as they are. Tomorrow we will have the trial, so we may deal with this threat."

Things happened quickly after that. Eica and Lucea arrived at the library. Leonine gave some whispered instructions to the young chronomancer, and she left. He directed Harper and Eica to sit at one of the rectangular tables set between some shelves.

Eica asked, "What is this all about, Harper?"

"You'll have to ask Leo— The king," Harper said. "But he wants you to do a divination and me to observe."

When the king did approach, he sat down at the head of the table. "Lady Eica, I called you here because Lady Harper says we are under attack by some supernatural being."

Eica's gaze went to Harper. "Supernatural being?"

The king repeated everything Harper had said, and when he finished, Eica looked frightened. "By the Vine." She turned to Leonine. "Sire, Harper and I should do a joined reading." Then to Harper she said, "Have you ever done one before?"

"Yes, with the woman who gave me my first deck."

"What do you mean, joined?" Leonine asked.

"Harper and I will divine together, and the spirits within our cards may draw strength from the both of us. It may help us in traversing the veils to seek more information about this Rot."

"This action doesn't sound safe," Leonine said.

"It isn't safe," Eica said. "Manipulating the veils is never safe."

"Very well," Leonine said, "begin."

"Sire, you should leave," Harper said.

"What? I'll do no such—"

"Leo." Eica dropped all pretense, "Harper is right. We may search for information, but there's no guarantee we won't attract the attention of some otherworldly being."

"It could attack you, possess you, do all manner of things," Harper said.

"I will not leave."

"You're being pigheaded as usual." There was more worry than anger in Eica's words.

Harper didn't like the idea either, but Leonine refused to listen. She withdrew her cards from their pouch. There was a familiar thrumming in her mind – the murmuring of their presence and that they were ready to speak. Eica felt the same way.

"When you did this last, what happened?" Eica asked her.

"Nothing worrisome," Harper said. "We divined some simple everyday things."

"You know how to open yourself up to another person?"

"Yes."

"Then let's begin."

Harper took some deep breaths, finding the spirits much easier to see this time. Not solid, luminous like the Match Girl in the ballroom. Harper only noticed that she'd laid out her cards in the Celestial Cross until after the last one had been laid down. Eica had done the same thing.

Necromancer.

Steel Driver.

Five of Swords.

Two of Wands.

Harlot on top. Martyr underneath.

Jack.

Knot.

Witch.

Something wasn't right. Eica's spread differed from hers. Harper caught Eica's gaze, and it mirrored her own distress.

Leonine broke the silence. "What is it? Dire portents?"

Harper moistened her lips and waited for Eica to speak, uncertain if it was her place.

"My cards," Eica began, "say that everything is well. That there will be peace and prosperity."

"But that's good, isn't it?" Leonine said.

"No," Eica said, "Harper's say the exact opposite."

"Harper?" Leonine said.

"I won't go into explanations." Did Leonine know about reading cards? Had Eica taught him anything? There would be misery, deceit, and a battle of the mind, the cards implied. No, they said it would be Harper who would have to fight. Her mind must remain her own, while everyone else risked being carried away. That was not what she wanted. Harper wanted to leave now and not be a part of this journey the cards had set her upon.

But there was no way to change the fate given to her.

Even if she left, this fate would follow her back to Above Ground and disrupt the lives of those she loved.

"Harper!" Leonine's voice broke through her gloomy thoughts.

Harper gathered up her cards. "I'm leaving."

"What?" Both Eica and Leonine said in unison.

"I never wanted to come here," Harper said. "You have Reynard. There is no reason for me to stay."

"There is," Eica said. "I know you want to leave, and you know it would be pointless."

"One of you had better explain!" Leonine roared, pushing back from the table and standing. "What is it, gods be damned!"

"Leo." Eica raised her hand in a silencing gesture. The King of Vale quieted.

"Harper," Eica said, "you won't be able to escape this."

"You are the more experienced one of us," Harper said. "Maybe your divination is correct."

Eica shook her head. "No."

"But Eica –" Leonine sat down again, "– you are the more experienced. I'm inclined…" he turned to Harper, "…please, I mean no offense, but I'm inclined to trust Eica's reading more."

"Because it's what you want to hear?" Harper said.

"Yes," Leonine said.

Harper's hands flew and continued to straighten and gather her cards. "That is on your head." She slid them into the pouch. "I'll need some transport. I can't very well walk to the gate. Do you have a donkey?"

"You can't leave now. It will be dark soon," Eica said.

"Fine, I'll leave in the morning." Harper strode off, and just as she moved out of the room, Leonine stood.

"Harper, wait!"

Leonine followed her into the empty hallway.

"Is it seemly for the king to pursue a commoner?"

"I don't give a damn about that!" Leonine waved his arm in a wide arc. "I don't want you to go."

"I will not—"

"You don't have to do anything," Leonine said, ran his hand through his mane. "I just want you to stay, be part of my pride. A queen."

"How can you even think about that now?" Harper would never understand royals.

"You will not need to do anything. I will be certain you are safe."

Harper blew out a breath. "You don't understand."

"No, I don't," Leonine said, "but if you remain, you will help me come to understand."

"Leonine, leave her be." Eica had joined them in the hall.

"Eica—"

Harper kept walking as Leonine and Eica started in on each other in a language that Harper didn't recognize. *Let them squawk like crows. I'm leaving this place.*

As she walked, the visions began.

Her cards whispered, but the visions, which had been brief, now hit her with the force of their will. She saw the veils as they slipped between them. She'd never seen the veils to this extent, and it frightened her. Harper broke into a run, but the images followed her. If anyone was in her way or saw her fleeing, she didn't see, for the veils were whipping as though caught in a torrent. Her card spirits continued to dart back and forth underneath and straight through them.

Arriving in her room made no difference. They were still there, although now the veils had ceased their flailing. The spirits had gathered, still and patient.

Waiting.

"No," Harper said aloud. "No, no, *no!*"

Harper threw herself onto the bed, burying her face into the plush pillows. *I am no gods-be-damned hero. I am a simple diviner. I will not devote my life to anyone but myself!*

The spirits remained, still waiting.

* * *

As always, Harper knew when she fell asleep, for now she was sitting in a library, but it wasn't the one in Leonine's manor. This one was much grander, the shelves reaching the bottom of a high-domed ceiling. She was, however, seated at the same type of rectangular wood table. The tables were all around, along with comfortable reading chairs and a line of windows allowing light to pour in.

"Hello."

The sudden voice and appearance of the beautiful, dark-skinned woman sitting across from her caused Harper to jump and give a squeal.

"I'm sorry. I didn't mean to surprise you."

"Who—" Harper began. "Wait, I know you. You're her! The witch."

She grinned. "My name is Isbet."

"Why did you fucking drag me into the ethers, gods damn it?"

If her language offended, Isbet didn't react. There was something serene about the woman. Not fiery like Harper, or at least that's how Pops—

Pops. Marcel. Osvald. Dear Vine, she didn't realize how much she missed them. How much she missed her old life. She'd been so taken in by this place she'd almost forgotten....

Isbet had moved closer and took her hands, squeezing them. Harper hated crying in front of a stranger, but fear filled her with what she would have to face.

"I know it's hard," Isbet said. She lifted her hand to Harper's eye level, and that's when Harper saw the tattoo of vines entwining Isbet's wrist.

"You too," Harper said. "The Vine marked you."

Isbet nodded. "You must not be afraid, dear Harper. Whatever plans we may have had, they are meaningless when you are beholden to the Vine."

"But I didn't ask for this!"

"Oh, but you did," she said, "although you may not have realized it. The Vine knew your desire, but it does not give freely."

"My friend Eica said the same," Harper said. "What is the Rot?"

Isbet's brow creased, and she pinched the bridge of her nose with her thumb and forefinger. "It is all that is unholy. Filth. Grief, hatred, loneliness, want...." She sighed.

"Is it us? Humanity? We spawned it?"

"No," Isbet said, "the others did."

"Others?"

"The Children, those born of the Vine?"

Harper nodded.

"Then you know about the others," Isbet said, "also born of the Vine, but they covet the shadows. How much do you know about the time before?"

Harper shrugged. "I've had no schooling, only what I hear around the den."

"Tragically, we lost most of the history. There are many theories about what transpired after the farm boy felled the Vine. Good cannot thrive without its opposite. For every Child that was brought forth in the light, there was one for darkness."

"I have been told in those times, humans weren't safe from either," Harper said.

"They were not," Isbet replied. "Humanity was just something to be tolerated. Although many of the light protected them. The shadows overwhelmed the land, so the Vine drove them down, deep into the earth, even beyond where the dead lay, and there they stayed."

"What stirred the pot?"

"Now, that *is* man's fault," Isbet said.

It wasn't hard to understand. "How did you find out about this?"

"I was called to Underneath and shown that the Vine was growing,"

Now Harper's brow creased. "That's a bad thing?"

"Yes, considering it is what holds the Isles together."

"Oh, dear Vine," Harper said. "You mean…?"

"And denizens from Deep Earth now want to return to Above Ground, their desire so fierce that they birthed the Rot."

"And it will keep coming." An eerie calm washed over Harper. "I have to do this."

"Your Reynard needs you."

"Reynard," Harper said, "was never to blame."

The scene was rent in pieces. The books were torn from their bindings and the shelves shattered into splinters while Harper watched as the Rot filled the room and reached for her with black tendrils. Isbet touched her in the center of her forehead, jolting Harper awake.

The Rot had almost taken her. She could only hope Isbet escaped. It was just coming into the dawn. Had she slept through the night? Soon they would put Red on trial. Harper realized how inconsequential this all was. Their petty grievances against Red were meaningless.

She had to stop them.

Harper didn't bother washing up and changing clothes. She ran from the room and down the hall, but only got a short way before she realized how eerily silent the manor was. At least the servants should be up and about preparing for the day's work. Where was everyone?

Her cards began their whispering, although they needn't have warned her. Harper stopped and drew them out. The first card was the Martyr, and she heard its cry once again. *Lament, lament!* She replaced it, knowing for whom it cried. Both the people of Vale and Above Ground.

Further searching proved futile. There was no one in the manor. Her heart dropped to her stomach as she ran until she came to the throne room, also empty, but lights were blazing everywhere. The doors stood open, and Harper saw what looked like the whole of everyone living in the manor heading towards town.

Harper broke into a run again and didn't stop, even as her sides ached and her heart hammered. She pushed herself on until she caught up with the group as they stood gathered at the town square. Leonine was standing on something she couldn't see, his sight above the crowd.

Their gazes locked, and Leonine smiled in a way that sent a chill through Harper. Even from where she stood, Harper could see his eyes were pools of black. Her cards were screaming now, their sounds filling her ears and her mind until she could no longer concentrate.

"Harper!" Even with the din, she heard when Leonine called her name. The group turned as one and the same eerie smile, identical to Leonine's, split each face. The crowd parted, forming an aisle. There was Red, on his knees before Leonine, who stood atop a large crate. "Come closer," Leonine called to her, "we've been waiting for you. No trial for Reynard. I have made my judgement."

The Rot had them all.

CHAPTER EIGHTEEN

When the phantom came again, Red knew he was done.

"They are coming for you."

"About gods-be-damned time." No one had come to the shed in what seemed like days, and it stank of his piss and shite. He would have vomited from the stench if his stomach wasn't empty. Dry heaves were all he managed.

When Red heard the movement outside, the sound was like a gaggle of geese. How many witnesses to his execution? Someone shoved the door open so hard it banged against the wall. Several forms tried to push in at the same time. A tangle of bodies, seeming to meld together as one deformed being. Red expected Isengrim to be the first to lay hands on him, but Leonine himself blotted out what limited light there was, seeming more massive than Red thought was possible.

Leonine gripped Red by the scruff, lifting him off his feet as claws dug into his flesh, and he couldn't stop from crying out. The group found that amusing, their laughs bordering on hysterical. They had the phantom voice behind theirs.

As they half dragged Red through the wooded area, his phantom took the form of a fox, or more accurately, the shadow of a fox, as it danced and cavorted, and the space in Red's chest pulsed, matching the rapid beating of his heart.

They came to the street. This early many of the citizens slept, but the eerie quiet lent an unnatural air to what was happening. The laborers should have been about their business, but there weren't any. They stopped at market square and Leonine stepped in front of the crowd and turned to face his bewitched subjects. Someone behind Red planted their hands on his shoulders and forced him to his knees.

"Bring me something to stand on that I may address you, my people!" Leonine said. After a time, they dragged a crate out and Leonine climbed atop it. "My loyal citizens, people of Vale! Would you waste time telling of Reynard's transgressions against you, or would you have me judge him now?"

"Judge him!" the crowd yelled as one.

Leonine laughed from deep in his chest. "What say you, my loyal subjects? Hanging? Tar and feather? Shall we bind him in his fox form until his senses leave him?"

The crowd shouted various methods of how to end Red's life. Leonine let his subjects continue, with mirth in his expression at each idea. Finally, the king raised his hands to silence them.

"Let us not kill him! I say to the Cesspit!"

"Yes! Yes! To the Cesspit!"

"Reynard of Vale, I sentence you to the Cesspit for the rest of your natural life," Leonine said. "There you will feed us and strengthen us."

Red didn't know what the Cesspit was, but it didn't bode well for him. And what did Leonine mean by feed us? Red recalled that his phantom had spoken of *us*, like there was more than one entity. Red's phantom had disappeared, but the piece in Red's chest filled him with a giddiness, like he'd consumed too much wine. He was grinning and not wanting to.

"Look at him!" Leonine was pointing at him. "He still believes he is better than the rest of you!"

"To the Cesspit with him!" The crowd's cheering rose to a fever pitch. As the first rays of the sun filled the square, Red looked at Leonine's eyes and how the Rot lived in them. He searched the crowd and found they, too, had black eyes and faces twisted in their want to punish Red. There was no hope. He looked skyward to see the last light and waited.

Then Leonine spoke and Red's blood ran cold.

"Harper," Leonine called out, "we've been waiting for you. No trial for Reynard. I have made my judgement."

Harper, gods be damned, no! "Leonine!" Red didn't bother with protocols. "Please let Harper return to Above Ground, and I will go willingly!"

They ignored him. "Bring him! Lady Harper will learn what is to become of him!"

"Harper!" Red hoped she heard him above the crowd. "Run! Run to Above Ground!"

Then Red was being pushed along with the wave of bodies, hands coming from everywhere, ushering him forward. They walked, Red barely able to keep up, but whenever he stumbled, someone would pull him to his feet.

It was full daylight when they left the city and came to the dirt road from where they first entered Vale. It seemed like forever ago. Now as Red struggled to keep moving along the road, trying to keep up with the crowd, hoping he didn't fall, he thought about everything that had happened since finding that damnable mask.

You walked right into that, you stupid cur! You'd still be free if you weren't so greedy.

They got to the doors and Leonine pushed them open with ease. The crowd started again, shoving him out into the cavern. To his horror, the Rot had infected everything. The stench was so vile it burned Red's nostrils and filled his lungs, causing a fit of coughing.

They walked deeper into the cavern, until they came to a clearing and there, a hole ripped into the ground like a knife wound. No light came from the place and if the stench in the cavern burned him with every breath, the smell of this place made him want to vomit. It was nothing like he'd ever experienced, and it gripped Red with a terror that spoke to him. *You cannot go down there!*

The crowd halted at the edge. Leonine raised his hands for quiet once again. "I have led us here by command of our brethren, who told us of this place and how it hungers for the souls of those who are unclean."

The Rot said he was unclean? Red would have laughed. "Leonine!" he called, "don't you see you are being influenced by this evil? The Rot has warped your mind and your souls." Red broke free of those who held him and turned to confront the crowd. "The souls of you all! You must fight its influence!"

Why was he even trying to reason with them? Were they so weak that they allowed this thing to take hold? Perhaps they deserved whatever fate the Rot planned for them. Still, he was a citizen of Vale and, as Pops had said, they were his kin. He knew what the Rot was, and it was not something he'd wish on an enemy, let alone these people.

But Leonine said, "After a century of freedom, we will punish you for your crimes. Goodbye, Reynard."

The crowd hoisted him up above their heads with surprising strength and carried him to the edge.

"No, don't do it!"

Harper. Could she still be here? Why, by the gods, hadn't she listened to him? "Harper!" Before he could warn her, the crowd pitched him into the darkness. No, not just darkness. It was absolute nothingness. Even when there was a new moon, one's eyes would still adjust, taking in what scant light there was until things took shape.

However, once he passed the entrance, everything vanished. There was no light, not even the memory of it, when Red squeezed his eyes shut. The absence of light was overwhelming. Even his cry as he fell seemed muted. Would he fall all the way to Deep Earth?

He plunged into an icy sludge that threatened to pull him down to his death. Red struggled, flailing his arms and legs until his natural instincts took hold. Still, it was agony, the cold threatening to stop his motions and his heart. He came to what seemed solid ground and pulled himself out of the muck.

Red lay there curled up and shivering like a newborn. What now? Would he lie there until he died by starvation or thirst? Or should he shift into his fox form and let go?

"You're a pathetic creature."

Red was beyond fear, beyond caring, so he didn't respond when the voice came out of the shadows.

"What will you do now, Reynard the Fox?"

Lie here and die, you bastard.

"You don't have to. Come to me and I will give you the means for revenge."

Did it even matter now? He just wanted to stay where he was and let whatever take him.

"Get up!" The voice of his mother caused him to bolt upright. "You lazy, worthless animal! What did I tell you? You are a fox! You are cunning and guile! Stop this shameful behavior!"

Red pushed himself up on his hands and knees. Had he heard his mother's voice? Now that he was on his feet, he saw something – brief flashes of cold white light, showing a sinuous movement like serpents twisting and entwining, expanding themselves forward and upward. This was the Rot devouring the green of the true Celestial Vine and feeding off all the ills of the world.

"Is humankind, is animalia so far gone that this is their fate?" Red said aloud. "To what ends? What do you hope to accomplish?"

The rotten vines crawled their way across the floor towards him. Red stepped back until he felt something on his neck, almost in a caress. He spun around to face more coming for him from his opposite side. Red placed himself in the center and took a few cautious steps back.

The vines joined in the center of the space, the cold light current still making its fleeting appearance as tiny streaks of lightning in a black sky. Continuing to entwine, they made a form, human. A woman who reached her arms out to Red as though asking for an embrace.

"Red." The sound of his name on the lips of this thing was an affront to him. Was this thing supposed to be Harper? The sight of it both sickened and infuriated him. How dare they do this to his memory of Harper?

"Red," the thing called to him again.

"No more. No more Red. I am Reynard the Fox!"

The change came, as he recalled it, fur bristling, muscles tightening, hands and feet now pawed and clawed. And he could see. There were no longer just streaks of light but the things from the bowels of Deep Earth. He'd seen some of them in his nightmare. Others Reynard couldn't tell what they were, but they had him turn and escape their reach.

As Reynard continued, he noticed his phantom was silent. And the hole in his chest, although not gone, seemed as if something was dampening its power. He thought, *Is this what the phantom wanted?*

Reynard realized something else – every time he was in his fox form, the Rot's influence lessened. He couldn't figure out why. Cunning and guile weren't a substitute for true intelligence. But wasn't that just another way of saying intelligence?

He stopped and sat, raising his snout to glean any scents besides that sickening bog stink that permeated the air. Their sense of smell was one of the fox's greatest talents. It didn't take him long to discover *something*.

There it was, a distinct scent that seemed to find its way through. Yes, Reynard focused on it. It was mild and like tilled earth and greenery. Reynard didn't know what he would find, but he would not allow himself to give up, at least not yet. He continued to move forward.

It wasn't long before Reynard saw a light shining like a beacon. It wasn't burning bright, but it was enough that it drew Reynard. When he came upon it, he found it was a seedling. He supposed that was the right term for it, a single stem with two rounded leaves. How it looked so green and supple and how it glowed with a warm light was beyond Reynard's understanding.

Reynard didn't know why, but the need to protect this small sign of life welled in him. It was the least he could do until death took him. Maybe the gods or the Vine would look on him, and he would end up somewhere nice.

Death was not a subject he'd ever considered, even when he faced it. He'd always been able to scheme his way out of it. But how long could one count on cunning and guile before fate just said enough? Reynard barked a laugh. Well, he was finding out now.

Reynard settled down, curling his body around and within the blossom of light.

The beings of darkness gathered near, filling the air with their growls and laughter. Reynard made it clear by how he gazed at them that the seedling was under his protection. If they found this amusing, to the nether-hells with them all.

No matter how many gathered, they never strayed too close. They played at who could come the closest before scurrying away like cockroaches surprised by daylight. When they dared touch it, it burned them, but they bragged as though they'd made some glorious act of bravery.

Reynard continued to watch, keeping one eye on the beasts and the other on the plant, never straying from his vigil.

"Red."

Reynard raised his head. "I am not—"

"…if you can hear me, I'm coming."

"Harper." Reynard came to his feet. "You can't. I'm not worth it."

The things chortled. Reynard was sick of the sight of the bastards. A part of him, and he knew it was the Rot's attraction, wanted him to attack, but that other part of him….

"Harper." Reynard settled back down. "I'll think of something, I promise. I will free you from the cost of my misdeeds."

CHAPTER NINETEEN

He was gone.

Afterwards, the crowd turned silent, their faces blank and their eyes still black.

"Wait!" Harper reached out to stop someone, but they pulled from her grasp. "Wait, you can't, damn you all!" The same thing happened, no matter who she tried to stop. They ignored her, intent on walking.

Harper saw Aislinn. She pushed her way through the group and grabbed her by the arm. Aislinn looked at her, no recognition in her expression at first. "Aislinn?"

"Harper?" She seemed confused. Black tears flowed down her cheeks. "Eica."

Aislinn shook off her grip and continued to follow the crowd.

"Leonine!" The king was the last to follow and cried black tears too.

Harper grasped his muscular forearm. "You've got to break free of its influence!"

He turned to look at her. Then he gripped her shoulder and shoved her to the ground.

"Go." He said the single word, but his tone was in obvious pain. Was he warning her? Telling her to leave Underneath as Red had begged him? The fox was thinking of her safety. It changed her perception of him and what his fate might be. Harper picked herself up, indecision gnawing at her. This was never any of her concern. Then she remembered Eica—

Aislinn spoke her cousin's name. Harper wondered, was Eica in the crowd? She turned towards the pit. "Red, if you can hear me, I'm coming."

Harper walked, not wanting to catch up to the crowd or risk

someone seeing her. Her cards had gone silent, which Harper found ironic since they knew she was going back into the lion's den. Harper chuckled at her own joke.

It was well into the morning when she reached the square. There were people outside. The shops were open, and everyone seemed to be about their business, but there was something...stoic in their movements. No one smiled or laughed, there was no bartering or arguing over prices. Their actions were unconscious. They were sleepwalking through the day. Harper continued walking and trying not to meet anyone's gaze.

No one seemed interested in her presence. She noticed they didn't have the Rot in their eyes. So, what was happening here? It was then the cards began their whispering. As discreetly as she could, Harper drew her cards again. A simple three. The Steel Driver, Ace of Bones, and the Trumpeter.

"You tell me a destiny I already recognize," Harper muttered aloud.

There was no one without when she arrived at the estate. She didn't know if she should walk in or find an alternate route. As she approached the threshold, the bitter scent of the Rot wafted out. Faint but recognizable.

Harper swore. She started forward and kept a grip on her card pouch. Where everyone had gone remained shrouded in mystery, but she thought she heard a voice speaking somewhere and she moved in that direction. It was in the throne room, where Harper found Leonine sitting on his throne.

Something else was with him.

Harper kept herself just out of sight. Leonine slumped down with his head rested on his fist. Something sat at his feet. Vaguely human but not flesh, a tangle of pale vines that moved from the whole. It was whispering, but Leonine didn't react. Harper noticed his eyes were no longer black, but his expression mirrored those of his subjects.

Harper stepped into view. Leonine glanced up at her, his eyes widening slightly as they darted back and forth. Something of him was hanging on. Harper nodded. She slipped away. She went in search of Eica.

Trying her room first, Harper came upon a sight that she found difficult to believe. There was a figure on their knees before Eica's door. A...how to describe it? Bubble of light. Strange symbols moved over its surface. As she got closer, she realized the figure was an old woman. Harper was certain she'd seen her before—

"Dear Vine." Harper reached out but did not dare to touch the bubble. "Lucea."

Lucea's expression was pained, as though she were fighting an inner battle. She didn't seem to notice Harper's presence. Since she had little knowledge of chronomancy, Harper decided not disturb whatever it was Lucea was doing. When she heard a sound in Eica's room, Harper didn't hesitate; she grasped the handle and pushed the door wide.

The room was in shambles.

"Eica?" As Harper stepped farther within, she saw—

Eica lay prone and sprawled by the table where they had lunch, it seemed forever ago, when her fellow diviner had helped her make new cards. Harper rushed to her side and knelt. She grasped her shoulders and turned her over. Eica's eyes were open, and her chest rose and fell, but she didn't seem to notice Harper was there.

"Eica?"

She blinked, and her eyes focused. "Harper."

"Tell me how I can help."

Eica flinched and moaned, as though struck with pain. "I'm trying...."

"I know," Harper said. She pushed her arm underneath Eica's shoulders and helped her to sit up.

"The cards."

Harper hadn't noticed them before, across the table.

"We're fighting," Eica said. "We're all fighting together, but we don't know how long —"

"Hush," Harper said. "Concentrate on that." Harper gathered up her cards and stacked them, then she went around the other side of the table and sat, her legs curled underneath her. Her cards came out.

"Reynard...."

"I know," Harper said. "As soon as I can figure out how to save him, I'll go."

Eica's hand shot out and gripped Harper's wrist with surprising strength. "You should go—"

"No," Harper said with a finality that surprised even her. "Talk to me, Eica, how is it you can fight?"

"Something inside...." Eica released her hand and it fell limp onto the table. "Your cards."

Harper wasn't sure what that meant, but she laid the cards.

King of Bones, Three of Wands reversed, Ace of Bones....

Something was creeping up on them. A pervasive chill entered the room.

The Deceiver reversed.

Harper was surprised when she drew the Match Girl and she appeared, with her Match burning bright, cradling the flame with her palm. The light was to keep her focused and to keep the Rot at bay. It seemed to work because the presence ceased its movement. Harper placed the Match Girl card aside from the others. She looked at Eica and noticed her eyes were closed.

"Eica."

"Tell me," Eica said, "tell me what they say."

"They talk about strength and power. A leader with..." she realized, "...animal instincts." Harper thought that meant more than just Leonine. Cards used people as references, but the other two spoke of inner clarity and rethinking an idea, intermixed with cold, hard facts. She told Eica and came to the Deceiver reversed. "But this makes little sense. We know the reversed Deceiver means someone is using your own weakness against you. That is about the Rot itself. And these," Harper motioned to the others, "are telling us that there are facts and truth that—" *Wait.* "Yes." Harper drew five more cards. They stayed Bones, Wands and for the first time, the Knight of Coins. Again, like the Ace of Bones, it referenced fighting with an animallike fervor. The deep-seated instincts of the hunter in humanity. "I see now. The animal part of you. It keeps the Rot from taking complete control."

Eica gave her a tired smile. "So that's what they were trying to tell me." Harper figured she meant her own cards. The Rot must have attacked as she was laying them out.

"Eica, what did you and Leonine fight about after I left the library?"

She didn't answer immediately. "May I have some water, please?"

"Of course." As Harper went to fetch it, Eica began speaking.

"I tried to tell Leonine to listen to you," she said. "He refused to believe. He wanted to meet with the prince and have his troops deployed throughout the kingdom, but I told him that would do no good."

"Is Tybert here?"

"I don't know."

"Lucea is sitting outside of your door." Harper returned to the table with the water and took Eica's hand, leading her to the glass. "She's aged far beyond her years."

"I told her not to!"

"But what is she doing?"

Eica took a sip. "Trying to keep the Rot at bay by…creating what she called a circle in time."

Harper's brow creased. "What does that mean?"

"If I'm understanding," Eica said, "she is keeping me…us and this room at the same time. It doesn't go forward or backwards. Did you feel something here just now?"

"Yes," Harper said, "the Rot was trying to steal upon us."

"That's as far as it got," Eica said. "But if you say she looks aged, then she is using every drop of her power and she will die if she keeps on."

"I've been told whenever a chronomancer uses their power, the realm takes back a bit of theirs," Harper said.

"That is the truth." Eica sipped again.

"I didn't want to disturb what she was doing," Harper said.

"That is the correct course of action."

"If the Rot hasn't taken Prince Tybert and his troops, I could use their help to rescue Red."

"You have the Rot's attention again. Once you leave this room, it may try to attack you, as it did me."

"All this destruction." Harper looked around the room.

"It was more than a mental battle," Eica said. "But Harper, you are the Vine's Beholden. Perhaps as it has been doing that it will protect you further."

Her voice faded. "I still wish you would go."

"I can't, and you know it," Harper said. "Leonine said the same. We must stop the Rot here or not at all."

She gathered up her cards, including the Match Girl. "Vine protect you."

Eica was asleep, or so it seemed. She didn't respond. When Harper stepped into the hall again, Lucea looked worse than before. Heavily wrinkled and emaciated, her clothes mere rags hanging off her skeletal frame.

"Gods be damned," Harper muttered. "Forgive me if this is a mistake, Lucea."

As always, she drew cards. The Reaper and the Necromancer. Harper muttered an oath. Of course, both cards didn't mean death on their own, but both together? Harper reached out and touched the bubble with her fingertips. The symbols wavered as her fingers stung with cold pinpricks. She drew them back and took a deep breath.

Harper plunged her hand through and screamed at the sudden icy daggers piercing her skin, but she continued, laying her hand on Lucea's shoulder, and shook her. The bubble shattered, spraying tiny shards of ice, which covered Harper. To her shock, her arm fell lifeless to her side.

"Dear Vine—"

Lucea toppled onto her side, unconscious. Harper pulled herself over to the girl and leaned in, pressing her ear near Lucea's face. She was breathing. Harper could only hope she recovered.

Her only problem now was getting out of the manor and finding

Tybert, if he wasn't already here. Harper started back down the hall but halted when she heard footsteps. More a click-click sound than normal footfalls. Harper did not like the sound, so she turned in the opposite direction and ran.

A howl filled the hallway, and the sounds came faster. Harper dared to look back to see –*Dear Vine*– Isengrim, or at least a deformed version of him, caught somewhere between his human and wolf self, as though undecided what form he should take.

The thing was coming for her. She had to do something. She would fight if it came to that, but she knew she didn't stand a chance. She was in an unfamiliar part of the manor now. She turned down a hall, hoping it led to the entrance, but even as that thought occurred to her, she knew she'd be out in the open.

She'd have to deal with Isengrim.

Another turn and she came to a heavy wood door, marred by use. The thing was almost on her, but she pulled the door open and slammed it shut, then pushed the heavy bar through its holders. The thing threw itself against it, but the door held. Harper found herself in the kitchen. Pots had been left boiling on the stove, and something burned in the oven, pouring out black smoke. Food left out on the cooking block was now a banquet for swarms of flies.

A crow flew in the window, scaring the shite out of her. It was too small to be a shape-shifter. It squawked at Harper, then picked at the half-eaten loaves of bread. As she was watching it, she noticed the silence. If Isengrim thought she would open the door to check, well, that was damned insulting.

It wouldn't take long for him to figure out she would not indulge him. The other door led outside to the gardens, with neatly arranged rows of vegetables and fruit trees. Before Harper stepped outside, she grabbed a machete hanging on the wall. She checked her surroundings; not seeing any sign and knowing she couldn't stay there forever, she started at a jog down the garden path.

Movement to her left alerted her almost too late that Isengrim had found her. In his current state, he couldn't take her by surprise, but it was enough that he caught her out in the open. What he didn't see was the machete in her hand. Just as he got close enough to tear her throat out, Harper swung the blade in a sideways arc, slashing across his chest. Harper barely jumped out of the way as his momentum brought him forward and he fell.

Isengrim pushed himself to his knees and twisted his head around at an impossible angle to glare at her.

"Isengrim, you must take your wolf form." Harper backed away as she spoke. "It's the only way to—"

Isengrim spun around and leaped. Harper gripped the haft of the machete, bracing it against her shoulder. Isengrim ran right into it. Again, momentum sent them both down. Harper was underneath him. She heaved with her body weight and pushed him off.

Harper crawled back. Isengrim lay there with the machete buried in his shoulder, his chest rising and falling, and a growl erupted with every breath. His eyes were wide, but his expression, like that of the others, was blank.

"I'm sorry." Harper climbed to her feet, sick at the thought of leaving him, but what could she do? She had to escape. There was no way of knowing if the Rot would send someone else after her. It could be Leonine next.

However, an added problem presented itself. She still didn't know if Tybert was anywhere near here. She didn't remember seeing him or his daughter as a part of the mob, so maybe they were free from the Rot? Right now, Harper wanted to put as much distance between herself and the manor as possible. Two roads branched off from the main. And as always, Harper consulted her cards. Deciding a path was quite easy in divination; they gave her the left road.

It seemed Harper walked alone on the road for hours. The light was in the center of the sky and Harper's stomach growled and her throat was dry by the time she crested a hill and saw a small castle. There was movement in the courtyard. Maybe she could find help there.

The cards started. Harper recognized the voice of the Lady of

Lies. So, she wouldn't find help there either. Maybe she should return to Innrone to get the guard? Or better yet, Pops could get her mercenaries in no time. Enough money and they'd do everything.

She turned to go and came face-to-face with a large black cat.

It growled, its green eyes glistening. It crouched, ready to pounce.

"Who are you?" Harper hoped it was a citizen of Vale.

The cat straightened, and it seemed to rise on its haunches.

"No!"

The cat froze, startled.

"Stay in your animal form. It's the only way to fight the Rot," Harper said. "Prince Tybert and his army—"

The cat tilted its head and hissed.

"I'm sorry," Harper said.

The cat, keeping low on the ground, crawled over to Harper. She tried not to scratch it behind the ears, which would have been insulting. Still, Harper laid her hand atop the cat's head. "I suppose we're both alone."

The cat straightened and made several chirps.

"I'm going to return to Above Ground and bring back help," Harper said. "Then I'm going to free Reynard."

The growl was more pronounced.

"I know, but we need help," Harper said.

The cat gripped Harper's trouser legs with its teeth and pulled her forward. It walked away and looked back.

"Where are we going?" It was moot, since the cat couldn't respond, so Harper followed it into a stand of trees and from there to a small brick hut. It was a curing hut. The sight of dried meat hanging set her stomach to fresh protesting. Harper grabbed several strips, but they didn't help her thirst.

The cat led her out behind the hut to a rain barrel, and Harper drank. When finished, she said, "Stay hidden. I'll return, I promise."

It was past midday by the time she was on the road again, hoping she didn't meet anyone as she retraced her steps. She could see the town laid out before her and the manor. As always, when faced with a decision, she consulted her cards.

The spirit of the Piper appeared before her. He raised the pipe to his lips and played a jaunty tune only Harper could hear. Then he started into the woods, which ran alongside the town. The notes led her like they'd done the children so long ago. She would disappear too, at least for a while.

CHAPTER TWENTY

The great doors stood open as Harper approached. She couldn't see anything beyond them, not even the late afternoon sun lighting the cave. Before she left, Harper sat by the side of the road and drew her cards again.

The Celestial Vine. Harper smiled. The Queen of Swords. Harper *hm*'d. The Knight of Swords. "So, you're saying you'll protect me," Harper said aloud. Yet the Queen also meant shelter for her subjects. The Knight was a protector. The Queen was a caretaker. The Virgin reversed? What in the nether-hells?

As Harper reached for the cards, a vision came.

The Rot, spreading its filth throughout Underneath, bursting through holes and crevices, crawling its way, an army of black snakes. It stole upon the people of Innrone, feeding itself with every soul, whether pure or tainted. The vision faded into a second as the Rot reached the manor.

Harper was in total darkness for a moment. Then a faint light grew ever closer, until the surrounding scene became clear. Reynard, curled almost protectively around a supple new vine.

"Reynard?"

He looked up and right at her. "Harper?"

Then the vision faded, or more accurately, a black curtain covered it. One veil? Had she done that? Either way, Harper understood what she needed to do first. She needed to free Reynard and that small offshoot of Vine. She gathered up her cards except for the Celestial Vine. That she kept in her grasp. Harper stood, brushed off the back of her trousers, and started walking towards the doors.

Harper stepped through and she thought at first the Rot had

swallowed her whole. Instead, a fresh scent filled the space and chased away the rankness. The scent was familiar, and when it strengthened, Harper smiled. In her hand, the Celestial Vine began a steady hum. Beneath her feet, new plants sprouted from the mud. They continued to spread, making a sudden sea of green, bringing new life to what the Rot had tried to destroy. The Rot did not withdraw. It tried to overwhelm the surrounding newness, infecting the greenery, but Harper would not allow it. She called on the Vine, drawing the living out of the places where it slept, and was surprised that she could.

She closed her eyes, yet she could still see the glow of the living things and her card spirits. As they moved, the light they created shone against the veils as they passed through them. Harper saw other things moving between the real and the ethers. And the things that watched her with hate in her expression dared not come near.

She wondered why they seemed to fear her. Harper looked around and noticed the Match Girl and the Piper still with her and after a few moments the tall and powerful Steel Driver, his hammer resting over his shoulder, his expression hard and menacing. Harper figured the things were more afraid of him than they were of her, which suited Harper just fine.

Since they could not touch her, some went to taunting her, which Harper didn't give a rat damn about. Others watched her passing. The most vicious of the denizens of Deep Earth, the greater – like the Red Caps, Black Agnes, goblins, harpies, lamia and basilisks, which she was careful not to look back at – glared at her with hatred, which only concerned her. At one point, one of the Red Caps made a bid for her and when she looked at it, the Virgin appeared, and the purity of her light caused it to vanish.

This fascinated Harper. From what she had learned, only a Light-bringer could destroy a Red Cap with its holy prayers. But then again, what was more holy and pure than the Virgin? She would have questions for Eica if she got out of this.

When Harper came to the wound ripped into the dirt, the first hint of uncertainty halted her. How to get down there? The beasts gathered round, chuckling and insulting. She was so used to the feeling of the Celestial Vine in her hand. It was now a genuine part of her. Harper walked with confidence and stepped over the edge. The beasts started chattering, likely expecting Harper to fall to her death.

The Celestial Vine rose out of the dark to meet her, several offshoots weaving an intricate web that thickened and stretched itself taut. The way was steep, so Harper held the Celestial Vine card in her mouth and got down on her hands and knees and turned with her back facing the hole and climbed down. Above her, the din rose as the monsters protested her success. When her feet touched solid ground, she found herself in a cavernous tunnel. The Piper, the Match Girl, and the Steel Driver appeared, and to Harper's amazement, she got a glimpse of the veils from where they came. Harper breathed in, fighting not to gag and to calm herself. She'd never tried to focus her power on a task and wondered if it was even possible.

She fixed her gaze on the way before her, reaching out with whatever gathered within her. She could just make out the shimmering curtains of magic and saw the unpleasant things that moved between them. Suddenly dizzy, Harper wrenched her concentration away and sat hard.

"What was that?" She wished she'd spent more time with Eica. Well, she was determined to, so she forced herself to stand and moved forward.

"Human."

Harper stopped and looked at where the voice came from. Against the wall to her left, something detached itself from the shadows. Harper was about to keep moving, but curiosity got the better of her. She watched until it moved not into the light, but so Harper could see.

It was her.

More to the point, a hideous caricature of her, as if the Vine had remolded her into something ugly. No, not the Vine, the Rot.

"Your precious one is gone. The wild has taken him. Give up and return whence you came."

Harper frowned, not quite knowing at first, then realizing—

"Red!" Harper broke into a run.

"No!" the doppelgänger cried, "not that way! Flee!"

Harper no longer needed the Piper to lead her. She knew, sensed Red's presence, and it was fading. The human part of him was escaping like his former wife, Hermeline, had done. But Harper continued to run through the corridors in the semidark, her double taunting her all the way. When she entered another cavern, it was alive with glowing, warm light.

In the midst was a wall of vines, woven together, dotted with pale gold trumpeter flowers to form a huge ball-like structure. Her heart, already thumping in her chest, beat faster. Whatever beasts were there huddled in the shadows. Harper watched a few come out, moving close to the structure. It reminded her of her friends daring her to look at the well.

Except here there were no friendships. They were the childish dares of the foolish, which was proved when one of the dark fey, an imp, came the closest when one of his fellow imps shoved him from behind and fell into the light.

He screamed and the sound of burning flesh accompanied by the stench caused an uproar of laughing and snickering. The imp, not amused, went to attack his kin, and it escalated into an all-out brawl.

"Dare you enter, human?" It was her doppelgänger again, standing so close its fetid breath brushed her cheek. "They will tear you apart."

"I dare them to try." Harper raised the Celestial Vine card and shoved it into the face of her tormentor. It was the one who screamed now and spat vile curses at her. Harper didn't care. She started across and the dark fey noticed her and went to attack, but before reaching her, new growth burst from the dirt, entangling them. When others tried, the same fate befell them. Others satisfied themselves by hurling clumps of mud and rocks at her.

It was then that the Steel Driver appeared with a cry of rage, swung his mighty hammer, and although a spirit, it still struck home, scattering them, and breaking their bones. Harper stood before the wall and laid her hand against it. "Please allow me entry."

A few of the smaller offshoots detached themselves and wrapped around Harper's wrist, while the larger parted, creating an opening, and pulled Harper through. Inside, the air was sweet and from somewhere came a soft breeze, although Harper couldn't tell where from.

In the very center of the sanctuary, Harper saw him, in his full fox form, as he lay curled around a single offshoot, almost as tall as Harper. She stopped as near to him as she dared. "Reynard?"

He came awake, alert, which didn't surprise her. His gaze fell on her with no recognition. A low growl erupted in his throat, his teeth bared, and his muscles tensed, preparing to spring.

"Reynard." Harper lowered herself to the ground and sat on crossed legs. The fox's gaze followed her motions. "You must remember."

His stance didn't change. Harper drew out her cards. "Listen to me. You are Reynard, you are the fox, but you are a mortal man."

She laid cards. "Do you recall when we first met?" The first card was the Reaper. "I drew this card for you. You thought I was saying you were going to die. I told you it could be a sign of change."

The fox seemed to listen, but remained tense.

"You have changed. Your life has changed."

Harper laid out the second card, Five of Wands reversed. "So much conflict in your life, but now you're realizing you didn't prove how cunning you were by your past actions. Ace of Swords. Your judgement is clouded although you've been rethinking your decision." Harper frowned over the next card. "Queen of Swords reversed."

There was an almost imperceptible change. He'd stopped growling, although he still showed his teeth, and he relaxed.

"Whoever she was that forced you into this, she is not worth your wanting to please her," Harper said. A vision was forming, but not in the usual way for Harper. It coalesced within the light of the offshoot. It was Reynard, as a child, looking for something to give him purpose. The vision showed her Red's misdeeds and the reasoning behind them became clear in his words and actions. Including the death of Chanticleer's daughters. Red in his full fox form was gravely injured, his fur matted with blood from wounds all over him. His eyes wild. The daughters were in their hen forms and when Red attacked, Harper understood.

"So, you were no more than a savage beast. Hungry and injured and the hens became the nearest available prey." The story, at least that part of it, was wrong. Afterwards the fox cried out in mourning or agony, perhaps on some level realizing what he'd done. He'd chosen this life until it turned on him and forced him to flee.

"The Match Girl reversed," Harper continued. "I don't believe I've ever drawn her that way. It's time for Reynard to decide in which direction you want to go."

His stance was relaxed now. Or it was until his muscles started to spasm. Harper reached for him but then she realized what was happening. He was coming back. With the transformation complete, he lay on his back, not moving except for the deep rise and fall of his chest. He was naked.

He'd lost his clothes. Harper couldn't guess how. She supposed he'd torn them off when he regressed. Harper didn't know how much time had passed before he drew himself up on his elbows and turned his head to look at her. "Harper?"

"Lie still." Harper gathered up her cards and moved near him.

"What happened?"

"You regressed."

"What?" He went to rise up, but Harper pushed him back.

"I said lie still."

"I remember…" Reynard began. "I'm thirsty."

Now that was going to be a problem. Unless…

Harper drew the Celestial Vine, laid it on the ground and touched a finger to it. "Please, hear me." She imagined water, cool and clear, swirling up from the ground, from beyond where the Rot flourished. A spider web of cracks appeared from underneath the card continuing to spread. The center sank and water bubbled up from the depression and spread along the cracks.

A second depression appeared but from there a fountain of water shot upward.

"By the gods." Reynard had turned over on his side and was watching.

"By the Vine." Harper smiled.

"Indeed," Reynard said. "Would you help me? I could use a washing up."

"Yes, you could."

Harper helped him to raise up on his hands and knees. Reynard crawled to the spout. He drank deeply at first, then splashed the water on his face and body, scrubbing with his hands. Harper watched, truly seeing him for the first time. She was captivated, as the water ran through his hair, darkening the color and as rivulets ran down his muscular form.

Whether he realized she was staring was unknown. It wasn't until he was finished that he moved away from the spout that he noticed her regard. There were no words. The look he gave her spoke volumes. He crawled again, towards her.

He kissed her.

Harper stilled at first, then parted her lips and welcomed his invading tongue. She was breathless. Reynard was a damn good kisser. She would have laughed if she was certain he wouldn't take it the wrong way.

"Harper, sweet Harper." He kissed her all over her face, went to take her mouth again. "You brought me back! How?"

Harper held up the Vine card before stowing it back into her pouch.

"Yes, I recall now." He nodded. "I heard your voice, speaking my fortune. Thank you."

"Red." Harper laid her hands over his.

"Reynard," he said. "I'm no longer Red."

"Reynard," Harper said.

"Why did you come for me?" Reynard demanded. His tone was more worried than angry. "Why didn't you go home?"

"There wouldn't be a home to go to," Harper said. "The Rot plans to infect everything it can and bring the monstrosities of Deep Earth into all of Underneath and Above Ground."

"I know," he said, "but that wasn't—"

"I would not leave you," Harper said, resolute. "Besides, I need your help. Who better to stop the schemes of the Rot than the greatest schemer himself?"

"No," Reynard said, "this is up to you. I will be by your side, but I just know it must be this way."

He sat back and smiled at her then looked down, realizing for the first time his state of undress. "Oh shite." He looked up. "I'm so sorry."

"Why?" Harper said. "How many times have I told you I'm not some swooning maiden?"

The look he gave her was a puzzle. She wasn't quite certain what it meant. "Indeed, I'm glad." He began examining their makeshift fortress. "When did all of this happen?"

"I have no idea," Harper said. "It was here when I arrived. I thought you would know."

Reynard shook his head. "The last thing I recall is…promising to save you."

His expression softened. "But you saved me."

"We're far from safe." Harper nodded to where she had entered. "They're still out there."

"But you got in," Reynard said. "Couldn't we just go the same way out?"

"Yes, but," Harper began, "to be honest, I'm exhausted and hungry. I used much of my power getting here and summoning the spirits."

"Spirits?"

"Of my cards," Harper said. "Likely I would have never made it without their help."

"We can't stay, especially after what you've told me." Reynard stood, stretching his muscles. Harper couldn't help but admire the view. "I may fight my way through, allow you to—"

"No." Harper shook her head again. "We go together or not at all."

"Why must you be so stubborn? Didn't you hear what I said before?"

"I heard you. Didn't you hear me?"

Reynard sighed and his shoulders slumped. "Then we must think of something."

"First we eat." Harper rose, brushed off her trouser seat. "There were flowers blooming outside. I wonder if...."

Harper laid her hand on the Vine again and closed her eyes. She thought nothing was happening until Reynard said, "Harper, look!"

Harper opened her eyes and found that not only were flowers blooming, but they continued their cycle until they grew into scarlet pear-shaped fruits.

"By the Vine," Reynard said. "No more will I doubt its power."

Harper plucked six fruits, brought them over and sat across from Reynard, trying and failing not to glance at his man parts. They ate two fruits each and set the rest aside.

"You should rest," Reynard told her. "When was the last time you slept?"

Harper was already settling down. "Night before last. Oh...."

As she lay, she told him about her dream and how she'd spoken to the witch Isbet.

"I knew it," Reynard said after she was done. Although he didn't elaborate, Harper understood what he was saying.

She went on telling him of her experiences trying to escape the manor and Isengrim.

"If he survived your wounding him, I swear I will kill him myself," Reynard muttered, in his half form.

"No," Harper said, "Isengrim doesn't matter."

"He does to me." Reynard drew his knees up to his chest, looking put out.

"We might need him." Harper fell asleep, although she could still see everything around her.

* * *

"Harper?"

Reynard was there, his hands caressing her face and hair. He held the same gaze, the one from before, and Harper recognized it. Harper reached out for him, her arms encircling his shoulders.

Reynard continued with his gentle kisses as he worked to undo the ties on her shirt. She needed no instruction as she raised her arms and he lifted it over her head, tossing it aside. He kneaded her breasts before taking one dark nipple in his mouth, causing Harper to draw in a sharp breath. The liquid heat pooled in her sex. Reynard then gave her other breast the same treatment, and Harper moaned as she plunged her hands into his hair.

He straightened. The hunger in his eyes burned through her. Reynard undid the ties on her trousers and pulled them down to her knees, exposing her to him. When he lowered his head, Harper gave a cry and gripped his muscular shoulders.

"Oh gods, Reynard!"

He raised his head, a look of male satisfaction on his face. He removed her boots and freed her of her trousers. "I won't be gentle with you." It was a feral growl.

"I don't want you to be," Harper breathed.

"I might..." he said, "...not be able to control...."

"Then don't."

"If I shift, I'll be part-animal. I may hurt you."

"I trust you, Reynard."

It was those words that made his decision. Reynard spread her legs wide, locking his arms underneath her knees, and thrust deep into her. Harper cried out, her back arching at the delicious pain causing her to burn from within. "Reynard!"

He stopped, pulling her to her knees. He guided her down onto his shaft again. Harper needed no urging as she drove him into her, while they held each other as though something might tear them apart.

"Gods, Harper!" Reynard threw his head back and with an animalistic cry, the change came, the fox part of him taking hold and bringing him to his half form. Still, he didn't cease, continuing to thrust deep into her until....

It was Harper who reached her end first, and as she did, she cried out Reynard's name, over and over. It drove Reynard over the edge. With one final push, he filled her. They both fell together, entangled in each other's arms. The only sound was their labored breathing.

Harper lay content. No one had taken her, like that in, well ever, and there were no regrets. She nuzzled against Reynard's chest. "You are an animal."

He chuckled. "Thank you." He was stroking her head. "Sleep, my beautiful diviner."

Harper did for a time. She didn't know how long, but when she woke, it was from Reynard entering her again. He took his time, and they enjoyed each other, learning what each one preferred and giving them that pleasure.

Harper knew it couldn't last. They couldn't stay here forever, but for now, she lay in their sanctuary.

CHAPTER TWENTY-ONE

Reynard watched Harper sleep. For the first time in forever, he was happy. Despite that, he knew soon they would have to face their common enemy. The dark fey outside their sanctuary would impede their progress if not outright kill them. Reynard did not know what to do when they left.

Some rescuer. My sweet Harper, you are the true heroine.

Harper had gotten here and pulled him back from the brink. That told Reynard how truly powerful she was. He hoped she realized it, because as much as it pained him to admit, he would have to depend on her.

I will do my best to protect you.

He wouldn't say that aloud. She'd likely give him a good crack across his head.

"Harper, love, wake up."

Harper muttered something before opening her eyes. She smiled at him. "Reynard."

He kissed her. "I wish we could stay here together."

She reached up and stroked his cheek. "So do I."

She sat up. "My cards?"

"Here." He'd been careful to set them aside during their lovemaking. He knew to treat them with the utmost care. "Will they lead us out?"

"Yes."

"Where shall we go?" Reynard asked.

"Back Above Ground. The Rot is too powerful here. We must warn the people."

Reynard nodded. "Will you go home first?"

"Yes," Harper said, "and then…I'm not sure."

"The cards will tell you."

"Yes." Reynard noted the confidence in her voice. He was proud of her. She'd always had the heart of a warrior. Now it was coming through.

"There are things I need to tell you," Harper said. "Shahir left Vale to return to Morwynne, but he said you were still beholden to the mask. The influence would diminish."

"Damn it." He'd almost forgotten about that blasted mask. "He didn't say how long he would be gone?"

"No," Harper said, "but when I saw him last, the Rot held him."

"Damn it to the nether-hells," Reynard muttered. "If he gets ahold of it again…."

"He hid it in his manor."

Reynard blew out a breath. "We— I have to find it."

Harper sat up, looking as if she might protest. Reynard took her hands. "I don't want to be away from you," he said.

"Neither do I, but you have to," Harper said.

"It's not just that I am beholden to it," Reynard said. "They placed something inside of me. It's like a taint in my soul that the Rot uses to control me, although…" Reynard rubbed his chest, "…I haven't felt its influence since finding the offshoot."

"The Vine will protect you," Harper said.

"Will it? I've had little confidence in its power." Reynard grinned and gazed around their sanctuary. "That is, until now."

"Trust that it will." Her tone was resolute. "But it may ask something in return."

"Then I will swear to my belief in the Vine and accept whatever task it gives me." It surprised Reynard that his words were true. He'd never sworn his allegiance to anyone, not even Noble the Second. The Vines that made up their sanctuary trembled for a few moments then stopped.

"I believe that means it accepts your oath," Harper said with a grin.

"I never thought the Vine was alive," Reynard said. He developed a new respect for magic along with his for Harper. Still, the Vine would need the help of those it considered its children. Reynard didn't know if he was one of them as an animalia, but if the Vine accepted him and he could assist Harper, then he was satisfied.

"So, what will we do now?"

Harper reached for her clothes. "We're leaving."

Reynard shifted into his fox form once again and waited while Harper dressed. "My cards," she said

He'd laid her pouch aside while she was sleeping. He retrieved it now, carrying it in his mouth. He watched as Harper drew them out, fascinated by how deftly she shuffled them and drew one, showing it to him. It was, of course, the Celestial Vine. When Harper approached the wall of vines, they untangled, revealing an exit. Harper was about to step through, but Reynard bounded in front of her. Whatever was out there, he wanted to face it first.

The glow from the sanctuary illuminated the cavern a few steps ahead of them. Beyond that was the all-encompassing darkness. *Are we alone?* Reynard wondered. As the thought came, there was movement in the shadows and suddenly demonic creatures charged at them. Reynard crouched, ready to spring and tear the throat out of whatever came near.

There was a flare of yellow light before them. Reynard couldn't quite see, but he thought there was a little girl kneeling, and the light emanated from her. The ones in front stopped, and the others fell over them.

This caused fighting to break out amongst them, which Reynard thought was inane, since their prey was supposed to be the two of them. Harper started forward, and Reynard trotted behind her. Out of the corner of his eye, Reynard noticed some beings had separated themselves from their riotous kin and were edging their way towards them. Reynard barked a warning, uncertain if Harper would understand.

She was still holding the Celestial Vine card in her left hand. The image of the girl still in front of them seemed to float above the dirt, still on her knees. The specter of a man appeared, tall and powerful, with a hammer resting on his shoulder. Then to his right, a beautiful young woman in flowing robes.

Reynard was in such awe he almost didn't notice Harper had stopped. In his mind, he frowned, wondering what was impeding their progress. He walked around to stand next to Harper. Someone – or more accurately, something – was there. A horrible misshapen she-demon that grinned with broken teeth and eyes burning with hate. Reynard realized what it was. It had many names, but the thing had dared to mold itself in Harper's image.

"You will go no farther," it said.

"Will you stop us?" Harper challenged. "I don't see how."

The thing began pacing. "You are a pathetic creature, not worthy of the power the Vine gives you." It crawled forward. "Give yourself to the Rot."

"No."

"You whore! You will—"

Reynard had had enough. He bounded forward with the speed given to him by his fox form, leaped upon the thing and sank his teeth into its throat, ripping putrid flesh and crushing brittle bone. It didn't have time to scream before it was dead. Then Reynard was back within the protective light.

What remained of the dark fey hurled vile curses at them, but Harper turned and graced Reynard with a smile before continuing. The fox shook his head, hoping to remove some of the taint. His stomach soured, but in his present form, he doubted it would have any ill effect. Foxes could eat carrion.

When they arrived at their destination, Harper put the card away. The specters waited to see what she'd do. Harper turned to Reynard once again. "I assume foxes can climb?"

Reynard huffed at her. A well-known fact was a fox's acrobatic prowess. Harper laughed and stepped aside. There was a crude vine ladder. Reynard backed a few steps up. He waited and looked at Harper. He hoped she knew what he was trying to convey.

"Go first," Harper said. "I have to continue to keep the dark ones at bay."

Still, Reynard didn't like it.

"Besides," Harper continued, "we don't know what's in the cavern above. Remember we're still Underneath."

She was right. He stepped back. Then, rushing forward, he used his powerful hind legs to leap and dug in with his claws, hoping he wasn't causing any serious pain or injury to the Vine. When he reached the top, he turned, sat on his haunches, and stared down. He could see the light as it rose from the depths until Harper appeared at the edge.

Reynard stepped back, wishing he could do more, but Harper seemed quite capable of pulling herself up. He was grateful she was all right and a little embarrassed when his happiness manifested into a squeal and his tail wagging. Harper tried but failed not to chuckle. Reynard wasn't the least bit upset by it.

Harper knelt before him. "Find the mask. One more thing, if you can get to the royal manor, look for Eica. She was fighting the Rot and helped me escape. You may also see Lucea but…she may be…." Harper didn't finish and Reynard saw her swallow and tears threatened.

Reynard whined and placed a paw on her thigh. He hated to have to leave her again.

"I know," Harper said. "I've thought of what to do. I'll go home first, then I'll go to the royal manor. Find me there if I'm not in the den."

All right. Please be careful. He could only sound his concern and frustration. He didn't want to take the time to shift. Reynard licked her over the face. Then, before he could change his mind and refuse to let her go, he made a dash for the great doors.

* * *

The weather had turned ominous. Clouds of slate blotted out the light and a freezing rain fell, making it difficult for Reynard to see more than a few steps down the dirt road. And, of course, nothing stank worse than wet fur. If there weren't more pressing matters, he would worry about catching his death.

The rain was not a detriment to reaching his goal. There were so many other instinctual methods at his disposal. Reaching Shahir's manor wouldn't be a problem. He knew the black panther didn't have a family, just a few servants to keep the place. One thing that did worry him was his sudden inability to tell the hour. Something again that was determined by his instincts. Reynard didn't know if the Rot had anything to do with it. It was light enough for him to see. He could only assume it was daytime. He didn't think the servants were up. If they were, then what? Walk up to one of them and ask, "Do you know where your master hid the mask that keeps me prisoner?"

Just get there first, Reynard.

Shahir had gone for a more modest look for his home. It resembled a country lodge, like the one where Reynard had found that gods-be-damned mask. It did not surprise him that there was no one about outside. But also, there were no lights in the windows, or smoke coming from the chimneys. Maybe it *was* early morning.

Reynard went around back to the servants' entrance. A crude wood door direly needed replacing from the worn-away boards. Reynard figured maybe someone would allow a poor drenched fox in for some food. Reynard scratched his paw against the door.

It came open.

His hackles rose, as wet and matted as they were. The Rot was here or had been, for that stench was unmistakable. Reynard set one paw inside and looked around. The kitchen was just like any other, except it looked like it hadn't been cleaned in ages. Stacked on the cooking block were dirty plates with half-eaten food, gone bad. Pots sat atop a cold stove, which should have had a fire burning to chase away the damp, if nothing else.

Reynard continued forward, his ears twitching and gaze alert. He'd never been here before, so he could only guess where the mask might be. If he harkened back to his thieving days— Reynard would have laughed aloud if he could. As if he'd given up his life of crime years ago. Something as valuable as that would be in the most private place in the home. The master bedroom.

The door to the inner rooms of the house also stood open. Not something usually done. Reynard tasted the air. There were people here, though he wasn't sure where they might be. The hallway he stood in branched off to his left, and even in the waning light, he could see what appeared ahead of him was the main hall.

He guessed the hallway to that led to the servants' quarters, and an idea emerged. Maybe by some miracle he could find dry clothes. He started in the hall. Three doors on his right were closed and Reynard found himself grateful. From them came an odor of unwashed bodies mixed with the Rot stench.

Just stay where you are, locked in your rooms. Don't come out.

The laundry was at the end of the hall. There was another exit, which Reynard noted. The first thing he saw were four washtubs filled with stale water and soaked clothing. It seemed like the servants had stopped what they were doing in the middle and left everything there. He found some clean clothes hung up to dry and others folded in baskets. There was a stack of towels in one and Reynard shifted to full human form and dried himself off. The clothes were those loose trousers and vests the panther liked to wear. They were too big, but Reynard shifted into his half form and that filled them up, if not completely. The fit was better.

Now for the mask. Reynard continued to make his way to the main hall. He couldn't see much in the gloom. He made out the shapes of cabinets and chairs, and portraits on the wall. There was an inner balcony at his left, accessed by a flight of stairs. Reynard climbed, choosing his steps. He just hoped Shahir was still away. At the top of the stairs was another hall in front of him, and the balcony continued right. Two more closed doors, but Reynard figured the house lord wouldn't have his room where everyone could see his movements.

The hall looked much too portentous. Reynard wished he had a light.

Somewhere there was a noise, a sharp crack like the splintering of wood. Reynard swore under his breath. Hurried footsteps, then a massive form rushed from the other room, spotting Reynard. It was hard to tell who or what they were, but there was the smell of Rot and the musk of animalia. He only knew it was massive, larger than anything he'd seen, human or animal, and it seemed the whole body was alive with wriggling things.

It opened its mouth wider than should be possible and it roared. The sound was guttural and unnatural. Reynard didn't wait to see if it was someone in their half form and bolted down the nearest hall. He realized his error when it ended at another door. He tried the latch, and of course, it was locked. The thing appeared, filling the space between the walls. When it saw Reynard, it came barreling forward.

He had no chance, with his back against the door. But a fox cornered can be a dangerous thing.

"Fuck it." Reynard ran straight at the monster and slammed into it head-on.

CHAPTER TWENTY-TWO

It was good to feel the true sunlight on her face again, but Harper had no time to enjoy it. After she emerged from Underneath, as luck would have it, a farmer was passing by, driving a cart full of goods for market square. Harper told him who she was and where she needed to go, and although he didn't ask for money, Harper offered to do a reading for him without charge the next time he came to the city.

If there was a city to return to.

Everything seemed the same as Harper hurried through the familiar streets. Her cards were silent, which was good because it allowed her to reserve her power. And she felt more powerful than ever. She didn't know if it was being Above Ground and the warmth of the sun, but there was a sensation like lightning running across her flesh.

It was late in the morning by the time she reached the den. She didn't take any time to celebrate being there. She strode right in. "Pops!" She needn't have said it. He stood behind the bar and looked up when Harper entered.

When he saw her, his face lit up. "By the Vine, Harper!"

Not only did Pops come from behind the bar, but Marcel, Osvald, and the patrons themselves left what they were doing to surround her and trade embraces. Pops was crying like a baby as he hugged her again, and although Harper no longer had doubts about her destiny, her love for these people would have sent them away.

"We were so worried!" Pops said. Then the questions started.

"Did that demon hurt you?"

"Where did they take you?"

"How did you escape?"

And on until Harper threw her hands in the air. "Listen, everyone!"

She'd never gotten such attention so fast. "I – we – have little time. I must go see the duchess now."

Pops, seeming to realize the dire situation, said, "Boys, get us something to fight with."

Marcel and Osvald rushed to the back and came out with a sword in a sheath, and two clubs. Those the brothers used on unruly customers, but the sword, which Marcel handed to Pops....

He noticed her look. "Did a bit o' fightin' in my day."

Harper grinned. Her father was full of surprises.

"Let's be off," Pops said as he strapped on the sheath. "You'll tell us on the way."

Harper nodded, turned, and walked outside. Pops and her brothers and all the patrons followed. As they walked, others called to them, asking what was going on. As much as she could, Harper told Pops where she had been and the danger to Innrone. She told him about Reynard and how he'd helped her. That he would join her as soon as he could. And about the people of Vale and her training with Eica. Pops didn't interrupt or ask questions, acknowledging with nods and sounds.

Although Harper was intent on their destination, she noticed more people were joining the group. Commoners like her, friends and neighbors who loved their city and kept it. There were men, women, and children. Some had armed themselves with various implements, swords, clubs, rakes, shovels, whatever they could get their hands on. How the story spread in the ever-growing crowd, Harper didn't know, but she heard the tales on everyone's lips.

They crowded the avenue, stopping coaches of the wealthy who yelled curses from out the curtained windows, but the citizens ignored them. There were others on horseback, forced to join the flow of the crowd. Some joined, either out of curiosity or the desire to protect Innrone.

They drew the notice of the guards, who stood outside of the crowd but didn't stop them, although they kept their eyes on the people. Harper later learned since no one was committing any violent acts, they were unsure of what to do, anyway. Because they received no orders to the contrary, watching kept them content.

Before anyone knew, Harper led what had become a small army. They arrived at the gates of the royal manor. The gates were open during the day, but the royal guards moved to keep them out.

A female guard, nine feet tall, stepped forward. She was of giantess blood. "State your business." Harper frowned. Where had she heard that voice before? She realized it was the guard who had come looking for her the night she met Aislinn. That seemed forever ago. The guard didn't recognize her, likely only having a description to go by, but she was glaring at Pops.

"I am here to see Her Grace on a matter of...." Harper faltered. What was it? Life and death? The invasion and destruction of Innrone? It was all and everything. "Innrone is at the mercy of a force that wishes to destroy it. I came to warn her."

"With an armed mob at your back?"

"Mob?" Harper said. "These are the people of Innrone who wish the duchess to protect them. Is that not her duty?"

"Go away, all of you!" the guard said.

But Harper wasn't looking at the guard anymore. She was looking at a robed woman striding down the courtyard path. Harper didn't recognize her but thought she might be the high chamberlain, rumored to be overseeing Innrone. She was ancient and emaciated, her skin stretched over her bones, giving her a skeletal appearance. The guard turned to see just as she reached her. She whispered something into her ear.

"You jest?" the guard said. She turned back to Harper. "You're the diviner Harper?"

"Yes," Harper answered, waiting.

There was a brief flash of something in her expression. What? Amusement? Respect? "Her Grace commands you into her presence, Lady Harper."

A murmur of surprise passed through the crowd. Harper was uncertain how the duchess knew her name. Her spirits were buzzing around her like angry hornets. Pops looked at her in shock, then turned back to the guard. "Let's go then."

The guard put her hand out. "Only Lady Harper."

Protests started in the crowd.

"Listen here, you giantess bitch—" Pops began.

"Pops," Harper said, "I'll go in alone. When Reynard comes, I'll need you to tell him what happened if I don't come out."

"Daughter." Pops hugged her close. "What type of father would I be if I let you go in there alone?"

"You're our sister," Marcel said, "we protect you."

"Pops. Marcel. Osvald." Harper didn't want to cry, but the tears came. She was back with her family again but knew what she might face if she entered that manor alone. "I love you."

Harper detached herself from them and turned back to the guard and the robed woman. "All right."

"If yer not out before sundown, we're comin' in after ya!" Pops yelled as Harper stepped through the gate with the sound of the ill-omened groan as it closed behind her.

Harper turned to face the woman, who looked down her nose. "I am High Chamberlain Reva Jourdain. Please follow me, Lady Harper."

Harper did so without responding.

"I don't know why Her Grace wants to meet with a commoner," Jourdain went on and Harper wondered was she was being influenced? Or was she just another lickspittle, only concerned about keeping up appearances? "I've been so worried about her as of late." Jourdain spoke more to herself, but just as they got to the entrance, she turned to Harper.

"Mind your manners, girl! You'll treat Her Grace with the respect she is due."

Before Harper could answer, Jourdain opened the doors and ushered her inside. Harper had never been in the manor, but it was just as she expected. Garish decorations and furniture, all made of the finest woods, metals, and materials. There was enough wealth there to feed a family of ten for several winters. That was the only thing Harper noticed. Jourdain was going on about how dare the rabble come to the palace gates and how she had a good mind to have the guards arrest them all.

Good luck with that. If the guards accosted the people, it would end in blood and death. Which was the last thing Harper wanted. But she doubted this old crone would care. Harper would bring it up with the duchess.

"Here." Jourdain addressing her brought her out of her thoughts. The chamberlain held open a door to another lavishly decorated room. Like when she visited Vale, there were foodstuffs and drink set out. The only occupants were two pretty maids in identical uniforms who stood stiffly at the food tables, neither smiling nor greeting Harper when Jourdain motioned her inside.

"Her Grace will see you at her leisure." And without another word, Jourdain closed the door.

Harper approached the table. "Good afternoon."

She expected to be ignored, but the two bobbed a curtsy in perfect time. "Good afternoon, milady. What is your desire?"

For the duchess to get her arse in here. Of course, Harper didn't say that. "Just some water will be fine." Although she thought she should eat something because she had had nothing since...when? The fruit in the sanctuary.

But they had little time for niceties. Although Harper was certain the Rot wasn't present, her cards continued to hum in warning. Maybe it wasn't too late to save Innrone and perhaps all the Riven Isles. Still, starving herself wouldn't do any good. Harper asked for two of the sandwiches. They'd removed the crusts and cut the bread in perfect triangles. As if making them look pretty would make them better. Vine, she'd never understand the whims of the rich.

Harper took a goblet of water and the sandwiches and sat on one of the many plush couches in the room. Whoever had decorated did everything in pink, from the walls to the carpets, to the furnishings and curtains. Harper rolled her eyes and set her lunch down on a low glass table. She nibbled one sandwich while she looked out the row of windows, each two man-heights tall.

She continued to wait. The chapel bell rung twice, although Harper didn't know what time she'd entered this room. It was long enough, and the two servants were also noticing the passage of time by the way they shifted their weight from one foot to another.

Harper had had enough. She rose, strode over to the door, and pulled the latch. It didn't budge. She'd not heard a key click in the lock. She turned to the girls. "Why is this door locked?"

Both girls looked taken aback and identical flushes colored their checks. One girl blurted, "It's locked?" then exchanged a glance with her companion. Neither looked contrite. In fact, they both seemed confused.

"We don't know, milady," the second girl said.

"Stop calling me milady," Harper said. "It's Harper."

The girls exchanged glances again. "I'm Chloe."

The second said, "I'm Gertie."

"Well, Chloe and Gertie, didn't anyone say anything to you?"

"No mil— Miss Harper," Gertie said. "We were told to wait here and provide service to Her Grace and guest?"

"Guest." Harper doubted that's what she was. She lifted her fist to her chin and looked around again. She could break one window and escape, but how far would she get? And she had to be certain Pops and the guards did not injure the others. The fact was she needed to see the duchess, so she couldn't – *wouldn't* leave.

"Damn it all." Harper plopped down on the coach again. "So, I guess we wait."

She felt sorry for the maids, who were just doing their jobs. They were laborers, commoners, just like Harper, and didn't deserve to be in the middle during this…whatever it was becoming. When the chapel bell struck three, there was the sound of the lock clicking. Harper stood.

But it wasn't the duchess who entered. It was the guard from the front gate.

"Lady Harper," she said, "by order of Her Grace Magdalen

Brigette, Duchess of Innrone, you are under arrest for crimes against the city government."

So, this is how it will be. "I see."

Behind her, Chloe and Gertie gasped and began an almost imperceptible whispering.

"You will come along," the guard said.

"So, the duchess lured me here to have me arrested?"

"I will take you by force."

Harper snorted, but she walked forward, surprised when the guard stepped aside.

"No shackles?"

"Of course not." The guard seemed offended by the question.

"I touch iron all the time," Harper said. "It's never bothered me before."

"Well, I wasn't aware of that." The guard calmed a bit. "I've seen what iron can do to fey."

"You don't have to be fey for iron to hurt you," Harper said. "It often depends on your Gift. But thank you for your concern."

The guard nodded.

Harper expected to be taken to some dank cell, but the guard led her up a staircase to the second floor, down a hall, and to some rooms at the rear of the manor. Another guard stood at the door. He moved aside and saluted, then took a ring of keys off his belt and used one to unlock the door.

The room wasn't as grotesque as the rest of the house but had all the essentials. Bed, dressing table, desk, and a washroom. All done in a staid brown. A guest room for less than royal guests?

Harper looked at the guard in confusion. "What is this?"

"This is where Her Grace said we should confine you. I do not question orders."

"Perhaps you should," Harper told her. "Tell me, what's your name?"

At first, Harper thought the guard wouldn't respond. "Sergeant Titania Falstaff."

"Would you do me a favor?"

She raised a brow and crossed her arms.

"Please."

"What is it?"

"The chamberlain was going on about having the crowd outside arrested," Harper said. "You know what will happen if she involves more guards?"

"The chamberlain is not in charge of the royal guard, but I will speak with my superior."

"Thank you," Harper said. "And one more thing?"

"That's two favors," but she said it with an amused tone, so Harper continued.

"Will you let Pops know what's happening, that I'm fine and not to start a fight?"

"Very well," Falstaff said. "Anything else?"

"Just one more thing," Harper said. "A man will come looking for me. His name is Reynard. Tell him to look after the people and make certain there is no bloodshed."

"I will tell him. You have my word."

"Thank you so much," Harper said, "and please, take care of yourself and yours. There are things happening and...."

Harper decided not to go further. She could tell the sergeant already knew there was trouble. In fact, by the look she gave Harper, she was already aware that something wasn't right in the manor.

"Stay here until someone comes to relieve you," Sergeant Falstaff said to the other guard, who looked both confused and frightened. Perhaps he had sensed something too.

Harper walked into the room and stood in the center. The door was locked behind her. She went to the bed and sat, drawing out her cards.

The Prisoner.

Seven of Wands.

Light-bringer reversed.

The Lady of Lies.

The Virgin.

The Jester.

"Reynard," Harper said, "I know you'll be here for me. Please take care, the Rot is here, but it's hiding itself. I don't know where."

There was nothing she could do now. No escape. Just wait for what was to come. But she would be ready.

CHAPTER TWENTY-THREE

The blood of the thing he fought was poison. Reynard knew this because it burned going down his throat and caused his stomach to spasm, and he had to fight to hold down his gorge. Despite his wounds, and the dizziness that claimed him, Reynard found the strength to continue fighting, even though it didn't matter.

He had the element of surprise, as the beast clearly hadn't expected Reynard to charge him. It gave the fox an advantage, however briefly, and he sank his teeth into…what? It ripped apart in strips of something that splintered in his mouth. The beast wrapped sinuous arms around his torso and squeezed while something snakelike wrapped around Reynard's throat.

He continued to rip at the wriggling things with his claws and tear at them with his teeth as his lungs cried out for air. The beast lifted him off his feet and crushed him against the nearest wall. As the last vestiges of consciousness faded, Reynard shifted into his fox form, slipping through his living bonds.

He took off running. To the nether-hells with the mask.

Something wrapped itself around Reynard's hind leg, snapping it back as he leaped forward. Muscles strained and he howled and stumbled. Fury erupted, spreading fire through him as he bit the thing apart, freeing himself, but before he could gather his wits, the monstrosity was on him again. It didn't stop; it kept coming, forcing Reynard back to the railing. When it reached for him again, Reynard took his half form, allowing his weight to carry them both forward. The beast roared, whether in protest or triumph Reynard didn't know, but with the crack of wood they were falling through space.

Their bodies twisted, the beast landed hard with a wet *thunk*, and chunks of wood flew everywhere. Stunned, Reynard lay in the tangle with blood soaking his fur. He heard the sound of movement in the other room. He tore himself from the tangle. His leg was in agony, but he half dragged, half crawled back up the steps.

"Vine protect me," Reynard muttered as he moved down the hall, hoping whatever it was didn't choose to climb the stairs. He sat down with his back to the door, waiting. Sounds of animalistic grunting came and more movement. He reached up behind him, grasped the latch, and his heart stopped when it clicked. He pushed the door open and hauled himself within, closing it behind him.

He was even more shocked to see the sparse decor. A single lamp with a trapped wil-o-wisp supplied a soft light. Once he found the mask—

And there it was, sitting atop of his dressing table, of all things. Reynard felt ridiculously annoyed. Didn't the panther believe it was important enough for him to lock it up, or at least hide it? But it was silly to be thinking that way. Reynard should be grateful he had no trouble finding it. Now that he had, he realized with trepidation that he didn't want to touch it. He'd not thought of the presence in his chest and realized he almost felt whole again. It had to be his vow to the Vine.

And it was the Vine that would give him the strength. "Please," Reynard said as he approached and reached out. He dropped the mask when he felt it shudder. Now what to do? The floor was stone. If only he had something to smash the mask with. "I could use a good pair of boots right now."

He picked the mask up, walked to the balcony and looked down at the stones below. He turned back to the wil-o-wisp. "What do you think?" Reynard expected some type of fanfare or lightning. Something as he dropped the accursed thing that had caused him so much misfortune. It fell and when it met with the stones it shattered.

And what remained of the thing in his soul dispersed.

"Thank the Vine." Reynard stood there for a moment, head bowed. He breathed in the chill air before stepping back into the room. He lifted the glass off the base of the lantern. The wil-o-wisp pulsed with light, brightening in its freedom. It followed Reynard back out onto the balcony. Reynard was about to jump to a nearby tree branch when he noticed something moving down below.

He shrank back into the room. The wil-o-wisp remained hovering where Reynard had just been standing. Then it dropped from sight, over the edge of the balcony. Far below, Reynard heard several cries. He walked onto the balcony and saw several figures chasing after the wil-o-wisp. "Well, I'll be damned."

He was out the window, on the branch, and down the tree. He stopped to see the mask ground into the stone, likely by the tread of the beasts. Again, he found himself disappointed. So much trouble, and destroying it had been done with…well, he would not say no trouble. He couldn't figure out why he was feeling this way. What was he expecting? Lightning? Thunder? Fire and great plumes of smoke?

He supposed he was angry at himself for letting such an insignificant thing lead him down this path. But had his life been so perfect before? He was doing something good and just. His mother would have hated it.

He needed to leave Vale and return to Harper.

Red continued to travel through the woods until he arrived back at the Great Doors. He was cautious as he entered, but nothing was there to accost him. He was relieved to see the sunlight once he arrived Above Ground. It seemed like the first time in years. He didn't know how much time had passed since he'd separated from Harper.

Harper, by the Vine. I hope she is safe and well.

Now how to get to the city? He wasn't keen on shifting to a fox because too many things could happen. He would have to find new clothes. His half form would scare anyone who laid eyes on him. So, human it was. Reynard started off at a jog to preserve his strength.

In the back of his mind, he couldn't help but think of the mask smashed on the stones with no fanfare. It came to him he wasn't so upset with that, more about nothing happening. How could he be certain the mask no longer trapped him? He wished he'd asked Harper what might happen. Maybe it was a cruel trick. That the blackness in his soul would come again, taunting him or driving him to violence.

Reynard stopped there on the road, unable to breathe, bent over, his hands pressed against his knees to steady himself as he fought to take in enough air, his chest squeezed tight. When his legs could no longer support him, he sat down hard in the dirt alongside the road.

What in the nether-hells is wrong with you? Get yourself together, Reynard!

But he couldn't. It came to him he was in battle distress. It went by other names, depending on what caused such paralyzing fear. The mere thought of continuing with normal life was impossible. He recalled an old soldier whom he'd met on his travels who was so scarred by his experiences he became trapped in a world where the battle never ended, whether asleep or awake. He only found peace in drink.

Was it happening to him? Was he becoming a mere shell of a man?

He still could hardly breathe, and the surrounding scene blurred. Reynard wondered if he had escaped the manor. If the beast still had him in its grip. Perhaps this was all a dream while he breathed his last.

Something changed in the air, a sweet scent that he recalled. When he felt a hand on his shoulder, Reynard leaped back with a cry. He lost his footing and sat right back down again. What he saw terrified him. Was he dead?

A woman stood before him, tall and imposing, yet here she wasn't there, her body translucent. She wore full armor and held a sword driven to the ground, her hands folded around the pommel. Her gaze was fierce, like daggers to his chest.

"Wait—" Reynard realized who she was. "Harper. Harper sent you!"

She smiled and nodded.

Reynard climbed to his feet. It was clear Harper had seen his struggle and sent help. "Thank you," he said. "Tell Harper I'm coming."

Another nod, and she turned and faded behind a veil as she walked away.

A sound caught his attention. A wagon came trundling down the road and Reynard waved the driver down. "Sir, may I beg a ride into town?" The man stopped the cart. He was ancient and stared at

Reynard with one eye milky white. Reynard didn't know if it was possible for him look nonthreatening, but he tried to.

The man spat off to the side. "Git in back."

* * *

The old man took him as far as the city limits. Reynard thanked him before rushing off into the crowds, which seemed to him less noisome than normal. There were the usual merchants, servants, and laypeople. It wasn't long before Reynard noticed the absence of the guards.

He first traveled to Pops' den, but found it locked tight. Not a good sign. There was only one other place for him to go. He hoped to the Vine Harper was there waiting for him. It wasn't until the crowd thickened that Reynard realized something was amiss. He made his way through those gathered, noticing many of them carried weapons. The mood was volatile. There were whispers of rushing the gate. Harper couldn't be encouraging that?

When Reynard came to the head of the crowd, he saw Pops standing before a giantess of a guard and giving her hell. He had to admire the old man. Now why was he…?

Reynard searched nearby but didn't see Harper. If he had been in his fox form, his hackles would have risen right about now. "Pops!"

Pops turned. "Well, about time you got here! Harper's in there!"

Now it was Reynard who approached as he shifted into his second form, and the crowd fell back with many exclamations of surprise. He still wasn't as tall as the giantess, but he could look her in the eyes, "Where. Is. She." Reynard bared his teeth.

"Are you Reynard?"

Put off by her continued calm, he growled, "I am."

"She has a message for you."

Confused, he said, "What is it?"

"She wishes you to stop any bloodshed from occurring," the guard responded. "She wants you to look after these people."

"Fine, but that doesn't answer my question," Reynard said. "Where the fuck is she?"

"Inside." The giantess nodded towards the manor. "In one of the guest rooms. Don't worry, she's safe."

"They arrested her!" Pops said. "On some gods-be-damned treason charge."

"They did what?" Furious, Reynard turned back to the guard. "Open the gods-be-damned gate!"

"No," the guard said, still calm.

Reynard leaped upon her with a growl, shoving her back against the fence, which wasn't as easy as he was making it seem. "Do I look like I'm playing games?"

Other guards approached with swords drawn. The people withdrew a few steps. Only Pops and his sons turned to face them and placed themselves between Reynard and their adversaries.

"I can kill you before your guards take a step!"

"No, I don't believe you will," she said. "You'll be doing the exact thing your lady begged you not to do."

Anger, frustration, worry all warred within the fox. Yet Harper had asked him not to let them hurt the people. If he killed the guard, blood would spill, and he would have failed her.

He released the guard and stepped back. "I...we will not leave without her."

"You are free to stand in protest, but I will not allow you inside."

"Then that's what we'll do!" Pops called out. He began giving orders to people, to bring food and water, whatever was needed from them to settle in. Reynard realized how well respected the man was to command such power. Harper got her warrior's spirit from him.

He wanted – *needed* to do more. Reynard didn't know all the laws of the Isles. In Vale, anyone was free to go before Noble to air their grievances and request to speak on behalf of anyone accused of a crime. Grymbart had once done that for him. Did they have something similar here? "Am I able to air my grievances by an audience with the duchess? Speak for the prisoner?"

"You are not a citizen of Innrone."

"Damn it all."

"We will do it!" Pops said. "We demand audience with the duchess, so says the queen's law."

The giantess motioned to one guard and gave him whispered orders. "Stand back," she commanded.

Reynard almost shifted to fox to rush the opening but thought better of it. These accusations were ridiculous, but why had the duchess accused Harper of treason?

The Rot.

"Giantess," Reynard said.

"Sergeant Falstaff."

"Have you noticed strange goings-on as of late with the duchess?"

The slight twitch of a muscle below her eye showed a response. But it was enough for Reynard. "There is something I must tell you. Innrone is under attack."

That got a seeable reaction, her expression one of shock. "Your Lady Harper said the same thing."

"You believe her, don't you?"

Pops stepped forward and said, "My daughter don't lie."

Falstaff opened her mouth to speak, then closed it.

"You're just going to ignore what's going on? Just follow orders?"

Falstaff's lips quirked. "Your Lady Harper said something like that too."

"Then listen to her, gods be damned!"

"And what would you have me do, shifter?" Falstaff inquired. "Disobey orders? She is still our duchess."

Reynard balled his fists. He wanted to lash out at her again, but what good would it do? "At least send a message to the capital. Let the queen know something is amiss."

"Without proof? The queen will want more than intuition."

Reynard growled from deep in his throat. He was about to walk away when a thought occurred. "What about the foreigners? Can we send a message to Rhyvirand asking for help?"

Reynard thought she would refuse again, but she said, "There's no assurance they'll respond."

"Or arrive before we're all dead, but it's something." Reynard asked the crowd if anyone would carry messages to Rhyvirand. There was a messenger present, so he and three of his comrades agreed to go, mainly to get away from the threat to Innrone. Reynard couldn't blame them.

It was after that the guard Sergeant Falstaff sent into the manor came running back. He stopped at the gate but didn't open it. "Sergeant?"

Falstaff moved closer and her subordinate whispered something.

"Damn it," Reynard heard her say.

She approached him but looked at Pops. "They denied your request."

"What?" Pops roared. He followed with words that even Reynard never uttered in the company of others. And he was in complete agreement. The crowd, just settling down for the night, roused.

Reynard turned back to Falstaff. "Please, there must be something...."

There was. Something caught Reynard's gaze over Falstaff's shoulder. Something like black snakes slithering up the fine marble walls of the manor. No, not snakes – vines, coal-black. They sprouted offshoots and thorns and continued their climbing.

"Oh, dear Vine," Reynard muttered.

Falstaff whipped around. "What in the nether-hells...!"

Everyone stopped and stared. There was an eerie silence. All sound was muffled, as though they all were underwater.

It was the sound of glass shattering that caused everything to come to stark clarity.

"Open the gates, now!" Falstaff yelled.

As the guard went to obey, he halted, his whole body seized up. His eyes bugged and his mouth opened wide. Black blood poured from every opening. Thorns burst from his eyes, his chest, and all over his body until they ripped him apart. Screams filled the air, and the crowd scattered in a panic, scrambling and pushing. Some fell and threatened to be trampled.

Reynard froze. He couldn't stop watching and the chaos continued around him.

"Reynard!" the familiar voice called.

Sergeant Falstaff was screaming orders to the guards remaining, but it all sounded like a foreign language in Reynard's ears. The guards arranged themselves in a line before the fence, their swords drawn, as if it would do any good.

"Reynard, come on!" It was Pops, gripping his arm. "Get back!"

"No!" Reynard tried to break his grip. "Harper!"

"Ya can't get ta her if yer dead!" Pops' words cut through his desperation.

Reynard allowed Pops to pull him away as a wall of thorns sprouted, following the length of the fence, even breaking through the packed stones where Reynard had just been standing. Pops had saved his arse.

The line of guards moved farther back. Falstaff stood in front. "Sergeant!"

She had to have heard him but didn't turn.

"Is that enough proof for you?"

"Pops," Marcel said, "what do we do?"

"Hope ya have an idea, Reynard."

They were looking at him. Harper's father and brothers expected him to think of something. But for the first time in his life, Reynard had no plans or grand schemes. He was lost. Harper was alone and a prisoner of the Rot. And there wasn't a gods-be-damned thing he could do.

CHAPTER TWENTY-FOUR

Something was very wrong.

Harper knew it when something jarred her awake. Still in a half sleep, it took her a few moments to recall where she was.

Yes, the royal manor. How long had she been asleep? Harper rubbed her eyes. It was dark out, but it wasn't...*normal dark.* And her cards were screaming. Harper closed her hand around the pouch and a vision caught her. There she discovered Reynard, in no physical pain but that of his heart. He sat miserable and alone on the side of the road, his thoughts going down a dark path. His fear and doubt were palpable even through the veils. The more she watched, the deeper he sank into the fugue state.

Harper tried to reach out to him through the veils, pulling them aside, but they fell back into their places. She wasn't strong enough to manipulate them that way. It was possible. She had seen other diviners do it, but like the veils themselves, something separated her from the power she needed.

"Damnable fox, I won't let you give up!" Harper drew a card and grinned down at it. There was her true strength. She held the card between her palms. "Go to him."

There stood the Queen of Swords, as tall and mighty as the Steel Driver. She was dressed in silver armor that made a direct contrast to her dark skin, yet her eyes shone like the precious metal. The spirit bowed to her and turned, parting the veils. She needed no instruction.

Harper replaced the Queen to see what happened. She walked around the bed and faced the window. With the curtains drawn, the wan light filtered into the room. Harper reached out and grasped the curtain edge, pulling it aside.

"Oh, dear Vine."

Covering everything were black vines and thorns. They entwined around every surface and choked out whatever plant life was in their grasp. They undulated like black worms on hot stone as they continued their growing and tangling until they blotted out the light.

Harper stepped back from the window just as a massive thorn forced its way through, shattering the glass. Had she tarried a moment longer….

The Rot came in, its taint climbing the walls, its offshoot looking for what? Her? Harper dashed to the door and began pounding. "Guard! Help! Let me out!"

There was no response.

The vines continued their searching, wrapping around the bedposts, crawling along the thick carpeting. They reached the dressing table and smashed into the mirror, lifting the bottles of perfumes and oils and cracking them with little effort.

"Guard!" Harper continued to slam her fist against the door. What could she do? She pulled her cards, drew one. The Celestial Vine. "Dear Vine, help me!" Harper could see veils, and behind them the Vine burst through where the Rot had filled the window. The healthy green of fresh growth whipped around the tainted vines of the Rot, splintering them into fleshy strips.

Harper drew the next card. The Steel Driver. She pressed the card against the door with her open palm. "Steel Driver, guide my Gift." Like the hammer itself, Harper gathered her power, brought it slamming down on the door with the strength of the Steel Driver behind it.

One, two, three, four, and nothing remained but chunks of wood. When Harper entered the empty hall, she heard a commotion nearby. She replaced the pouch but kept both the Steel Driver and the Vine cards in her hand. She wasn't certain where she needed to go, since she'd not been paying much attention while following the sergeant. She recalled the long hall, which she guessed went the length of the manor.

There was a center opening separating the walls. Harper could see a carved wood banister and as she walked past the end of the wall, there was a double staircase she recalled climbing, which led down to the main hall. The opposite side of the room had the same. Harper figured there were rooms farther down each hall, away from prying eyes. The hall was rectangular, with ten tall windows, five on each side of the staircase. Heavy canary-yellow drapes blocked out the sunlight. The entire room had been done in the same gaudy color. There even were yellow tiles.

Seven jeweled chandeliers hung from a high ceiling and cast light. The source infuriated Harper – imprisoned wil-o-wisp. She would see them freed if she had something to say. The great double doors made of smooth ivory were closed.

Chaos reigned down below, with the chamberlain in the middle of it all. She tried in vain to calm people and give orders at the same time. Dozens of servants coming from the inner hall were running around in a frenzy. Young men carried various articles of furniture that were being piled against the main doors. Others lugged armloads of weapons and stacked them against the far wall, where members of the Royal Guard equipped themselves with as many as they could carry. A group of people were stacking crates. Harper saw after a servant opened one that they were packages of rations wrapped in paper.

Rations often held salt fish or sausages, hard bread and some type of pickled vegetable. If the soldier was very lucky, they would get some honey or dried fruit. Others brought waterskins. Everyone knew they would settle in for a battle.

She wasn't leaving that way. Even if she could make it to the outer hall without drawing attention—

"You, diviner!"

The chamberlain was standing at the foot of the stairs, red-faced, with her hands on her hips, trying, Harper figured, to look imperious, but she only looked absurd. "What did you do?"

Harper descended the stairs until she faced her. "What did *I* do?" *You highborn bitch!*

"I know you're behind this!"

"Get out of my way, pissant!"

"You crude little slut!"

Harper slammed the heel of her hand against the chamberlain's nose, smashing bone.

The chamberlain spat out a litany of curses while blood flowed over her mouth and dripped from her chin. Her voice was a nasal whine. "I will have you killed!"

Harper turned and walked away.

"Don't walk away from me, commoner whore!" Despite her order, the chamberlain didn't follow.

"Miss Harper!" It was Gertie. "Please help!" The girl was distressed.

"What is it?" Harper asked.

"I can't find my sister!" Gertie wrung her hands. "We got separated when— What's happening, Lady Harper?"

She knew she couldn't take the time to explain things to Gertie. "Listen, I need to find the duchess. Do you know where she is?"

"But—"

"It's important. I promise I'll help you find Chloe. Right now, for all of this to end, I need to see Magdalen."

The girl's shocked expression was likely caused by Harper using the duchess's first name. A terrible breach of protocol. "I believe she's in her suites?"

Harper put her hands on Gertie's shoulders. "Is there a place you can hide? Your rooms?"

Gertie sniffed and nodded.

"Good. Don't let anyone in until I come for you. Now, where are the royal suites?"

She pointed to the other staircase. "Left at the end of the hall."

"There she is!" It was the crone again, with two harried guards. "Arrest her!"

Before the guards could react, there came the sound of glass shattering. All eyes turned to the windows, where a thorn ripped through the drapes. Ignoring Jourdain's orders, the two guards rushed forward, drawing their swords to meet the new threat.

The chamberlain looked at the thorns and back at Harper. She graced Harper with a look of disgust before joining the soldiers. Yet she stayed far back while screeching supposed orders, which did little to encourage or command.

Harper had to do something. If the Rot consumed everything here, speaking with the duchess would be moot. Harper chose a spot under the stairwell and drew her cards, but she didn't know what to do next. The Steel Driver and the Vine were still in her hand. She'd almost forgotten they were there, even when confronting the chamberlain. "I've called on you so much." She held up the Vine card. "I am your Beholden, but I don't know what to do."

She laid both cards down and drew a third, frowning over the Piper. The Harlot and the Virgin came next. And one she hadn't drawn yet, the Nightingale. "Let's see, the Piper leading astray. The Harlot, immorality, and its opposite the Virgin. The Nightingale reversed."

After she laid the Nightingale, everything around her faded into a vision. Through all the panic, something moved among the bodies, gliding with a sinister grace. It was vaguely human but made of shadows and serpents.

No, not those things. It was the Rot. A construct of pure evil. The shadows were real, but the serpents were vines twined to form a mere semblance of humanity. It turned and looked right at Harper. Then the true visage of the Rot replaced it. The same Harper saw so long ago in the country house.

The vision faded when Harper sensed something nearby. Some of the younger servant children had joined her in her hiding place. Harper smiled at them. "This is a good place."

They were terrified and didn't speak, but the one who appeared the oldest nodded.

Harper wasn't certain what the vision meant or who she'd seen, although she had an inkling. Right now, she had to prevent the Rot from pressing any further. She lifted the Piper to eye level. She reached out and moved the veil aside, and he appeared. He played and those in the room, while not seeing him, heard and reacted to his music. They calmed and moved along with the notes of the pipe. Even the chamberlain, with blood on her face and clothes, started an odd sort of dance that would be amusing if they weren't in such a dire situation.

The children in hiding crawled out to join the others as they cavorted to the music as the Piper's tune increased in fervor. Harper wondered at the morality of it all. It was not a pleasant sight, seeing all the helpless people under her control.

The vines were reacting too as their movements slowed. Harper called on the Vine and, like before, new green shoots burst the rotted vines, overtaking them and forming intricate webs of green over the broken windows, like the Vine did in their sanctuary.

Reynard. Harper hoped he'd arrived, and Falstaff had relayed her message. She hoped he was thinking of a way to get to her.

Harper had work to do in here.

Now the Nightingale was still puzzling her. Reversed it could mean several things. Humility, sincerity, and the want of approval. It would have made more sense if it were upright. The Virgin and Harlot combination was also a puzzle. These cards joined in a common purpose or warred with one another. She had to figure out what they meant.

The people were still dancing. Harper would have to call the Piper back before long because the dancers would drop from exhaustion. Then again, that would keep them out of her way, giving her time to find the duchess. If she were even alive anymore.

A streak of black moved amongst the dancers, drawing Harper's attention. She replaced her cards and moved from underneath the stairs. Whatever it was, it stood in the far corner of the room. More movement near the entrance and there was something else. Harper pushed around the dancing bodies. It took her a moment to realize the shadowy beings were being spawned by the rotted vines, growing in gray pustules that burst open like overripe fruit, each dropping another creature in the room, covered in ichor. When one went to shake it off like a dog, Harper saw what they were. Ghouls.

"Stop!" Harper cried out. The Piper halted, and the dancers did in kind. For a moment, all eyes were on Harper. Their labored breathing was the only sound. A scream arose from the rear of the room, followed by many others. They drove forward, past people still standing, dazed by the sudden halt of their dancing. They ran in a wave of bodies, trying to push their way into the narrow outer hall. Something stopped them and caused the people in front to tangle with those behind them. Harper soon saw why. Goblins forced their way into the middle of the mound of people. They pulled hair and ripped at flesh with their teeth and claws.

A voice rose above the panic. "To arms!" Those who heard responded by fighting their way to the weapons. Those who fled for their lives proved a hindrance.

Harper watched, sickened by what she had caused. The ghouls pounced on those not quick enough to escape. They feasted, although normally they only devoured corpses. They were not being as exacting now. Harper stepped back, retreating to the shelter of the stairs, but by moving, she made herself a target. One goblin saw her and grinned with its green rotted teeth and took its time as it crossed the room, its attention on her.

It was almost upon her when Harper wrenched her dagger from its sheath and slashed out, but the goblin saw it and danced away. Other goblins gathered, goading their friend on. Harper held her dagger out, walking backwards until her back was against the wall.

She used one hand to get her pouch open, a feat, but she managed. As stupid as people said goblins to be, the beasts wore a wary expression. Then, Harper supposed, the one attacking her decided whatever she was doing didn't matter. It squatted and kept the grin on its face. Drool dripped down the scraggly beard on his chin. Its clawed hands flexed.

Harper didn't know what card she drew until she heard it whispering over the din.

Fire engulfed her, or at least a sense of fire coursing through her blood, filling her with a force that was familiar.

Let me in.

The goblins screeched as a white light washed over them, coming from Harper herself. The goblin rushed her, whether in fear or anger Harper no longer cared. She swung, and the blade sliced the goblin's neck. Its head was absent from his body. Harper raised the weapon to eye level, a dagger no more.

It was a sword.

CHAPTER TWENTY-FIVE

"You're going to burn it?"

"Have you another suggestion?"

Reynard balled his fists. "How will you control it?"

"As best we can." Falstaff turned away to approach the group of laborers who arrived on the scene with carts carrying several large barrels of water.

"That isn't a proper answer," Reynard muttered. He had an ill feeling that burning the rotten vines and thorns would only cause further damage.

Pops walked up behind him. "You gotta do something."

"I don't know what to do." Reynard's calm was hanging by a thread. "They're going to burn it."

"Everybody get back!" Falstaff ordered. "If you're not part of the operation, you're in the way."

"No." Reynard didn't move. "This is wrong. It won't work." He wasn't sure how he knew. He just did.

Although Reynard was talking to himself, Pops said, "Then we better do what the giantess says."

Another group of laborers moved as close as they dared, carrying buckets, the contents of which were splashed on the wall of thorn vines. Reynard recognized the smell of the liquid. Grain spirits.

Reynard drew Pops back. He could see the vines and thorns quivering. Did they know?

The citizens who followed Harper remained gathered. Reynard didn't know if they cared or just wanted a spectacle. He supposed he couldn't blame them if it was the latter. At least now everyone realized Innrone was in danger. Reynard could only hope Harper could speak with the duchess.

They brought lanterns and placed laborers along the length of the fence and, Reynard guessed, also on the sides. Waiting for the order.

When it came from Falstaff, each man tossed their lanterns at the fence. The spirits caught almost at once. The fire spread, licking at the vines and thorns. It looked like it might work until Reynard saw the fire was burning the liquid but not the vines and thorns.

Something else was happening. Gray sacks were forming from the flesh of the vines. At first Reynard thought they were filled with liquid. He could see movement through the skins. One sac burst apart, and something came out, covered in ichor. It stretched itself out to a spindly, human shape, hunched over as its clawed hands dragged on the paving stones.

"What, by all things holy, is that?" Falstaff and her soldiers drew their weapons.

"That, my dear sergeant," Reynard said, "is a ghoul."

Another sack burst; more followed. The wet sound of the sack skin rending was all anyone could hear. Then one ghoul howled, a guttural sound that sent a shudder over Reynard.

The screams and shouted oaths began, and the crowd turned and fled as one. Goaded by this sudden show of fear, the ghouls charged, and Sergeant Falstaff, with a cry, sent her troops to meet them. Reynard had always heard that ghouls were mindless abominations, so they caught him and the troops off guard when they scuttled and danced out of their reach and instead, focused on the fleeing citizens.

"Son of a bitch!" Reynard dashed towards the nearest ghouls, just as one grabbed a terrified woman by her hair. He leaped on its back and slashed his claws across the ghoul's throat, tearing it open. The ghoul fell dead with a grunt. The woman, upon seeing Reynard in his half form, screeched like a banshee and ran. *So much for thank you.*

Reynard saw Pops and his sons engaging the ghouls. The old man was quite good with a sword. He'd lost track of Sergeant Falstaff, but he had little time to dwell on it before another ghoul tried to get past him.

From then on, all was a mess of blood, torn flesh, and feral cries. Reynard had never considered himself a fighter. He'd always used cunning and guile to get out of any situation. It only worked with beings who could reason. But the ghouls were only intent on killing. So Reynard continued to fight.

It ended when Reynard heard Pops screaming. Reynard turned to see Pops' son Osvald lying bloody on the stones, a sizeable chunk of flesh ripped from his chest. Thinking of Harper, knowing it would devastate her, Reynard howled and threw himself back into the fray, fighting at Pops' side, until there were no more ghouls left alive. They'd killed both soldiers and civilians. Marcel and Pops wept over their lost family. Somehow, killing the ghouls didn't seem to mitigate the loss. Reynard left them in their mourning.

Reynard approached one soldier to ask about Falstaff and was relieved to find that she survived and was in one of the nearby eateries. Someone was trying to find a healer for her injuries. The only healers he knew were Shahir and Asta, and he couldn't fetch either.

Reynard found the sergeant. They'd moved a chair close to the door. She sat, looking out onto the scene when Reynard came in. He saw there were piles of cloth on her left leg. She was in great pain.

"Sir Reynard." She forced a smile. "I am glad to see you are alive."

"The same," Reynard said with a smile.

"You were right, and I am sorry."

"There was no way of knowing. You shouldn't waste time with self-pity."

"Would you know a talented healer?"

"Not Above Ground," Reynard said.

"I'll be dead before you can bring them here."

Reynard hadn't known the beautiful giantess for long, but he felt sorry for her. "I want to do something for you…."

"Don't you worry about me. Focus your energies on getting to your lady," Falstaff said.

"If I had any idea how, I would." He was exhausted and took the nearest chair, sitting down hard. He shifted into his full human form.

"Amazing," Falstaff said, "we are alike, you and me. Two misfits trying to survive in a world that considers us outsiders."

"Yes, here." But in Vale, he was home, amongst his kin, lost to him though they were. He would lose Harper if he didn't think of something.

"I've sent to the capital for military help."

Reynard turned back to her. "Truly? I took you for someone who preferred the heat of battle."

"Do I look like some glory-hungry warmonger?" Falstaff said. "Shut your mouth."

Reynard laughed. It had been too long. "We are not prepared for more. I suggest you evacuate the city."

"To where?" Falstaff adjusted her gigantic frame in the chair, and her face twisted with the pain. "And if we can keep this contained—"

"Damn it!" Reynard stormed from the home. There was no containing the Rot, and as soon as the dark fey regrouped, they would attack again. They needed help, and they needed it fast. Reynard walked closer to the manor, past the people gathering the bodies of the dead and helping the injured, and approached, as close as he dared.

"Harper." Reynard bowed his head. "I'm going to do what you did. Gather an army, but this time they will not flee. Please take care."

Reynard returned to the home and Falstaff. "Sergeant, I am sorry."

"I understand," she said. "I'm going to call out the militia and order the citizens to stay in their homes or they can leave if they wish."

"I'm sorry, this has all been placed on your shoulders."

Falstaff shrugged. "Can't be helped."

"Listen," Reynard said, "I'm going to see if I can gather more fighters from my home, but there's a chance I won't return. Please don't ask me to explain."

"I won't," she said.

"If I don't come back, please tell Harper I went home. She'll know what that means."

"All right."

"Good fortune to you, Sergeant."

"And to you, Reynard the Fox." Her smile was rueful.

Reynard didn't ask how she knew that he was *the* Reynard the Fox. He just grinned before taking his leave.

Once outside, Reynard found himself in a quiet alley and shifted to his fox form. He surprised many people when they saw a fox running down the road. Getting to the entrance would take a long time. There was only one other way to get to Underneath.

The city was silent with no one about, so he guessed Falstaff didn't need an edict commanding people to stay in their homes. Word traveled fast in cities. The thought almost made him chuckle. When he arrived at the bottom of the hill, he noticed the witch-fire was gone, likely because the caster of the spell was now out of reach.

Just run. Keep running and fighting.

Reynard ran up the hill with single-minded determination as the pit loomed closer. When he came to the edge, he didn't stop. He leaped forward into the darkness. His paw pads came down on the slick vines, sinking into the flesh, and the vines reacted, reaching for him and twining around his hind legs, but Reynard tore into whatever vine was nearest, ripping strips of it out. When it didn't release him, Reynard began tearing with his teeth and claws until he felt it falter. He had to take care not to allow the full animal in him to take hold, but he allowed enough of that wild part to lend him strength.

Reynard leaped again. The vines lashed out at him and scored hits that removed fur and left marks. But the pain was inconsequential. At one point, something tripped him, and he went rolling down until he struck against the hard earth. He didn't hesitate. He broke into a run, a blind dash to get far away.

His chest aching and his muscles screaming, he halted. There was some light coming from the glowing mushrooms. Reynard didn't know where he was. He had to get his bearings. *Calm yourself, fox, use the skills the Vine gave you.* He smiled. It was the first time he'd admitted the Vine gave him his talents.

He closed his eyes, using his instincts and his nose to catch any familiar scents. *There!* The very faint scent of fresh growth. And something else, like smoldering embers? He wondered if someone was nearby. It was possible he was near another world or an entrance. He'd visited a few of them, so he hoped this was a place he recognized.

He continued and let his senses lead him. After a time, he saw a glow up ahead of him, brighter than the plant life, and as he moved closer, he realized what they were. Wil-o-wisp. Enough to light the tunnel he now found himself in. He walked forward, not wanting to injure them. Wil-o-wisp were quite docile, but they were Children of the Vine and, if threatened, they could deliver a shock that would leave a grown man paralyzed. Another favorite trick of theirs was leading mortals astray until they became lost or stumbled into a dangerous situation.

So, when the group moved as one, Reynard sat waiting, and his head tilted to one side in confusion when they stopped. Reynard started walking again, choosing each step, and the wisps went before him. Were they leading him astray? To his doom?

Reynard didn't notice that they'd surrounded him and were pressing him forward. They seemed to know where they were going. Their light, which many thought eerie, was welcome to him.

"Well, I'll be damned." There was light at the end of the tunnel. He chuckled at his use of such a cliched saying, but, well, it was the truth. The wisps separated, clearing a path. "Thank you!" Reynard hoped they understood. Not about to press his fortune, Reynard dashed out of the cave.

He was on a hill, easy enough to climb down. Spread out before him was the small town of Belltide.

He was so achingly near Vale that he swore he caught the scent of his kin. Vale was the human town where he'd gone and played so many of the tricks he'd became famous for. Well, he'd better be about his business. If any of the humans saw him in his fox form, they would have no way of knowing he was a shifter, unless he shifted back, and Reynard was quite certain that seeing a naked man appear before them would be enough to send anyone into a faint.

Reynard kept to the wooded areas between the human and animalia. The sun shone bright in a blue sky at Belltide, but the closer he came to Vale, the darker it became. It was as if both day and night were conjoined. It was not a normal cloud cover as one might see during a storm as it made its way across the heavens, but a stark line where blue met slate-gray clouds that floated low over the landscape. An alien sight, and it made Reynard shudder.

Still, he pressed forward. When he came upon the familiar road, Reynard, regardless of what might happen, ran again. He noticed no one was about, but it wasn't his concern. He felt for his kin, but to save them, they had to drive the Rot out of Vale and Innrone. So, with thoughts of Harper guiding him, Reynard came to the city.

The people here were shells of those he knew. More like the people of his nightmare. How long ago had that been? When Reynard came close to someone, he realized their eyes were closed. Sleepwalking? Perhaps it was a good thing that no one was paying him attention.

He came to the royal manor. The air held an icy chill. The stench of the Rot was still present, although not as strong. Reynard figured this was because it was focusing all its attention on Innrone. Moving with care, Reynard made his way to the throne room.

There was Noble, slumped over on his throne, dressed in all his finery, his circlet lopsided on his head. He didn't stir even as Reynard approached and sat before him.

"Your Majesty? I have come home. I need—"

He saw movement out of the corner of his eye, too late for him to react. Isengrim, in his full wolf form, charged at him, and slammed his snout into Reynard's rib cage, sending the fox sprawling. Pain erupted where Isengrim hit, and Reynard heard the sickening crack of bone.

"How dare you?" Isengrim snarled "How dare you show your face here, you traitorous whoreson? Are you so eager to die? Very well then, I shall oblige you."

CHAPTER TWENTY-SIX

"Isengrim, you have to—"

But the wolf was mad with vengeance. He charged, his eyes burning with hate and saliva dripping from his mouth. But as though they were in the arena, Reynard dodged.

"Stand and face me, you coward!"

Reynard continued to evade him. He knew as before, Isengrim would get hold of him eventually. And there was no dust to throw in his eyes. The next time he dodged, he focused on Noble, who had not moved from his position. He was asleep for all Reynard could tell, with his eyes open.

"Sire, please hear me!" He leaped upon the throne itself and, as he'd done with Harper, Reynard bit the king in his hand.

"How dare you!" The wolf leaped, trying to get at Reynard, but only succeeded in knocking Noble's inert body from the throne. Either the bite or falling must have worked, because Reynard noticed Noble's fingers curl.

"Fight!" Reynard begged the king. "Take your true form!"

Isengrim was on him, but Reynard didn't move, and the wolf sank his teeth deep into Reynard's shoulder. His bite ripped through sinew and crunched bone and Reynard couldn't help a scream of agony. He fell on his side, his front leg now useless. He'd never survive on his own. Neither as a man nor a fox. He ground his teeth hard around the pain and forced the words out: "It no longer has you."

Isengrim released him, which was rather surprising, and stepped back. Reynard's blood dripped from the wolf's lips, and he rolled on his side and vomited. His head spun and the surrounding scene was fading, and he feared he would faint right there. That would be humiliating. "Uncle, please help."

Was he dreaming? There in the total darkness was a flicker of green light, and Reynard felt himself floating towards it. It was the offshoot, looking like Reynard had first seen it. Why was it here? He knew the darkness would never end. He set down beside it and watched as it quivered, then grew. Again, his head tilted back and forth. What was it doing?

Instead of growing straight up, it was crawling towards him. It touched his right paw, which Reynard realized wasn't there, or at least he couldn't see it. Yes, Isengrim had bitten it off. The Vine was spreading, forming an intricate web of tiny offshoots that continued up and around his shoulder, and Reynard felt an odd pull he couldn't quite describe.

Now what?

The light returned and with it the agony again, but the pain was brief as his eyes opened. Isengrim had backed away, standing next to the king's body, fear in his eyes. Reynard had no idea why he had that look. Reynard was at his mercy. Still the wolf stood and stared, and Reynard noticed the crack in the floor, and then there was the Vine entwined around his leg. It was hard but Reynard could see the tangle of vines piercing his shoulder, taking the place of his bones and tendons, until it had recreated his paw.

It's no wonder Isengrim looks like he's about to shite himself.

"Is that...?" Isengrim lowered his head.

Reynard turned over and lifted himself up. "Thank you." He bit at the edge of the Vine, separating it from the base.

"How?" Isengrim rose on his haunches.

Fearing that he'd shift, Reynard cried out,

"Don't shift!"

Isengrim sat. "Why not?"

"Do you remember anything before you came here?" Reynard asked.

Isengrim tilted his head. "I...." Reynard saw the realization in his eyes. "Something had me."

"It has everyone," Reynard said. "The Rot. Do you recall?"

"Yes, I do." Isengrim's hackles rose. "An evil presence— No, there were many."

"You must wake Noble and get him to shift," Reynard said. "Only in our animal forms can we rid ourselves of its influence."

"But we can't stay this way forever!" Isengrim whined. "You know what will happen."

"Yes, and that's why time is short," Reynard said. "We must leave Vale and go Above Ground."

"But—"

"I promise to explain all, but right now, I must find Eica. Then we need Asta. They need a healer in Innrone."

"I believe you're sincere for once in your life," Isengrim said. "Very well, I'll see to the king."

The girl was no more.

When Reynard saw her lying in front of Eica's room, he thought Lucea was dead. What remained of her was a dried-out husk, withered and gray, her skin hanging from her bones. *Damn it to the nether-hells.* He was powerless to help her as a fox. He washed her face with his tongue. When he moved back, he saw tears escaping from her eyes.

"Don't worry, I'll be back—"

A screech had Reynard jumping back while his hackles rose. He recognized the woman, who was in her half form, and although her eyes were normal, her stance and expression left no doubt she planned to attack.

"Aislinn."

She let out another ear-splitting screech, which Reynard felt right to his bones. Then she was coming for him. He didn't want to hurt her, but she was leaving him with no choice. Still, Reynard gave ground as she snapped her beak at him, trying to spread her wings in the narrow hall. She halted as she came close to the girl, her neck twisting sideways, much like Reynard and his kin tilted their heads when they were trying to understand something. Reynard took advantage of her moment of inattention to attack. Leaping, he only meant to push her back, but when he hit, he slammed her onto her back and slid several feet across the marble floor.

"What in the nether-hells—"

If his feat of strength surprised Reynard, Aislinn was stunned. She wasn't so injured or frightened that she couldn't climb to her feet.

"Aislinn, you must remember yourself!" Reynard cried. "Take your full animal form!"

Aislinn hissed at him. He couldn't fight again, and he didn't want to lose another limb. When she charged, Reynard braced. *Take out the wing, watch the beak and talons—*

"Aislinn, stop!"

Reynard whipped around, expecting Aislinn to claw his eyes out, but when he turned back, she was stock still.

"Aislinn," Eica said in her hawk form, "you know me."

Something moved past Reynard, an ethereal shape. He wasn't certain who it was, not being familiar with all the Major and Minor Arcana. He thought it was the Virgin. She reached out and brushed her hand down the arch of Aislinn's head. Reynard sat and expelled a breath of relief as Aislinn took her full animal form.

"Reynard," she said, "why – how?"

"That's a tale for another day," Reynard said. "We must find our people and convince them all to take their animal forms."

"It was like being trapped in a nightmare outside my body," Aislinn said. "That thing— The Rot wants to devour all."

Her gaze moved to the girl on the floor. "Is that Lucea?"

Both women moved closer.

"I told her not to do it!" Eica sounded near tears, although she couldn't cry in her form. "Is she…?"

"No," Reynard said. "Look, she's crying."

"We have to help her," Aislinn said.

"We can't," Reynard said, "you know we can't."

Eica screamed. It was a cry of guilt and frustration, but she knew Reynard spoke true.

"I left Isengrim with Noble," Reynard said. "If he wasn't able to convince our king to shift, we may have a serious problem."

Aislinn said, "Go to *our king*. I will find the pride."

"Eica?" Reynard said.

"I-I will—"

"We need Asta." Reynard bobbed his head. "And we need Tybert and his army. The Rot has invaded Innrone, and it has Harper prisoner."

"Harper?" Both women spoke as one, and the cries they gave were not ones of guilt but fury.

"I will not return without Tybert," Eica said.

When they parted ways again, Reynard dashed back, hoping he made it to the throne room. The roar was so loud that his fur stood up. He'd not heard it in decades, and it sent a cold lance of fear to the pit of his stomach. For a moment, paralysis had him. The animal instinct to flee made him tremble. But no, he couldn't. Even if he died by Noble's teeth and claws, he would not leave Isengrim alone. Reynard forced himself to move. A second roar stopped him again, but he pressed forward. When he came to the throne room, his heart near stopped.

Noble stood, drawn up to his full height, still in his half form. He stalked towards Isengrim, whose haunches were against the wall. Noble had scored a vicious hit and blood matted the wolf's fur. Isengrim looked ready for Noble's next attack.

"Leonine!" Reynard shouted. Upon hearing his name, Noble turned, and, like Aislinn's, his eyes were normal but filled with the wild of his people. "You are king of Vale! Remember!"

Noble went down on all fours, his tail slashing the air behind him, one paw forward. Reynard swore he was smiling. It was not a good sign.

"Shite," Reynard muttered. *Well, time to die.* At least now he'd found help, and maybe they could rescue Harper. Reynard growled low in his throat.

Noble laughed.

What Reynard didn't expect next was Isengrim leaping upon Noble's back and biting down on his mane. Noble turned around, shook his head, tried to throw Isengrim off as Reynard, as humiliating as it was, went for his flank, and was near crushed when Noble fell on his side.

"Leonine!"

The king's chest rose and fell. Isengrim didn't move. Reynard moved around to face the king. "Become what you are!"

When the change began, Isengrim released him and moved to stand beside the king. In this form, he was still a massive beast.

"Reynard."

Reynard went down on his forepaws. "My king."

Leonine looked at him. "How—?"

"Sire," Isengrim said, "we must not tarry. Reynard has promised to explain."

"That thing..." Leonine said, "...the Rot. I could not fight it. I no longer deserve to be king."

Reynard came to his feet. "Stop it!" Surprised at his own tone, Reynard continued, "We were not immune to its power. It held us all in its sway."

"But it is different—"

"Sire!" They didn't have time for this. "Do you wish to save your kingdom? Your subjects? Would you abandon us because of your wounded pride?"

The fire lit Leonine's eyes, and Reynard was happy to see it.

Reynard explained what had happened since they'd thrown him into the Cesspit. He received no apologies and expected none. Leonine first led them to the royal quarters, where he had ordered the pride cloistered before the Rot had taken complete hold. So, it did not surprise them when they met Aislinn coming from the opposite direction.

"Majesty!" Aislinn could not bow, so she inclined her head and spread her wings. "My king, I am so glad to see you."

"And you, Aislinn."

"I cannot get to the pride."

"Yes, I had them locked within." Leonine pawed at the fine marble. "Stand clear."

Leonine made quick work of the door, and Reynard's admiration for him grew. He strode in first and Reynard thought it was a good idea if he stayed outside. Despite them being larger than normal, he was still the smallest of their group. A commotion followed and when it was all finished, Leonine emerged, followed by his pride.

"Reynard," the king said to him, "what is our next step?"

A momentary shock, then Reynard said, "Eica went to fetch Tybert and his army. We must meet her there."

"Should we summon the militia?" Aislinn asked.

Another shock when Leonine looked at Reynard. "Yes," Reynard said. "It should be easier to bring them back. The people I saw are entranced. Perhaps it won't be difficult to awaken them."

They decided Aislinn and Isengrim would go into town and fetch the militia and spread word of the coming battle, while Reynard and Leonine would travel to Tybert's castle.

"There is one more of our kin I wish to find," Reynard told the king when they were alone. "Finnick."

"He should be in his room," Leonine said. "I will tell you where. Go to him and I will wait for you."

Reynard bobbed his head again. "Yes, sire."

Finnick's room was on the same floor as Eica's, at the rear of the manor. Reynard only hoped he could convince his fellow fox, who had so much hatred for him. But he knew how he might bring Finnick back.

When he came to the door, he clawed at it. Between barks and howls, he called out, "Finnick!"

Nothing moved in the room. It tempted Reynard to shift into his half form, but he didn't want to take the chance. Reynard continued scratching and howling, like any pet begging for entry, but he wasn't worried about his dignity. He just needed to know—

The door opened as though pushed by a gentle breeze.

Reynard would have preferred anything else, it splintering with the force of a mighty blow or being ripped clear off its hinges. Reynard would not go in.

"Finnick." Reynard took several steps back. "I know you're there. Come out, or are you a coward?"

Finnick was there in his half form. He slammed a fist against the door. He stared at Reynard with black eyes.

"Damn it," Reynard said.

"I. Will. Kill. You," Finnick growled.

"Will you, boy? You will kill your better?"

His words had the desired effect. Finnick growled and went to reach for him, but Reynard dodged. Finnick stumbled and hit the opposite wall.

"Clumsy boy," Reynard said. "What would your mother think?"

"Don't you dare!" Finnick made a reckless grab for Reynard, and the fox bit him.

Finnick cried out and shoved his hand under his shoulder. "You bastard!"

"Think of Hermeline," Reynard said. "What would she think of you? Allowing yourself to be manipulated?"

"Hermeline." His tone was sorrowful. "Mother."

"Take your fox form and fight me proper," Reynard challenged.

The hateful gaze returned, and Finnick fell to his hands and knees, shifting. "I will make you pay for what you have done."

"Finnick, listen to me! There's no time for this!"

"You expect me to just forgive?"

"I expect nothing of the sort," Reynard said, "but Vale, all the Riven Isles, are in danger. You know this! You know the Rot wishes to destroy all who dwell in the light."

Finnick took several deep breaths. "I saw my mother in my nightmares."

"I'm so sorry," Reynard said. "If you wish retribution once we're victorious, I'll not protest, but for now, our king waits for us."

"Noble," Finnick said. "Is he…?"

"Yes, he is free of the Rot," Reynard said. "He waits for us in the throne room."

Finnick walked before him, then looked back as if he wanted to speak further but changed his mind.

"I spoke true. If you still wish for me to be punished, I will accept it."

When they reached the throne room, Leonine had not moved from the spot. He waited while Finnick paid him reverence.

When they were outside, the sun shining through the gray made Reynard happy. And for the first time, he had hope. As they raced to Tybert's castle, it took all their muscles to keep up with Leonine as they ran. Reynard forced himself on. When they crested the hill that overlooked Tybert's castle, Leonine stopped. Reynard supposed they shouldn't just rush to the gates.

The king roared, and although Reynard still trembled, it was out of respect for his king. Nothing happened at first, then the gates opened. Out marched in perfect formation, with Tybert and Asta at the lead, hundreds of cats, and above them, Eica circled, her wings spread wide before landing before the king.

They spoke, and Tybert and Asta approached. Reynard moved forward, but he didn't step out of the king's shadow. However, it was enough for Tybert and Asta to see him.

"Your Highness." Reynard dipped his head.

"I thought I would never see you again," There was a bitter edge to Tybert's voice. "So now you are our savior?"

"I am the Vine's Beholden, and I have sworn an oath to protect its children."

"Such fine and flowery words," Tybert said.

"Tybert," Noble warned.

"I beg your forgiveness, Your Majesty," Tybert said. "Eica has told me of this dire situation and my army and I are at your service."

"With any luck, Aislinn and Isengrim have the militia gathered," Reynard said.

"Go forth, Reynard, Finnick, and Eica," Noble commanded them. "We will join you."

It was easy to keep up with Finnick, and something about running with the kit gave Reynard an unexpected strength. He supposed it was because Finnick was of the same blood. When they came to the center of town, Reynard allowed himself to look towards the future. Aislinn and Isengrim had gathered the militia. Now they only awaited their king.

But when Noble arrived, he did not take control of his soldiers. He turned to Reynard and said, "You are my general now. Lead my army."

The old Reynard would have refused. Made excuses about his unworthiness. Anything not to be under the watchful eye of the king or have any responsibility. But he was a different beast now.

"Yes, Your Majesty," Reynard said. "I am at your service."

CHAPTER TWENTY-SEVEN

Possession.

Now Harper recalled Eica's words, *If you choose this path, prepare yourself for the consequences.*

The Queen of Swords remained at the forefront of her conscious thoughts. They shared quintessence, but Harper felt the pull of the Queen to draw greater power from Harper's self. This was what Eica had warned: that the more powerful spirit, in their quest to fulfill whatever duty the realm had given them, would seize control of their host.

As Harper lifted the sword again, most goblins had sense enough to flee. The great shining blade came down and cut one of the remaining goblins in half. It screamed and exploded in fire and ichor, and chunks of its flesh splattered over Harper's face. It burned, but she wiped it away with one hand and pursued the second goblin. As she walked, her goal became clear, her thoughts single-minded, as she watched the veils beat with an unseen wind. It gave her glimpses of the surrounding mayhem.

And the fire continued to burn her inside. Sweat trickled down her face, into her blouse and between her breasts. It would consume her if she didn't do something. When the last goblin could run no more, Harper speared it straight through its heart. Like its comrade's, its body blew up.

Her gaze locked on the other dark fey, which appeared as muddy stains against the translucent veils. The mortals had the glow of life, their quintessence a mixture of various colors. When someone died, their light would fade until a mere spark remained. That went out as quickly as a breath on a candle flame. It happened all around her as the once-living made their journey to Up Above and far beyond. She had to stop this as the Queen continued to draw from her.

More dark splotches appeared out of nowhere, and Harper knew them all, the worst scum of Deep Earth. More goblins and their kin, the Red Caps. Ghouls, basilisks, and some that Harper didn't even recognize. She guessed the larger denizens she saw in Underneath could not move through the rotted vines. Or at least, she hoped not. Their only purpose? To maim and kill.

Harper moved through the veils; some she had to push aside. She glimpsed things that most mortals should never meet, and she would not forget. Yet she took it as good fortune that they remained trapped. Some stared with malicious intent while others clawed at the veils, but despite their delicate look, the veils held firm.

The sword cleaved through each of the dark fey. No soul traveling to Up Above marked their deaths, but their filthy quintessence – if it were that – simply dissipated into nothing. The darkness began gathering in one spot. Harper frowned. What were they doing? When she saw them charge at her, she gripped the sword with both hands. With a single motion, it ripped through the shadows, dispatching them. The basilisks proved more difficult as she had to close her eyes and allow the Queen's supremacy.

Screams and weeping reached her from somewhere far away. The room spun, and her stomach roiled, and Harper felt she would vomit. It was like being mired in quicksand, sinking ever deeper. With the last of her will fading, she said, "Stop," the words a croak from between her dry lips. She trembled. "Stop!"

The Queen of Swords continued dragging Harper along. She opened herself to the fire and allowed it to feed her anger. "I. Said. *Stop!*" She snatched the pouch from around her neck and drew the Queen of Swords. She held the card between her palms and imagined sending fire into it and to the spirit. The Queen screamed and Harper screamed, and the spirit left her body. And Harper fell into blessed darkness.

★ ★ ★

As always, Harper knew when she dreamed.

The main hall was empty. The darkness behind the tall windows was so absolute that light from the chandeliers reflected off the glass. Harper had the sense that something, though she couldn't see what, was observing her. All was peaceful save for that.

"What do you want to say to me?"

Whatever it was, it had not expected Harper to address it. The emotions coming from it told her that much.

"You know nothing of the powers of a diviner."

It came from the darkness at the other end of the hall. It stank of the long-dead. Harper recognized it as the thing she'd glimpsed walking as chaos went on around it. It made its body up of a tangle of writhing, rotted vines. It walked within inches of her. If it expected Harper to move or back away, it was going to be disappointed. The face was the Rot's, but the body itself was the shape of a woman wearing a ball gown made of black leaves.

It continued to hold Harper's gaze, and she didn't blink. The vines that made its hair were moving as though it were Medusa; they dared to reach out and stroke Harper's face. Harper stayed still. It hissed in frustration, likely because it couldn't get Harper to react. If she showed fear, if she tried to flee, it would feed on those emotions. Harper would not give it that satisfaction.

The construct lifted its hands and grasped Harper by the throat. Now she needed to concentrate. If she panicked and *thought* she was choking, she would indeed choke. It was difficult for her not to pry the hands off. Harper grew tired, and she closed her eyes and pushed away with her Gift.

When she woke up, Harper almost wished she was still asleep. Her entire body was in agony. She was certain every muscle stretched to their limit and then some. Her head was pounding and there was a sour taste in her mouth and her throat was stripped raw.

The first things she saw were massive shelves reaching two man-heights stacked with bottles. She was in the wine cellar, but how the hells had she gotten there? The bottles reminded her of her savage thirst, so she bit down on her lip and pushed herself up. The pain was so intense it brought tears to her eyes.

A rat ran across Harper's field of vision, and when she turned, she saw the bodies.

Harper stared, and her stomach lurched again. She slammed her hand over her mouth and forced the bile back down. There was dead everywhere. The bodies had been strewn without care around the room. Many were mutilated, unrecognizable as men and women. Some were missing limbs, others were disemboweled, or had their hearts ripped out. The limbs of those who still had them were bent at unnatural angles, broken, some with the bones stabbing through the flesh.

Dear Vine, they've left me here with the dead!

Had they assumed Harper was dead? Or did they just want her out of the way? Harper could do one thing, dredge up anger. She grabbed one bottle and pulled it from its place. Liquor was the last thing she should drink and she knew it would not quench her thirst but only make things worse.

She broke the wax seal by tapping it against the side of the shelf. When it crumbled, Harper sniffed at the lips of the bottle. The scent was strong and leathery, with a hint of burning wood. Harper tipped the bottle up and choked as the bitter liquid ran down her throat. The rush of warmth was immediate and went right to her head. It did some good by dulling her headache.

Harper moved to rest her back against the shelves while she took another drink. And she thought of Reynard. "I hope you're here, fox. I doubt there's much else I can do." When she felt herself dozing, Harper set the bottle aside, gathered herself up and stood, using the shelves as leverage. Looking at the bodies again, she felt shame at their inhumane treatment, but there was no changing the situation.

Harper found the stairs out of the cellar, but it seemed to take forever to climb them. Several times she had to stop and support herself by laying a hand against the rough stone wall. When she came to the heavy wood door, she was relieved to find it unlocked.

When she pushed the door open, she was in the kitchen. It was enormous, larger than anything Harper had seen before. The staff was hard at work, tending to boiling pots and cauldrons. A group at one of the cooking blocks was preparing more rations packets. The smell of frying food nauseated her again.

A screech made her jump out of her skin, followed by a crash and clattering. The maid who had dropped the tray of crystal was staring at Harper in fear. The entire kitchen focused on her.

"The dead are rising!" the maid screamed and turned and ran from the room.

Oh, for fuck's sake!

One of the kitchen matrons picked up a cleaver. "Get back, you damned demon spawn!"

"What's wrong with you? You put me in the cellar with the dead!"

The matron said, "You are not undead?"

"Don't you know a living person when you see one?" Harper said. "If I were—"

Three guards stumbled over each other to get into the room after a rush of footsteps.

"There!" It was the maid screaming. "I saw them carry her down!"

"Wait," one guard said, "you're that diviner."

"Yes."

"We thought you were dead," the guard said, "after that display. Come with us. Chamberlain Jourdain will know of this."

Harper realized she was still holding on to the door for support. "I'm not sure I can."

Perhaps the guard noticed what a state she was in, for he approached her and offered his arm, which Harper took. Like with the chamberlain earlier, she paid little attention to where they were leading her, but the guard took care in walking.

"Tell me what occurred after I lost consciousness," Harper said.

"Well…." The guard seemed uncomfortable. "You – that is, the apparition – dispatched many dark fey. It gave us an advantage."

"The Rot. Does it still have us trapped?"

"The what?"

"The vines and thorns," Harper said. "It's the Rot."

"Aye, that's a good name for the devilish things."

When they came to the main hall, Harper was greeted by another unsettling sight. The casualties of war. No one had come away unscathed from the event. They had set up a makeshift triage, and the injured were being treated by more young maids and manservants. Others were running back and forth, likely to and from the kitchen or where they stored medical supplies. One thing that broke her heart was the people, soldiers and civilians, huddled in corners or under the stairs. What they'd witnessed shattered their sanity.

They'd boarded the windows up, although not all, but the Rot retreated. The vines and thorns were gone. Harper wasn't certain if she should be relieved or more suspicious. She doubted the Rot would give up.

When those present noticed her, the stares and whispers started. Harper didn't care. The guard led her to sit against the wall underneath one of the boarded windows. "Stay here."

Where did he expect her to go? Harper answered with a nod. She was dozing off again when a familiar voice said, "Miss Harper!"

It was Gertie. Harper graced her with a wan smile. "Hello."

"I thought— We thought—" Gertie began, then she threw herself at Harper and embraced her. "Chloe is dead."

"Oh, dear Vine, I'm so sorry." She was furious with herself that she hadn't been able to stop it. "Please forgive me."

"What for?"

"I wasn't able to help you—"

"Nonsense," Gertie said. "After what you did – I've never seen such a thing."

Harper smiled again.

"You're exhausted," Gertie said. "I'll bring some rations and water."

"Thank you, Gertie." Harper admired the girl's bravery after facing the loss of a loved one. And that brought Pops and her brothers to mind. How were they faring? Were they fighting the Rot too? She supposed she could do a reading, but she didn't have the strength or wherewithal to try.

"Diviner!"

Oh shite—

The chamberlain had obviously found a safe place, because – barring her broken nose – there wasn't a hair out of place or a scratch on her.

"We thought you were dead," she said matter-of-factly.

If I hear that again….

Then the chamberlain said something Harper wasn't expecting.

"We need your aid and your power, diviner," Jourdain said. "Would you be our champion?"

CHAPTER TWENTY-EIGHT

Harper was certain she had lost her senses. "What's this? You want me to fight for you?"

"We saw the power you wield." Jourdain, of all things, knelt before Harper and arranged her skirts around her legs. "We would be fools not to take advantage."

Take advantage? That put her out, but Jourdain didn't seem to notice.

"You are loyal to the duchess, are you not?"

The duchess. "Where is she?"

Jourdain's brow creased, likely at Harper's tone. "Her Grace is safe in her rooms."

"And she's asking this of me?"

"Yes, of course."

"How could she even know me?"

"She knows of your power."

"I wish to speak with her."

"Certainly not!" Jourdain said. "It's not your place to demand an audience. She gave you the honor of defending the people."

Harper didn't feel like she was demanding. She did wonder if the chamberlain had spoken to the duchess recently.

"What I did doesn't come easily," Harper said.

"That is obvious by the aftermath," Jourdain continued, "so we will see to your care until you regain your strength."

Gertie approached at that moment, carrying a packet and a waterskin. "My Lady Chamberlain, if I may, please?"

The chamberlain scowled at the young girl, but Harper said, "I would rather have Gertie see to my care."

"Very well." Jourdain reached out her hand to the nearest guard, who helped her up. She walked away.

"Here you are, Miss Harper." Gertie handed her the packet and the waterskin.

"Gertie, could you help me out?"

"I can try."

"I need to find out what's happening outside."

Her eyes widened. "But I can't—"

"No, no." Harper waved her objection away. "I don't want you to go outside. You're the only one I trust, and I need to know what the situation is."

This brought a grin to her face. "I will do my best, Miss Harper."

Harper opened the packet and found a tiny fried fowl and fresh biscuits with honey-butter. Although she appreciated Gertie's effort, she felt like an absolute hypocrite, eating well while others had to do with rations. On the other hand, she didn't want to hurt Gertie's feelings. She rectified the situation by sharing it with two of the injured servants nearby. Although shocked, they were appreciative.

Still nervous about her experience with the Queen of Swords, Harper drew out her deck. They were silent, considering the situation she was in. She shuffled them well, but the first she drew was the Queen. Harper blew out a breath, holding the card between her palms as before. "I'm sorry. Please forgive me."

No response. Not even a quiver.

Harper drew the second. The Reaper. She didn't bother drawing another.

She was dozing again when something caused her to come awake. She sat up. Uncertain what was happening, Harper looked around. The injured were lying on bedrolls on the floor. Soldiers spent from fighting slept standing leaning against walls, while others just lay where they were.

The Virgin was whispering to her.

The cards had not abandoned her. Harper listened. She noticed some soldiers, both male and female, tossed in their bedrolls, their expressions distressed. Harper looked at them, and the veils appeared, and she saw....

"Damn it all!" Her exclamation brought all attention to her. "Wake those soldiers up, now!"

Everyone stared at her.

"Damn it all, didn't you hear me? Wake the soldiers, they're being attacked!"

Harper drew the Virgin. The light of her purity filled the room and revealed what no one else saw. These dark fey, unlike the others, could mask their forms. Their power was invading dreams and feasting on souls while bringing carnal pleasure to the sleeper. None suspected their life was being drawn out of them.

The incubi and their counterpart succubi caressed and whispered endearments, but it was all false. But now that Harper had revealed their presence, they left off their dark seduction and screamed, their gazes full of hate at being brought out into the light.

Two of the incubi came for Harper, while the others, thinking she was not worth their attention, or not caring, continued in their evil deeds. Harper didn't know what the incubi guessed they were going to do. The Virgin stood between her and them. She was the direct contradiction of what they were.

Her Gift protected her, but others remained enthralled.

"Help them!" It was the chamberlain yelling and at first Harper thought she was talking to her, but she was ordering the soldiers, who hesitated.

"Do as she says! They can't hurt you, only those asleep!"

The soldiers fell on the demons and ended their existence. The two who threatened Harper fled before the Virgin. Their companions wakened those attacked. Harper hoped that was the end of it all. It wasn't.

"Fire! The city is on fire!"

"Everyone, remain calm!" It was the Chamberlain. "We are safe—"

Something – Harper had never seen its like – crashed through the boarded window, making splinters of the planks. The screaming started anew. It was goblin-sized and vaguely childlike, but its skin was blood-red and its entire body covered in barbs, oozing ichor. Other things followed it in, some winged – harpies. Yes, Harper knew them, and from somewhere, the lamia slithered inside. Harper stood and pulled out her deck.

"Harper."

The voice was a whisper. As if someone was standing right next to her. When she turned, she caught sight of the construct. It was smiling at Harper and motioned her to follow.

Harper snorted. "When I get good and ready."

Harper drew, and it was the Steel Driver. The big man appeared, and Harper opened herself up to him. Unlike the Queen, the Steel Driver threw himself into fighting the evil before him. Now her dagger became the hammer, and she used it to crush the skull of whatever bloated thing had come through the window.

The voice came again. "Harper!"

Harper ignored it, and its cry born of frustration and anger carried across the room. How dare Harper ignore its summons? The reason was clear. She was not loyal or in their sway. She was Harper. Witch. Diviner.

When she found her body straining under the Steel Driver's influence, she asked to be released and he complied. Harper had to save some of her Gift for what was to come. Certain the soldiers could handle what survived of the dark fey, she approached the stairs. The construct turned and walked to the right. Towards the duchess's suites.

At the end of the hall, two more constructs stood guard. The doors opened without their help and Harper stepped inside. The suite might have once been luxurious, but all the finery was covered in the Rot and the whole place stank of it. All too familiar to her now. The construct that led her there walked into the next room. Harper thought it had previously served as a sitting room, but the furniture was in the same condition, cracked and molding. There was a table laden with spoiled food. The construct sat arranging its makeshift skirts and motioned Harper to sit on the opposite couch.

Harper faced the construct.

"Greetings, Lady Harper. Diviner. I have wanted to speak with you." The voice was pure venom, its words a snake's hiss. It was an affront to Harper's ears.

"Please allow me to introduce myself, although as my loyal subject you should already know me," it said. "I am Magdalen Brigette, Duchess of Innrone."

"No, you're not," Harper said. "Where is the duchess? Did you kill her?"

"I am Magdalen!" The construct came to its feet, balling its fists.

"Last I heard, Magdalen is human."

The construct huffed and strode into another room. Curious, Harper waited. The construct came back, sat down again, and placed something on the table. It was a signet ring with the royal crest.

Harper shrugged. "That means nothing."

"How dare you!" It slammed its hands on the table, palms flat. "I am she!"

"Let's say that you are," Harper said. "What do you want from me?"

That seemed to calm it a bit. It leaned back in the chair. "I want to know the future."

"Really."

"We...I need to know if we will succeed. It has not gone well but if we have you with us, to tell us all –" it smiled, but it looked grotesque, its teeth splinters, "– I can use the information. My people are losing heart after all these years."

"The citizens of Innrone or the dark fey?"

It chuckled maniacally. "I like your fire, Lady Harper."

"First tell me, what started this?"

"You wouldn't believe me."

"Try me."

"You."

Harper lifted a brow. "Me."

"Not you personally. Mortals." It gestured with its arm. "You drew on the magic that held us, the Celestial Vine –" it said the word with disgust, "– fought us. But it opened the way for us to leave Deep Earth. Humanity continued to draw on that power, but for avarice and hate." The construct tapped a finger on its chin. "I suppose we should thank humanity instead of killing them all."

"You think that humanity will allow themselves to be wiped out?" Harper said. "You see what's happening here now?"

"Yes, I know," the construct said. "I admire humanity, to be honest. They weren't quite so…." It stopped, its expression pinched as it searched for the right word.

"Thriving?"

"Yes, I suppose that works."

There was a noise from outside the room, drawing both their attention.

"Oh, what is all that racket!" The construct stood. "Now, don't go anywhere."

It strode from the room. Harper drew her cards out of her pouch. *Perhaps for the last time*, she thought.

The construct returned and resumed its seat.

"My apologies. I'm afraid we have visitors, but they'll not disturb us." It made a swift motion with its hand and a wall of black vines and thorns grew across the doorframe.

"Anyone in particular?" Harper continued to shuffle her cards.

"Oh, the fox," it said. "My guards will see to him. Now." The construct stared at the cards with hunger in its eyes. "Will you read for me?"

"Only if you spare Reynard."

It rolled its eyes. "I have no intention of killing him. He is so beneath my notice now. I thought for a time he would be mine but…." It shrugged. "Does that trouble you?"

"That you wanted Reynard?"

"Yes. You love him, don't you?"

Harper appeared to consider for a moment. Of course she loved Reynard, but not in the sense the construct was thinking. Harper supposed it took her silence as a yes.

"I knew it!" The construct clapped its hands like a giddy schoolgirl. It was a complete change in its attitude. "Has he made love to you?"

"That's personal, don't you agree, Your Grace?" Harper finished shuffling and sat her deck on the table.

"Oh, of course," the construct said, embarrassed.

They both looked at more noise coming from the other room.

"Honestly." As Harper placed the card, the construct yelled, "Kill them already!"

"Harper! Are you there?"

"I am," Harper responded, but her eyes didn't leave the construct.

"I'm coming!"

"I suppose we should hurry," the construct said. "I won't kill you if you tell me my future."

"Very well."

The construct sat on the edge of its couch, hands clasped in its lap, its gaze eager.

"How familiar are you with the cards? Have you ever had a reading before?"

"No." It bounced a little in its seat.

"Shall I explain as I read?"

"Yes, yes, of course."

"I will do three spreads," Harper said. "I will begin with the Celestial Cross."

Harper laid out the cards. "The first represents you. The person who's having the reading." She laid the card in the center. "The second is the obstacle." Harper set this card over and across the first. "Above the first and second is influences. Below is bringing darkness to light, unless reversed. Reversed means the card drew upside down."

The construct was leaning over the table, its gaze intense, nodding every time Harper spoke.

"To the left and right of the center," Harper continued, "you have things of the past and the immediate future." She pointed. "These four stacked to the side represent attitude, environment, your hopes and fears, and the eventual outcome."

"Yes, that's it!"

"Now...." Harper called her Gift to her as she closed her eyes and hovered her hands over the cards. She didn't need to do so. It was a ruse, a distraction. Her movements were to draw aside the veils. She turned the cards.

The Jester.

The Celestial Vine.

The Lady of Lies.

The Knight of Swords.

Harper continued, while manipulating the Vine. She couldn't change the future, only a sorceress could do that, but she could show the truth and destroy the construct's dreams.

The Prisoner.

The Match Girl.

The Knight of Wands.

The Witch.

The Necromancer.

The Giant reversed.

Harper sat back. She looked at the construct, who didn't seem to realize she'd finished. Its eyes were still on the cards. It looked up at Harper. "Tell me, tell me all!"

Harper drew in a deep breath. "You will fail."

The construct leaned back, its eyes wide, its hands gripping its skirts so hard Harper could hear the crack of the leaves as it crushed them. "No, do it again."

"There is no point."

"Do it again!"

Harper did. The outcome was the same.

"Again!" With each card laid, the construct trembled. It came out of its seat and paced, its hands flexing. Harper remained calm and laid the Celestial Cross one more time.

"This is the last time," Harper said. "I said three."

"Shut up!" the construct said. "You'll do it as damn well many times as I say."

Harper shook her head. "Why did you choose such a child to be your host?"

"What did you say?"

"I wasn't talking to you. I was speaking to your master. The devourer, the Rot."

"I am the Rot!"

Harper laughed. "You're nothing more than a spoiled child who knows nothing of true power." Harper overturned the last card. And the hand refused to change. So did the future.

"You fail."

The construct cried out, a wail of pure defeat, and the vines and thorns around them writhed and undulated in response. Harper sat watching, calm. The construct threw a tantrum like a babe who had a favorite toy taken away.

It turned on Harper, its face a mask of loathing. "I hate you!" It rushed at Harper, but something made it stumble. Harper couldn't see what, but as the construct pitched forward, she snatched up the Knight of Swords in one hand and her dagger in the other.

The dagger became a sword and Harper thrust it deep into the construct's chest.

The construct didn't die. It came apart, the leaves shriveled, the vines loosened, and the face flashed between the Rot and the woman. Shock, despair, anger all passed over its face before going slack. Harper held on to the sword, placed the Knight down, and picked up the Match Girl. She appeared with her fire of light and life and touched the flame to the construct's forehead.

The fire consumed it, almost silently, until it was nothing more than ash.

To Harper's left, something ripped away the wall of thorns. Reynard pushed through the opening despite the cuts.

"Harper, dear Vine!"

"Reynard!"

He grabbed her, kissed her face, his hands all over her, caressing as though he'd forgotten how she felt. She had to stop him with two fingers on his lips. "Reynard."

"What happened? Where's the duchess?"

"She's dead," Harper said. "And I believe she's been dead for a while. That thing was not her, but what remained."

"It killed her?"

"I don't believe so. I believe she gave herself and now that thing is gone."

"Dear Vine, I don't care anymore. I'm just glad you're safe."

What remained of the Rot dried out and, like the duchess, became dust, while Harper and Reynard watched.

CHAPTER TWENTY-NINE

There was a battle being fought Underneath.

With Reynard at the lead, the citizens of Vale marched. They made an impressive sight. Never did Reynard believe he would stride alongside his king as an appointed general. Reynard the Fox. Once hated and looked upon as a traitor, now admired by the very kin who wanted to destroy him.

They walked through the center of town. The people came out and stared with blank expressions. Noble stopped in the middle of the square, opened his mouth, and roared. It had the desired effect. The people, shocked out of their stupor, took their animal forms and joined the procession. Those with families said their goodbyes and followed behind. Eica and Aislinn had flown ahead, visiting the outlying farms to spread the news.

Reynard's mind always stayed with Harper.

I should marry her, he thought. He doubted she would agree, and, in all honesty, he felt no desire for a mate himself. A nice thought, though. His instincts inherited from his ancestors thousands of years ago told him Harper waited for him.

Because they had to remain in animal form, they feared a confrontation with the humans of Belltide. They tried to stay within the confines of the woods. It had been easy for Reynard as one fox, but an entire army of wild beasts? It came to pass that the curious approached. Some clutched farming implements, but no one made any threatening moves towards them. Perhaps they knew these were animalia, and they had a mission.

When they entered the cavern, Reynard stared in awe at the sight of what seemed to be hundreds of wil-o-wisp floating there. A few approached and bathed Reynard with their light.

"Friends of yours?" Noble said.

It was the first time they'd shared such a camaraderie, and it made Reynard ridiculously happy. "I hope so."

The wil-o-wisp escorted them again, but when they reached the opening to the cavern, they halted. Even so, Reynard and his kin looked at the myriad of dark fey and waited.

"They are expecting us," Noble said.

"So it seems," Reynard said. "Then we shan't disappoint them, Your Majesty?"

"Indeed."

Noble's roar filled the cavern with its terrifying power. Many of the dark ones fled before it. Others took it as a call to battle. With the exceptional eyesight of the animalia, the darkness of the cave proved not to be a detriment as the Vale army charged forward, Reynard and Noble at the lead. Reynard engaged a nearby goblin, a bloated, hideous thing. It seemed determined to fight, although its movements were sluggish. Reynard moved in, ducked underneath its strikes, then danced back to tease it. Some of his old mischievous side was returning. "So, is that your best, oh bloated one? Had too many vermin for your supper?"

This, of course, enraged the beast, and it rumbled after Reynard like a great fleshy landslide. Reynard dodged around and leaped on its back and sank his teeth into the back of its neck. The goblin flailed around for a time and Reynard held fast until it fell prone.

He took a moment to determine how others fared. Noble and his females did the most damage. Humans always thought males fought, but not so with lions. No dainty maiden-like women were these. Of course, Isengrim held his own, and Bruin, who always loved a good fight, stood on his hind legs and roared as he batted them away like a child's kickball. When he saw Finnick dashing and dodging before going in for the kill, the fox's heart obviously swelled with pride.

Reynard allowed an inward smile before throwing himself into the fray again.

Someone shouted a warning and Reynard turned to look. Cockatrices in their midst. Not wanting to meet that terrible gaze,

Reynard turned his back to them and followed the others away while a group of the only animal who could defeat a cockatrice rushed forward – the weasel. He would have liked to see that fight, but he wouldn't dare look.

Besides, he had his paws full. The dark fey seemed endless, born from the Rot or the depths of other caves. His kin continued to fight. Another problem arose. Red Caps. Though tiny, the wretched beasts caused casualties. The only way to destroy a Red Cap involved pure light or prayers. For a time, it seemed the tide of battle turned until the wil-o-wisps converged on the Red Caps, burning them to oblivion with their light.

A ghoul jumped on Reynard, shoving him to the ground. It clung to his back. Reynard dropped, rolled, but it refused to let go, its claws sinking deep. Something swooped down and Reynard found himself aloft. As the ghoul struggled, it released Reynard. He felt a moment of panic, but Eica dove in and saved him. It wasn't easy for the hawks to maneuver, but they did enough to help their comrades.

Once on the ground, enraged by being surprised and in pain from his wounds, Reynard charged the nearest enemy, a lamia who screeched and tried to escape but Reynard grabbed her by the tail and dragged her along while she writhed and tried to get purchase with her claws. She was unprepared when Reynard released her and pounced.

Reynard noticed those bulbs again where the dark fey came from. He leaped onto a rock shelf and called out to Eica and Aislinn, telling them to rip apart the bulbs and to get any animal with sharp teeth and claws to follow.

It seemed with that, the rotted vines produced no new Children. They did not protect the source of their allies, and their numbers dwindled. Reynard continued to fight. The enemy fled before the people of Vale, realizing they were on the losing side.

"Leave none alive! Allow no escape!" Reynard commanded, and Leonine took up the call. The citizens chased them down.

When they were certain no dark fey lived, they took a moment to rest, but everyone knew they could not tarry long. Of the citizens, twenty-eight of his kin lay dead. As much as they wanted to mourn and give proper burial, it wasn't possible, but Reynard hated himself for not seeing to it.

Although bruised and battered, they continued. When they saw the light from Above Ground, they found the hole had become larger. There were definite signs of beasts climbing to the surface, shredding and crushing the rotted vines that Reynard had battled through on his way home. They lay there dead and shriveling. He was worried about what was walking around in the daylight. That had not occurred in the Riven Isles since the felling of the Vine.

Reynard looked at the king and he nodded. He was the first to climb. The branches and vines held the weight of the larger animalia.

Reynard saw it first, and he couldn't stop the howl of distress.

The city was in flames.

Fury burned like the smoke and flame reflected in his eyes and Reynard snarled before breaking into a run. His kin followed, with no need to be warned. And although many citizens ran about in a panic, others were working together to save what was theirs. *This is what kin should do for one another,* Reynard thought. But his real concentration was on getting through the city and past people who did not stop to stare although some ran. Even these humans knew the animalia had a purpose as they leaped and dashed, caught the wind above their heads.

They saw the city was in chaos. It was what they feared. The dark fey were everywhere, hampering the efforts to save lives. As much as Reynard wanted to get to Harper, he knew they had to help. Noble called out to their kin with wings and ordered them to fly on ahead to the manor and bring word that the Vale was coming.

The dark fey realized what trouble they were in with the animalia. They left off the humans to focus their attention on Reynard and his people. Although the last battle had exhausted them, the wildness filled him and was in the forefront of his soul.

And another miracle occurred. The humans came to fight as well. Animalia and human. It was a glorious sight. Reynard never thought he would see it come to pass. It wasn't just those experienced on the battlefield; it was the common citizens and laborers who wielded anything they could as a weapon. Their fervor caught most of the dark fey by surprise. Humans can be quite volatile when someone threatens what they have worked so hard for all their lives.

Reynard continued to fight, but also to move forward. When they could, his kin followed. Their ultimate aim came into sight – the royal manor. There was a large concentration of dark fey there who got the shock of their miserable lives when the animalia joined the battle. Reynard was no longer concerned with anything else. His Harper needed him.

When he came to the fence, he hesitated. He wondered, could he leap at it? Would the vines try to stop him? Reynard swore, his curses coming out in growls and yips. He had to get in there. Reynard dashed around the fence, running its length, but still saw no way inside. A shadow streaked over him, and he looked to see Aislinn. She landed before him, her eyes saying everything. She shifted.

"No!" Reynard cried.

She grabbed hold of him and took to the air again, carrying him over the fence. An offshoot separated itself from the rest and reached up, extending its length until it twined around Aislinn's leg. She released Reynard, and the Vines dragged her down.

"No! No!"

"Go, damn you!" Aislinn cried as the Vines imprisoned her.

Reynard turned from the sight and ran. Vines and thorns were all around the building. Some had pierced the windows, although they had tried to board them up. There had to be a way in. Reynard dashed around the side of the manor, until he arrived at the servants' entrance. There had to be something. Then he saw it.

The coal chute. No vines or thorns were around it, but was he too large? One way to find out. Reynard dove for it. He slid down the metal, coal dust rising around and sending him into a fit of violent coughing. It coated his fur. When he came out, he landed in the full coal bin. There were no vines or thorns here. Reynard made for the door, hit it with the force of his elbow, and it sprang open.

People were running around. Reynard wasn't concerned about any of them. He continued running, and although the fox got some strange looks, no one made any move to stop him. Somehow, he found his way to the Great Hall. He was looking for Harper amid the fighting.

He howled but knew even if she was in the room, she wouldn't know it was him. *All right, Reynard – concentrate!*

He shifted.

The strength of his second form filled him. He sensed the Rot, but it was very far away. Reynard kept enough of his mind on the evil. "Harper! Harper, where are you?"

All his yelling did was attract the wrong attention. Reynard was no longer concerned with the filthy bastards. He needed to find Harper. Two staircases. Which one?

He needed time to think. He would not get it here. *Vine, please help me find her!*

Then he saw her. A beacon in all the chaos. The Match Girl.

Reynard didn't hesitate. He ran, shoving aside anyone who got in his way, killing anyone who tried to attack. He took the stairs and rushed down the hall. At the end, there were two guards standing before a door made of carved ivory.

But they were not human, although they had the vague form of humanity. They were like the thing he'd fought in Shahir's manor, constructs made of the rotted vines and thorns. Without a doubt, Harper was on the other side of that door. But what did she face?

No time to consider. He needed to get past those two. Reynard said, "Fuck it."

"Reynard!"

He turned at his name. Isengrim, in his half form, approached. "Surely you would not fight those vile things by yourself?"

"I had planned on it," Reynard said. "How did you get here so fast?"

"This will teach you not to rush ahead." His gaze went to the guards. "Our king made quick work of those rotted things and freed Aislinn. Is that where your Harper is being held?"

"Yes."

"Very well then."

It was Reynard who reached them first. They didn't move until Reynard was within striking distance, and then they did so with amazing speed. Gigantic thorns were their weapons. Reynard and Isengrim both knew they could kill just as easily as any weapon made of steel. Also, there wasn't much room to maneuver in the hall. But the guards wouldn't be led out into the open.

"This won't work," Isengrim said. "We must face them as they are."

"Yes." Reynard bolted forward, squeezing himself as close to the wall as he could.

"Reynard!"

The guard closest to him stabbed forward and Reynard shifted direction, leading with his shoulder, which was re-attached by the Vine. The thorn pierced it right through. The other guard turned to watch and Isengrim was on him before he could react and tore him to pieces.

Reynard ground his teeth against the pain as the guard, unsure of his next action, took two steps forward while Reynard pulled back. The thorn slipped out. Isengrim barreled into him so hard, it forced him into the door. Reynard limped in after him. Isengrim had torn the thing apart in a heartbeat.

When he was through, black bile dripped from his fangs. He turned to Reynard. "Why in all the nether-hells did you do that?"

"I didn't want to take time explaining." Even as he stood there, he could feel the Vine mending his torn flesh. Isengrim saw it too.

"By the Vine," the wolf whispered.

Reynard's attention returned to the doorway to the next room, blocked by another thorn wall.

"She's in there, with the Rot. I can smell them both."

"I'll make an opening and you go for your woman."

"Uncle? Thank you."

He grinned. "Just be ready."

With teeth and claws, Isengrim tore away at the Rot and Reynard, too impatient, joined him. With the smallest of an opening, Reynard shifted to his fox form.

"Reynard, wait!"

Reynard no longer cared. Let them rip his body apart if he could get to Harper. His fur was little protection, and he felt the thorns pierce his flesh, felt his own blood matting his fur. When he appeared, he saw her standing there as though the entire world was right again. With much effort, he went to his half form. "Harper!"

Everything was going to be all right. As she turned to face him and smiled, speaking his name, it was all Reynard could do not to lose control, and he took her in his arms. Nothing else mattered.

CHAPTER THIRTY

"There will be no celebration until we mourn the lost."

Reynard waited while his Harper wept with her father and brother at the loss of family. There were losses in animalia as well. Noble was mourning the loss of two of his pride. Reynard would even mourn the people who tried to kill him.

But seeing Harper this way made Reynard wonder was this all worth it. Had they left things, the Rot would have destroyed Innrone. They had no illusions that the Rot was gone. Where would it slither its way from the Deep Earth next?

Sergeant Falstaff approached him, healed and quite put out by being left out of battle. "How is your lady faring?"

"As well as expected." To be honest, he didn't know how Harper was faring. Although, after knowing her all this time, she would be strong.

"Please give her my condolences," Sergeant Falstaff said. "The chamberlain has summoned me."

"I hope I will meet you again soon," Reynard said.

She managed a smile. "You will."

They told Reynard that she was now the senior ranking guard member since the dark fey had killed her superiors, which would mean a hard-won promotion. Reynard didn't envy her the position. He continued to watch Harper with her family, keeping a respectful distance.

Eica approached him. "She will be fine. Will you stay with her?"

"I'll do whatever she asks of me."

Harper moved away from her family. Despite her tears, she was smiling. "Reynard." She was in his arms again and Reynard was content.

"What shall we do now?"

"If I may?" Eica said. "Harper, I would like to continue to be your teacher."

Harper stepped away and looked at Eica. "Yes. There's so much I need to learn, especially about possession."

"Then you'll be returning to Vale?"

She looked at Reynard and smiled. "Oh, yes."

"Are you sure?" Reynard said. "I don't want to keep you from your family, especially now."

"You won't," Harper said. "I can come and go as I please, can't I?"

"Well, yes." Reynard felt his cheeks warm. "I didn't think you could do it."

Harper laughed. Reynard loved the sound.

* * *

The Duchess Magdalene Brigette was dead. Assassinated by the enemy, along with her guards. At least that was the official report. The chamberlain didn't question their explanation of what had happened. Until they could notify the queen, the chamberlain now ruled Innrone. She did not seem pleased by this, but she accepted it.

Reynard found he couldn't feel sorry for the duchess. Why she chose her path was a mystery to him. Then again, he never understood why some humans did anything. For now, Reynard was going home. Harper would join him as soon as she was able and start her training with Eica, spending time in Vale and Innrone.

The first thing Reynard did when he returned to Vale was take care of young Lucea. She had regained her youth but still lay in the hallway. Noble gave her a suite, and a caretaker was brought in to see to her needs. When she regained consciousness, Reynard was the first to visit, telling her of everything and how Harper would return soon, which delighted her.

Noble wanted to pin a medal on him, but Reynard refused. He was past such material things. He'd proven his courage. What he wanted was a pardon, but he didn't ask for it. In fact, he advised Noble that if there were still people who wanted him punished, he would accept whatever they decided.

Noble shook his shaggy mane. "This does not become you, Reynard. You are a hero, and you will have to live with it."

They didn't speak of Reynard's past after that, and since no one seemed inclined to bring it up, Reynard didn't either.

Reynard asked for one boon. Maleperdius. His own estate, which had stood empty since he'd left, and he invited Finnick, who suffered injury but survived, to share his home, and the kit agreed. It would take some work, as the estate had fallen into disrepair. Some humans from Belltide gave him a fair price for repairs.

None of this was as important as him seeing Harper again.

When it was time for her visit, Aislinn went to fetch her. The tunnels and passages of Underneath still weren't safe, as the occasional dark fey showed its ugly face only to be dispatched. But Reynard was certain Harper could handle anything now.

He was at the manor with Eica, enjoying a repast in her parlor, when Harper arrived.

"Harper!" they both said in unison, but it was Reynard who reached her first, and they shared a hearty kiss.

"I'm so glad to be here."

Reynard kissed her again until Eica cleared her throat. "Sorry, Eica." Harper grinned and hugged her. "If you don't mind, I'd like to visit with Lucea first."

"Go right ahead," Eica said. "We'll be right here."

Reynard gave her a quick peck on the cheek. "No rush." He was going to have her alone soon.

★ ★ ★

Since his residence wasn't ready yet, Leonine gave Reynard rooms in the royal manor and Harper spent the night, but she got little sleep. It suited them both just fine, so Reynard caught her trying not to yawn as he walked to Eica's room. As always, Harper's fellow diviner had food ready.

"Join us, Reynard." Eica motioned to the food.

"Are you certain? I'd rather not be in the way."

"You won't be. Right, Harper?" She winked.

"I want you here," Harper said.

Reynard sat and watched the training session, but not long after, a knock interrupted them.

Eica asked, "Who in all of Vale is that?"

Reynard and Harper watched as she walked to the door, muttering all the way.

"Who are you?" she demanded of the visitor.

"I am Isbet, and I am here to see the diviner Harper."

"Well, you can't. She's in training—"

"Lady Isbet?" Harper stood. "It's good to see you."

"And you as well."

"Wait, you know this woman?" Eica asked.

That of course led to more food being brought and more explanation, but when Harper asked what brought Isbet to Vale – and how'd she gotten there – Isbet's response was, "I have friends in Underneath. I am here because as a Child of the Vine, you and I are bound to serve it. You will return with me to Rhyvirand, and I will teach you how to use the Vine's power and your Gift to their full potential. You will come to where I trained."

"Stop!" Eica said. "I am Harper's teacher, and she will stay here."

Isbet looked at Harper. "Is that your choice?"

"Yes, it is," Harper said. "I appreciate your offer, but my place is here."

"Why don't you stay for a bit?" Reynard suggested. "It appears there are things you know too?"

"If it is fine with our hostess?" Isbet nodded to Eica.

"Very well."

So Isbet of Rhyvirand stayed for a time and the three Gifted women discussed magic and Isbet imparted her wisdom. Harper seemed to be enjoying herself, which made Reynard worry a little. Who was to say Harper wouldn't change her mind and decide to continue studying with Eica, then go with Isbet? How long would it be before he saw her again?

When the hour was late, Isbet stood. "I have enjoyed my time here very much. Thank you for your hospitality." The three followed suit.

"It was a pleasure having you," Eica said.

"Please visit again soon," Harper said.

They walked her to the door.

"We will meet again, Lady Harper."

"Indeed," Harper said.

Once it was just the three of them, Reynard released a sigh of relief.

"Don't worry." Harper grasped his hands. "I'm not going anywhere."

Reynard embraced her. It was enough for him.